On the Nickel

A CLEOPATRA JONES MYSTERY

ON THE NICKEL

MAGGIE TOUSSAINT

FIVE STAR
A part of Gale, Cengage Learning

GALE
CENGAGE Learning

Detroit • New York • San Francisco • New Haven, Conn • Waterville, Maine • London

GALE
CENGAGE Learning

LIBRARY OF CONGRESS CATALOGING-IN-PUBLICATION DATA

Toussaint, Maggie.
   On the nickel : a Cleopatra Jones mystery / Maggie Toussaint.
   — 1st ed.
      p. cm.
   ISBN-13: 978-1-59414-954-2 (hardcover)
   ISBN-10: 1-59414-954-2 (hardcover)
   1. Single mothers—Fiction. 2. Golfers—Fiction. 3. Women accountants—Fiction. 4. Maryland—Fiction. I. Title.
PS3620.O89O5 2011
813'.6—dc22   2010048399

First Edition. First Printing: March 2011.
Published in 2011 in conjunction with Tekno Books and Ed Gorman.

This book is dedicated to my mother, who has always encouraged me to follow my dreams.

Thanks to Deni Dietz, my editor, for all her help.

CHAPTER 1

Numbers flowed in satisfying streams through my ink pen onto the Sudoku puzzle. A nine here. A two there. I scribbled a possibility in the corner of a grid square and sipped my coffee. Patterns emerged. I inked a seven in the top row, leading to three other filled-in numbers.

Without warning, Mama upended her oversized purse on the kitchen table. Junk clattered. Loose coins clinked. A tube of mulberry-colored lipstick rolled on top of my folded newspaper. Alarmed, I studied her as she pawed through the mound of personal items. A can of hair spray tottered on the edge of the table, and I caught it a moment before it fell.

"Lose something?" I asked, placing the can squarely on the table.

Mama muttered out of the side of her mouth. "My car keys."

Her color seemed a bit off. I set aside my puzzle to help sort through the jumble. I lifted the umbrella and plastic rain bonnet and moved them to the side. Her wallet was large enough to give birth. No keys hiding under it. I checked beneath her new hairbrush, a tube of toothpaste, and a pack of breath mints. Nothing under the mini photo album, tissue packet, or her dog-eared credit card bill.

"Don't see any keys," I said. "Where did you have them last?"

"If I knew that, I wouldn't be looking for them," Mama huffed.

Was something else wrong? I chewed my lip and replayed the

morning in my head. Mama ate a good breakfast. Her buttercup-yellow pantsuit appeared neat and tidy, as did her mop of white curls. Her triple strands of pearls were securely clasped around her neck. So, her appetite and grooming were fine, but her behavior was off. Probably not a medical emergency.

I breathed easier. "What's wrong, Mama?"

"What's right, that's what I'd like to know."

There was just enough vinegar in her voice to make me think I'd missed something big. Like maybe a luncheon date with her. Or broken a promise. But I hadn't done those things. I pulled out a chair and invited her to sit down. "Tell me what's on your mind, Mama."

"The price of gas keeps rising." Mama sat and enumerated points on her fingers. "World peace is a myth. Social Security isn't social or secure. And Joe Sampson had no business dying on me."

She'd run out of fingers, but I got the message. Guilt smacked me dead between the eyes. I had forgotten something. The anniversary of daddy's aneurism. Usually we took a trip to the cemetery on August 21. I gulped. "Oh, Mama, I'm so sorry. Why didn't you say something yesterday?"

"I didn't want to make a big deal of it." Mama's voice quivered. "It's been three years, Cleo. I should be able to go by myself."

I reached over the kitchen table and covered her hands with mine. "You don't have to do that. I'll drive you to your meeting, then we'll swing by Fairhope on the way home."

Mama sat up soldier straight. "That will eat up your whole morning."

"No problem. We mailed all the quarterly tax payment vouchers to our Sampson Accounting clients last week. I can't think of anything at work that won't keep until this afternoon."

Half an hour later, I was sitting in the hall at Trinity Episcopal while Mama attended her Ladies Outreach Committee meeting. I'd brought a magazine to read, but there was something else about Mama this morning that worried me. Something more than our delayed cemetery visit. I wished I knew what it was. Even though I'm good at puzzles, I couldn't put my finger on what was wrong. Knowing Mama, I wouldn't have long to wait. I dug my magazine out of my purse and flipped through the glossy pages.

In a little while, the gentle murmur of conversation from the meeting room rose to an angry buzz. Mama's sharp voice sliced through the fray. "Mark my words. If you don't change your ways, Erica, someone will change them for you."

My heart stutter-stepped at the heat in her voice. This was not good. How should I handle it? Mama would not appreciate me trying to straighten this out. My intervention would be the equivalent of waving a red flag in front of a penned bull. I hesitated, hoping that the women resolved their difference of opinion on their own.

"You threatening me, Dee?" Erica's nasty tone ruffled the hair on the back of my neck and spurred me into defense of my mother.

I stashed the magazine in my shoulder bag and hurried down the pine-scented corridor, the soles of my loafers smacking against the hard tile. After their years of insulting each other, would the hostility between Mama and her arch nemesis turn physical?

I entered the back of the meeting room in time to see Mama stride up to Erica's podium. Ten seniors sat transfixed by the live drama. I had a very bad feeling about this. As emotional as Mama was today, her patience wouldn't last for long. And Erica seemed to be spoiling for a fight. That wasn't going to happen on my watch. I hurried forward, edging past the U-shaped log jam of tables and chairs. My eyes watered at the thick cloud of sweet perfume.

Mama planted her hands on her hips. "I'm saying what nobody else has the guts to say. You are despicable. That outreach activity was supposed to bring joy and laughter to those dying children. You crushed their hopes. Worse, you gave them false hope. They were crying, Erica. You caused those dying children to suffer more."

Except for the red stain on Erica Hodges' rigid cheeks, I couldn't tell she was upset. Next to Mama's sunny yellow suit and old-fashioned pearls, Erica's sleek jewel-toned slacks suit, gold-threaded scarf, and apricot-colored hair looked fresh, contemporary, and on point.

Looks could be deceiving.

"Errors happen, Dee," Erica said.

Mama huffed out a great breath. "This one could have been avoided. Francine was doing a good job with scheduling before you horned in and messed it all up."

Across the room, Francine gasped at the mention of her name. She slid down in her seat, covered her face, and ducked her white-haired head.

Erica surveyed the room, staring down the other matrons, before turning back to Mama. Her back arched, and her thin nose came up. "You think you could have done better?"

"I know so. All that hard work the committee put in. You wasted it. You hurt those kids. Those circus tickets were nonrefundable. You threw away money we worked hard to raise."

"Don't worry about it." Erica barked out a sharp laugh. "We'll find more needy kids to show our civic merit. The hospital has a never-ending supply."

A collective gasp flashed through the room. My stride faltered as distaste soured in my stomach. I couldn't believe what I was hearing. A glance at Mama's flame-red face and I knew Mount Delilah was about to erupt. I hurried forward.

"That does it. I demand your resignation as chair of the Ladies Outreach Committee!" Mama shouted.

"You're out of order, Delilah Sampson," Erica shrilled. "Sit down and shut up."

Mama's mouth worked a few times with no sound emerging. She clutched her heart. I stepped up and planted my hand on her shoulder. "Mama?"

She glared at Erica. "You can't talk to me that way."

"Think again." Erica smacked her open palm on the podium. "This is my meeting, my committee, my church, my town. I can talk to you any way I want."

Mama turned to face her friends. "Say something."

Brittle silence ensued. Not a single eyelash fluttered on the downturned gazes. Disbelief flashed through me. These women were Mama's friends. Her best friends, but they were all intimidated by this big fish in our tiny pond. Poor Mama. We needed to get out of here before both of us did something we'd regret.

I tapped Mama's shoulder again. "I'm sorry to interrupt, but I have a family situation and have to leave. Please come with me now."

Mama nodded to me and inhaled shakily. She narrowed her eyes at Erica. "This isn't over."

"Don't start on me, Cleo," Mama said once we were in my Volvo. I'd had to buckle Mama's seat belt because her hands were shaking so badly. "That ugly woman has pushed me around for the last time."

I donned my sunglasses and backed out of my parking space behind the parish hall. The cemetery visit would have to wait. Mama needed to be home with her heart medication. "She certainly is pushy. And her face is stretched so tight. How many facelifts, tummy tucks, and boob jobs has she had? She looked

13

my age, for goodness' sake."

"She's fake. A complete fraud. I hate the way she treated those poor children."

I turned east on Main Street and headed home. If Mama still wanted to go to the cemetery, we'd go, but only after we picked up her meds. "Tell me about it."

"We've covered for that power-hungry fool for years, but she went too far this time. She cancelled Francine's buses, said they were too expensive, and neglected to schedule other transportation. And it wasn't like we could fit all those kids in wheelchairs in our cars, even if we wanted to. It took six months to set that activity up through the hospital. Six months of everyone's time and the church's money. We tried to keep her out of it, but she elbowed her way in, like she always does. Erica has so much money and influence, everyone is afraid to stand up to her. Everyone but me." Mama wrung her hands. "God, I hate it for those kids. If you'd seen the disappointment on their faces, you'd want to kill Erica, too. I can't take it anymore. I can't take her anymore."

A brown delivery van in front of me signaled a left into the bakery parking lot. I slowed until my lane cleared. "I don't understand. If you guys always cover for her, why didn't someone double-check the buses?"

"We tried. Lord knows we tried. She yelled at Francine and told her she was an incompetent fool. She made Francine cry. Erica is a heartless bully. I'm fed up with her. Why does a rotten person like her even come to church? God, forgive me because I have no love for her. I want nothing to do with her."

"That's easy. Stay away from her."

Mama flung her hands up in disgust. "Walk away from my entire life? She's not just in my church. She's in the garden club, bridge club, and the hospital auxiliary. There's more overlap, and I could remember it if I weren't so danged mad.

Basically, the woman is a walking photo opportunity."

Unfortunately, Erica's picture sold lots of newspapers. There were definite perks in descending from the family who founded our town. I couldn't resist handing out a bit of advice. "Don't elect her to be the group leader."

"She's a Crandall. All she has to do is show up and she's automatically in charge."

"She's powerful because you ladies let her bully you around."

"Spoken like a pro." She eyed me speculatively. "What's your 'family situation,' Cleo? Got another hot date with what's his name?"

I ignored her comment about my blossoming romance with Rafe Golden. "My 'family situation' is you. I stopped your argument before things got further out of hand. Granted, Erica is not a nice person, but nothing good ever comes from showing your behind in public. You can thank me later."

Our Wednesday golf league special event required each golfer to use only three clubs and a putter. I'd selected my driver, my nine wood, and my trusty seven iron. With that winning combination, I'd thought my bases were covered. Wrong. I'd been in three bunkers without a sand wedge. Consequently my shoulders ached, my concentration was shot, and my score resembled the national debt. This round couldn't end soon enough for me.

My third putt on number nine screamed past the hole and tumbled gleefully off the back slope. It wasn't like I could go to my bag and grab my pitching wedge for this next shot. It wasn't there. This game stank. Worse, I stank at this game.

I trudged off the green.

I glanced up, hoping for inspiration. Any sign from above that might result in my next shot holing out would be welcomed. Instead, the soaring watercolor perfection of a cloudless blue sky of late August mocked me. Who needed picture-perfect weather when they were playing lousy golf? Shouldn't there be lightning bolts or hailstones coming my way?

How about a rogue tornado?

If a whirling funnel plunged down, surely it would toss this worthless putter all the way to Kansas. Crows cawed in the cornfield beside the green, their plaintive calls adding to my sense that it wasn't just my golf game that was in the toilet.

My name is Cleopatra Jones and shooting a round of par golf is my goal. I'm out here every Wednesday playing in the Hogan's Glen Ladies Nine Hole League, working on my game, and more importantly, trying to beat my friend, Jonette Moore. We've been best friends ever since elementary school. I've forgiven her for her bounty from the breast fairy. She's forgiven me for being tall and slender.

I studied my next shot. The tip of the flag was visible over the rise.

"How much you paying for those golf lessons?" Jonette's pixie-like face lit up with a devilish grin. She didn't look like she'd been fighting gravity all day. There was a bounce in her step and a sparkle in her amber-flecked eyes.

Maybe if I wore vibrant, formfitting tangerine golf gear like Jonette, this game wouldn't beat me each week. Today, my worries about Mama weighed heavily on my knee-length navy blue shorts and white polo.

"Nothing," I muttered, hunching my shoulders in anticipation of her witty comeback.

"That's your problem, Clee," Jonette crowed. She could crow because she'd already holed out. One tap of her ball, and it had disappeared into the cup. "You got exactly what you paid for. Nothing."

I tried to pay Rafe Golden for my private golf lessons, but he wouldn't take my money. He'd been generous with his instruction, but my swing thoughts vanished once he touched me with his magic fingers.

Bottom line, he scrambled my circuits. The sizzling attraction took my breath away. It thrilled me. And it frightened the daylights out of me.

"You're strangling that putter," Jonette said. "Loosen your grip. Don't be so uptight."

Easy for her to say. Holding on tight helped me keep my mind on the game. As long as I gripped a club, I stayed in the here and now. I had all of next week to replay the wild shots and near misses in my head. I didn't need them haunting me during play.

I shot Jonette my patented death glare, and she giggled. She, of course, had only used three strokes to reach the ninth green. Her tap-in putt gave her a par for the hole.

I dreamed about pars.

Birdies and eagles too.

They were endangered species in my double-bogey world.

I squeezed my eyes shut and contemplated the trek to the cart to get my stupid seven iron. I didn't want to expend the effort. Golf was angles and loft, numbers basically. As an accountant, numbers were my forte. I should be able to make my putter into a wedge if I got the contact angle right. I moved the ball up in my address to add loft to my flat-faced putter. The ball needed to fly over the long tufts of grass between it and the green so that its direction stayed true.

Ignoring the doubts in my head, I whacked the ball. It sailed over the apron as planned and trickled to a stop six inches from the hole. Satisfaction hummed in my veins.

"Nice up," Jonette said.

"Thanks." I tapped in for an eight, wishing I'd turned my brain on nine holes ago. I bagged my putter and plopped into the passenger side of the golf cart.

Jonette drove us toward the pro shop, where we would turn in our score card. The pro shop. Rafe was in there. I snatched off my red Titleist ball cap and tried to fluff my hat-flattened hair. Why didn't golf carts come with vanity mirrors?

"What's the damage?" I asked, not really wanting to know my golf score but needing closure on this round of golf.

"Not bad, not bad." Jonette whipped our score card off the steering wheel and waved it in my face. "Double-check my math. Looks like forty-five for me and sixty-two for you."

I reviewed the scores, summed the numbers in my head, and signed the edge of the card to attest the scoring. "These check out." My heart sank at the total, even though a sixty-two was eight strokes better than my score had been earlier this summer. I crushed my hat in my hands.

In my wildest dreams I'd never imagined a handsome, sought-after hunk like Rafe Golden would be attracted to a small-town woman like me. While we weren't professing our undying love for each other, the "L" word lurked in the back of my mind. Scary thing that, especially when I didn't know if the feeling was mutual.

Jonette veered off the sunny cart path into the shade of the leafy *Ligustrum* hedge between the course and the pro shop. She hit the brakes and shot me a razor-sharp glance. "You gonna tell me what's eating you, or do I have to wring it out of you?"

"It's Mama," I admitted flatly. My conscience warned me to keep my mouth shut, that this might blow over. Then again, it might not. But if I kept this worry inside, I would surely end up in the nuthouse. I needed to tell Jonette. "She got into a fight with Erica Hodges at Ladies Outreach meeting two days ago."

Jonette's jaw dropped, forming a perfect O in her heart-shaped face. "Your mom beat up that old biddy? And you didn't call me?"

"It didn't come to blows, but they were inches from it." Now that I'd opened the floodgates, words bubbled out. "Mama moped around Monday afternoon and Tuesday, too. She didn't watch her soaps, and she hasn't said a word about the food I've served. She went straight to bed after her hospitality meeting last night. It's like someone reached inside and turned Mama off. I'm worried."

Jonette's amber-flecked eyes rounded. "I see what you mean. Ordinarily, Delilah would be breathing fire and plotting ways to get back at Erica by now. Shutting down isn't her style."

My head pounded something fierce. Using the heels of my hands, I massaged my throbbing temples. "If that isn't enough to worry about, Charlie has been helpful lately. He drove both girls to the office supply store and endured their back-to-school shopping without complaint."

It took me two years to put my life back together after my divorce from Charlie Jones. I'd finally come to terms with my new existence. But the rules of life kept changing on me. I didn't know how to handle a nice Charlie or a quiet Mama.

Jonette inhaled sharply and went statue still. "What's he up to?"

"He's sucking up to me. To make me think he's changed."

My friend's hand went to her throat. "You're not buying his con job, are you?"

A twosome from our golf league whizzed past. I leaned close to Jonette. "Get this. He paid his child support check a week early this month. I didn't have to remind him about it."

"Something is definitely up with him. Watch your back and your front, too." Jonette frowned. "Are the girls okay?"

"Charla and Lexy are fine. They love this extra parental attention. Charla talks nonstop about getting her driver's license in a few months, and Lexy plans to join the high school yearbook staff."

"How's Madonna?"

I inherited my very pregnant, short-haired Saint Bernard from a friend who'd been murdered. "She's rounding out. Sleeping all the time. I still can't believe we're having puppies."

"I can hardly wait."

Jonette wanted one of the puppies, but I had no idea what to do with the rest of the batch. "Sell them," the vet had said. My immediate reaction had been: *No way!* Making a profit on Madonna's offspring was coldly wrong. Especially since she'd saved my life.

"What about the hot affair?" Jonette asked. "What's the word on that?"

Heat streamed from my cheeks. "A few scheduling problems, but hot just the same."

A big grin lit Jonette's face. "All that sneaking around put pep in your step this summer. And the man absolutely lights up when he sees you. I wish Dean reacted the same way to me."

Dean was Jonette's sixth try at finding true love. It tore me up that she was unhappy again. When was it going to be her turn? "I thought things were better between you two."

Jonette's expressive face fell. She seemed fascinated with the card clip on the steering wheel. "I'm thinking about leaving Dean, but I can't afford to lose my job, too."

Dean owned the Tavern, where Jonette worked as a barmaid. If Dean couldn't see how special Jonette was, he was toast as far as I was concerned. "Ouch. Tough call there."

"No kidding. But, it's not like either one of us is interested in someone else. Dean and I are comfortable together, like a pair of old shoes."

Another cart of lady golfers motored past on the sun-dappled cart path. I wished I knew what to tell Jonette. My experience with males was limited to two men, Charlie and Rafe. Charlie was oatmeal to Rafe's Belgian waffle. Inspiration struck.

Maybe Dean was oatmeal, too. "You deserve new shoes. If

Dean isn't up to par, you need to go shopping."

"Good morning, ladies. What are we shopping for?"

My head whipped around to the source of that deep voice. Built like a fireplug, Detective Britt Radcliff gave the impression bad guys didn't stand a chance against the mighty forces of law and order. His thunderstorm-gray eyes danced with laughter.

"Shoes," I said, chewing my bottom lip.

"Definitely shoes," Jonette echoed with mock solemnity.

"Right." Britt's grin faded. But his cop face didn't scare me. He'd been my Sunday school teacher and self-proclaimed protector ever since I could remember. "I need to talk to you, Cleo."

My throat constricted as possible implications of a visit from a cop leaped into my head. I had visions of twisted metal and precious blood spilled. I jumped out of the golf cart in alarm, my red Titleist cap tumbling to the ground. "My kids!"

I'd moved too fast, and the world went dark. Temporary blackouts were an annoying side effect of low blood pressure. I clawed my way out of darkness to find Britt holding me by my forearms and Jonette at my side.

"Your kids are fine." Britt's scowling face filled my field of vision. "You sure you're not in a family way?"

Giddy relief flooded my foggy brain. My daughters were safe. I pushed at the strong, capable hands that supported me. "I'm not pregnant. Why did you scare me like that?"

"But she could be." Jonette poked me in the ribs with her elbow. "She has an active sex life these days."

"Shush, Jonette." I stepped out of Britt's reach, leaned against the cart, and hugged my arms to my chest. "If it's not the girls, is it Mama?"

"Delilah is fine, as far as I know." Britt shoved his hands in the pockets of his tan slacks. "I'm here because of the trouble at the Ladies Outreach Committee meeting on Monday."

My stomach clenched and my breath hitched. "I don't understand. Is there an official complaint against Mama?"

"I'm afraid so. Erica Hodges filed an incident report yesterday. Two witnesses confirmed that Delilah threatened Erica during the meeting. Do you know what's going on?"

Fire brimmed in my veins. But before I could get a word out, Jonette beat me to it. "I'll tell you what's going on," she said. "Erica Hodges is a trumped-up, royal pain in the ass, that's what. She lords her blue-blooded heritage over the rest of us peons. If Delilah threatened her, she deserved it."

I tried to breathe normally. The girls were okay. Mama was okay. Erica was a puke, but that was old news. Bending down, I picked my cap off the grass and snugged it on my head. "I was there and overheard the exchange. Mama didn't threaten Erica. She suggested Erica should mend her ways. Mama was upset because Erica ruined the circus outing they'd spent months planning. For sick children."

"Upset or not, Delilah can't go around issuing terroristic threats. Can you talk some sense into her?"

I managed a choking laugh. "Mama is practically a force of nature. She marches to her own beat."

"She better watch what she says. Erica is pretty stirred up about this." He studied me for a long moment. "Those guns still under your bed?"

My breath caught in my throat. "How do you know about that?"

"It's my business to know these things. Keep the guns away from Delilah until this settles down. Let's be smart about this."

The guns weren't the problem. Mama was. She didn't take direction well. Never had. Never would. "I'll see what I can do."

"Be assertive. And nosy," he said.

A short blast of air puffed out of my nostrils. "You didn't think my nosiness was good a few months ago. You told me to keep my nose out of police business."

Britt's weight shifted onto the balls of his feet, his shoulders went back, and his arms tensed. His police detective eyes pinned me to the golf cart. Potential energy hummed in the air. "Should I take Erica's complaint seriously?"

A deep chasm opened between us with that question. I respected law and order, but family loyalty put me squarely in Mama's corner. If Britt came after Mama, he'd be coming after me, too.

Dread constricted my chest. I hated being on the wrong side of the law. But I hadn't done anything wrong. Neither had Mama. Unless you counted her shooting her mouth off, which was an everyday occurrence.

"Of course not." I blinked furiously. "Jonette's right. Erica's a bully. She participated in the argument one hundred percent."

He held my gaze until I squirmed. Britt trusted me to tell him the truth. Every accountant knew that increasing the number of data points increased precision and accuracy. I didn't have enough data points for this conflict between Mama and Erica. All I had was the sinking feeling that my life was about to get messy again.

In the sudden silence, Britt's radio on his hip squawked. I startled at the burst of noise. Britt's focus shifted as he responded. I leaned forward, straining to decipher the abbreviated police jargon. Britt uttered a terse response and turned to face us again. Waves of tension radiated from him. Harsh lines etched into his rugged face.

"What is it? What happened?" I asked.

"Police business downtown. Go home and stay out of trouble." Britt fixed me with another stern glare and hurried away.

Reasons for Britt's urgent summons tumbled through my head, none of them good. The possibility of more mayhem in

Hogan's Glen sent my stomach on a terrifying roller-coaster ride. Flying too fast. Free-falling too long.

Nervous heat poured off my body. Cold sweat beaded in my hairline, pooled down the rigid channel of my spine.

"You all right?" Jonette asked, touching my shoulder.

"Not exactly."

"You look like you've had a terrible shock."

"Gee, thanks." I studied my two-toned shoes. "The police radio. That sound of electronic static." I took three deep breaths. "I feel like I'm standing outside in that moment before a storm when the light thins. That twilight moment is upon me."

"Wow. That's deep. I never thought about a storm that way before."

"I can't shake this feeling. It feels like . . . you're gonna think I'm crazy."

Jonette implored me to continue with a wave of her hand.

I hated this helpless, skittering feeling. I tossed my hat back into the cart. My fingers sought a hank of hair and held on tight. "I can't shake this awful feeling in my gut. That call Britt just got, I can't stop thinking about it. What if that call is something terrible?" I met Jonette's anxious gaze. "Britt was headed downtown. Did you hear anything else?"

Her face scrunched. "Something about the Episcopal church."

The pounding in my head turned to thunder. My family belonged to Trinity Episcopal. Worse, Mama, Francine, and Muriel were meeting at the church this morning to plan the Sunday school hostess schedule for the fall.

I stilled. "You going home like Britt ordered?"

"Hell no." Jonette snorted. "Detective Dumb-as-Dirt can't tell me what to do. I'm headed to the church. Aren't you?"

I managed a breath and climbed in the cart. "You bet. But you drive. I can't think straight."

Chapter 2

Jonette zoomed out of the golf course parking lot, turning right in front of a speeding pickup truck. My life flashed before my eyes. Images roared through my head in horrifying succession.

A scream ripped from my throat. I braced for impact. The blue truck honked loudly and swerved onto the grassy shoulder to avoid hitting us.

She glanced at me over the top of her leopard-print sunglasses, her expression the picture of innocence. Her right hand fluttered through the air. "What?"

My fingers were embedded in the arm rest. "Get us there in one piece."

Jonette grinned. "He missed me by a mile."

I glared at her. "He missed us by inches. Pay attention."

"Don't be such a wet blanket, Clee." Jonette's hands came off the wheel to emphasize her point. The car veered toward the fog line. "I'm a good driver."

My stomach lurched. "You're an accident waiting to happen. If that truck hit us, we'd be goners. Not even the Jaws of Life could save us."

"Hey. This is a fine car." Jonette patted the dusty dashboard. "Don't you go knocking my two-thousand-dollar car. It gets me where I need to go."

I glanced at the stalled traffic before us, and my heart stuttered. "Slow down. That van up ahead is turning."

She slammed on brakes at the last minute and stopped short.

Behind us, tires squealed on the pavement. If we got hit from behind, we'd need firemen to put out the flames.

"I thought you'd be less bitchy once you got laid on a regular basis," Jonette said. "You ought to ask your doctor about a prescription mood enhancer."

My blood pressure spiked. Jonette had no right to criticize my moods. Sure, I was wound tight, but I had good reason. Living with two teenaged daughters, a pregnant dog, and an independent woman would wind anyone tight.

"You're driving like a maniac. Cool it," I said. "Charla will be driving on this road in a few months. Do I have to ground you every time she gets behind the wheel?"

Jonette's lower lip jutted, but her hands stayed put on the steering wheel. "I'd never do anything to hurt Charla. You know that."

A mail truck pulled off to insert letters in a roadside mailbox. Jonette accelerated around the mail truck, scooting over the double yellow lines into the lane of oncoming traffic. My feet jammed into the floorboard. I closed my eyes and prayed aloud. "Dear God."

She veered back into our lane. My eyes popped open. "I'd like to live long enough to see my children graduate from college."

"We're almost there, 'fraidy cat."

Jonette parked on Main Street a block away from the church. I pried my fingers off the vinyl armrest and stumbled from her death trap of a car. My heart raced faster than an Olympic athlete's.

I rolled my eyes at my friend. "You ever put me through that again and I'll kill you with my bare hands."

She tossed her sunglasses on the dash and flashed me a megawatt smile. "Promises, promises."

I turned my attention to the imposing stone church. What

had happened in the shadow of the tallest steeple in town? *Please, dear Lord, don't let Mama be in the middle of this.* My uneasy feeling grew at the sight of the two uniformed officers guarding the driveway entrance to Trinity Episcopal.

Jonette wormed her way through the crowd as I held on to her car and tried to steady my racing heart. Britt was nowhere in sight. I spotted my elderly next-door neighbor, Mrs. Waltz, headed my way. She was eighty going on a hundred and ten, with her gray bun coiled tightly on top of her head. Her pale green polyester slacks outfit reminded me of pistachio ice cream. "What's going on?" I asked, sounding calmer than I felt.

"Car wreck in the church lot." Mrs. Waltz leaned heavily on her wheeled walker. Her breath came in short huffs. "What happened to your hair?"

"Golf hat." I ruffled my limp hair self-consciously. I should have left my hat on. "Was anyone hurt in the crash?"

From attending this church all my life, I knew the layout of the rear parking lot intimately. If there was a car wreck back there, it couldn't be too serious. There was only one place, the circular loop connecting the back paved rectangle to Main Street, where there was any room to go faster than a crawl. While I was thinking this, a part of me was also thinking, *Please don't let Mama be back there.*

"Don't know, and I'm not waiting to find out." Mrs. Waltz maneuvered her walker around the island I made on the sidewalk. She muscled it over a bit of grass and back onto the concrete. "Got to keep moving or my joints will seize up."

"Nice seeing you," I called to her back.

Jonette returned, looking puzzled.

"Well?" I asked.

"I didn't get much. No one is allowed on the church property." Jonette did an empty-handed gesture. "I spoke to two of your mother's friends. Muriel and Francine were working in

27

the church office when the police evacuated the building. Muriel is miffed because they won't release her car from the rear parking lot."

That shaky feeling in my knees returned. The hair on the back of my neck stirred. "Muriel is always miffed about something. She'll get over it. Did you see Mama?"

Jonette shook her head. "She's not here. Muriel and Francine said Delilah stood them up today."

Relief flashed through me, closely followed by annoyance. "Where is she?" I hoped she wasn't over at Erica Hodges' house beheading Erica's chrysanthemums again. Or over at the newspaper spreading rumors about Erica to the gossip columnist.

"I asked her friends. They don't know where she is."

Another thought broadsided me. What if Mama hadn't made it because she'd been in the parking lot accident? I shivered. "Is her car parked back there?"

Jonette patted my shoulder. "Chill, Cleo. Delilah's not here. That's good news. Let's not invite trouble."

"You're right." No need to invite trouble; it came whether you wanted it or not. But I couldn't shut down my worry machine. Dread crept from my bones into my blood.

I shook my head to clear it. "Why is our entire police force here?"

Jonette shrugged. "Don't have a clue."

"Mrs. Waltz said it was a car wreck. Did you hear anything about a collision?"

"Not a peep."

The stone front of the church looked cold and forbidding, no easy feat in the heat of August. It's normally welcoming red double doors reminded me of spilled blood. My knees wobbled, and I willed them to hold me. Don't borrow trouble, I reminded myself.

Except for the driveway to the rear parking lot, the structure of Trinity Episcopal filled the block on the Main Street side. It was maddening to be so close and still be clueless. "Let's sneak around back."

Jonette's eyes widened knowingly. "Sounds like a plan."

We skirted the edge of the crowd, past the dense tree line that blocked the church parking lot from full view of Linden Avenue. We continued around the block on Schoolhouse Road until we came to the thicket.

Every Trinity Episcopal kid knew their way through the thicket. Navigating the dense foliage was a rite of passage like baptism and communion. The reward for such courage was an unobserved, secret hiding place with a clear view of the church back yard. The thicket was the ultimate place to spy on the church ladies who hid Easter eggs.

I led the way through the narrow kid-sized passageway, swatting drooping branches and taut spider webs away from my face. A large black spider dangled in front of my face, and I choked back a scream.

"Are we there yet?" Jonette whispered in my ear.

"Shh," I cautioned. "Britt will skin us alive if he finds out we're spying on him."

My nerves wouldn't settle. If anything, they were worse back here. My numb fingers and toes barely worked. If Jonette told anyone how crazy I was, I'd deny it with every breath in me.

When there was only one row of bushes between me and the Trinity grounds proper, I raised a hand to halt our forward progress.

Jonette squatted beside me, her amber-flecked eyes sparkling with excitement. I rationalized our position. We weren't being nosy. We were gathering information. Perfectly logical.

I parted the branches, and the church lot came into view. A knot of police officers stood twenty feet away. Their grim faces and hushed voices added to my unease. The entire parking lot was decked out with yellow police tape.

Oh no.

Crime-scene tape.

They didn't put that up for fender benders. My investigative nausea had been right on target. A crime had been committed back here. But what crime?

This area was off limits. It would look bad if we got caught. So we wouldn't get caught.

I studied the length of the parking lot. No wrecked cars in sight. There was, however, a heavily draped mound just off the pavement near the paved back loop. With this many cops called to the premises, that had to be a body under the tarp.

Not another one.

"Oh God," I said under my breath. My heart stilled as memories of finding Dudley Davis dead on the golf course flashed through my head. Sightless eyes, rigid limbs, dark blood-stains, and an odor that stopped me in my tracks. I didn't need to see another dead body. I still had nightmares from the last one.

"What? Let me see." Jonette pushed past me for a better view, throwing me off balance and sending me sprawling through the bushes onto the gravel covering this overflow sec-tion of the parking lot. Dismay choked the breath out of me as I flew through the air.

This was going to hurt.

My arms, which I instinctively raised in protection, scraped along the sharp, spiky edges of the trimmed branches as I sailed through the vegetative cover. Gravel rocks sliced my face, arms, and knees. My teeth crunched the gritty gravel dust. I tried to scramble back to safety, but I wasn't fast enough.

A uniformed officer detained me. Officer Eddie Wagner. I'd babysat for him twenty years ago. Below his mirrored sunglasses, his lips pressed into a thin line. He hoisted me to my feet and clamped my hands behind my back. "Detective Radcliffe," he said. "A present for you."

It felt like I was standing on roller skates, my knees were trembling so badly. Looking down, I discovered my navy shorts had split from mid hip to hem on the right seam during my fall. Lacy black underpants were visible, along with a swath of blinding white skin that the sun never saw.

Mortification lit my cheeks.

This couldn't be happening to me.

I was a sensible woman.

A pillar of the community.

I did not wear black undies as a rule, and I never flashed my privates in public. I was a good role model for my kids.

I don't know who groaned the loudest, me or Britt Radcliffe.

Britt stared into the woods. "Come out of there, Jonette, or I'm coming in after you."

Jonette squirmed through the hole I'd made. She shot me a wry smile. "Oops."

Oops indeed.

My jaw clenched. Oops was for dropping a penny when you counted out change at the supermarket. Oops was for putting a run in your stockings. Oops didn't cover falling into an area crawling with cops.

"What the hell are you two doing in my accident scene?" Britt asked.

Air whooshed from my lung. My gut had been right on the money. Being right sucked.

My physical equilibrium waffled. Officer Wagner strengthened his grip on my arms. I fought the encroaching mental fog. I needed a clear head to talk myself out of this mess. Although my mouth was so dry I didn't think I could even croak a word out right now.

Jonette recoiled from Britt's question. "I didn't do it." She raised both hands in surrender. "Cleo had to see what was going on. I followed her. That's all."

I groaned again. "Thanks a lot, Jonette."

"Didn't I tell you to go home and stay out of trouble?" Britt's angry gaze locked on me.

I nodded my head and hoped for the best.

"Then why are you here?" he growled.

"I needed to know what all the fuss was about."

"Why didn't you wait and read it in tomorrow's paper like the rest of the world? Why contaminate my crime scene?"

"Cut us some slack here, beefcake, and call your muscle-bound friend off of Cleo." Jonette dug her index finger into Britt's chest. "It was an accident that Cleo fell through the thicket."

Tendons strained in Britt's neck. Clearly, our fate hinged on his goodwill. "If you let us go, we promise to stay out of your way," I said. "We didn't mean to intrude."

Britt considered my impassioned plea for a second. Then, he growled at the officers behind us. "Cuff 'em."

I gasped as metal bands secured my wrists. My face itched, and a stray strand of hair tangled in my eyelashes. Could I do anything about it?

No.

Between the unyielding cuffs around my wrists and the beefy hand gripping my forearm, I was pretty well stuck. I blinked away my tears. We'd pushed Britt too far, and he'd snapped. Brand-new problems tumbled through my head.

How much jail time would I serve for contaminating his crime scene? Would I have to submit to a body cavity search? I quaked with fear.

Britt caught Wagner's eye. "Escort them out the front way, Wagner. Make sure everyone sees them in handcuffs before you turn them loose." Britt turned to me, his granite face cold and harsh. His sharp teeth flashed before my eyes. "If you do this again, Cleo, I will arrest you for obstructing a police investigation. Consider this your one and only warning."

Wagner shoved us forward.

I stumbled into motion, doing my best not to inhale the thick miasma of death clogging the parking lot. Like a sponge, my senses registered each environmental cue, from the pungent smell of crushed leaves in my hair to the trickle of blood down my leg to the heat boiling up from the asphalt pavement.

Adrenaline surged into my bloodstream, demanding release. Trussed up like a Thanksgiving turkey, I couldn't fight or run. I glanced over at the draped object, my unfortunate curiosity the only outlet for all that energy.

Who was under that tarp?

A glittering object to the left of the tarp caught my eye. I squinted to identify it and wished I hadn't. A chorus of oh-Gods shrilled through my head.

There was no mistaking the gold-sequined sandal on the grassy lawn. That flashy shoe belonged to a woman I knew well, a woman whose ancestors had founded Trinity Episcopal. A woman with enough blue blood to start her own social register.

My empty stomach twitched, turned, and heaved. The hairs on the back of my neck electrified, and my heart hammered in my ears. I couldn't feel my feet strike the ground, though when I looked down my legs were moving.

Run, my subconscious urged. *Get as far away from here as you can.* I strained forward, but a two-hundred-pound tether held me to a turtle's crawl. My lungs burned.

We passed the back entry into the Sunday school and strolled under the portico entrance of the parish hall. With each step, my body grew heavier. Everything blurred together like an impressionist painting. I tripped over the uneven sidewalk, startling my frozen lungs into action.

Air.

I needed air.

The sea of swimming faces parted to let us through. Prying eyes penetrated my soundless bubble. A car horn blared from down the street, and I jumped. Behind me, overloud laughter pealed above the murmured voices. Were they laughing at me?

"What's this?" Joan stepped out of her beauty shop, scissors in one hand, a black comb in the other. With her short, razored haircut, dark coloration, and ruffled sundress, she looked part elf, part gypsy, and thoroughly angry.

"Police brutality." Jonette tried to wrest free from our beefy captor. He held fast to the squirming tangerine dynamo.

"The long arm of the law finally caught up with you?" The mayor stepped in our path and sneered at Jonette. In his dark suit, white shirt, and narrow red tie, Darnell Reynolds looked like a permanent advertisement for the Fourth of July.

Jonette's chin shot up in the air.

Darnell waggled a pudgy finger in my face. "I told you to watch the company you keep, Cleo."

"It was an accident," I explained, humiliation and embarrassment heating my chilled skin, triggering a shudder. The body tremor knocked me off balance again, and I would have fallen without Officer Wagner holding me up.

"Step aside, sir," Officer Wagner said to Darnell. The mayor oozed out of our way.

"Let them go." Buck sounded breathless after running across the street from the gas station. Grease dotted his thin face, hands, and jeans. "If you arrest my accountant, who'll do my taxes? And the Tavern wouldn't be the same without Jonette."

Officer Wagner maintained silence.

My personal trainer, Evan Hodges, hove into view. His blond curls were the constant envy of someone with straw-straight hair like me. His white running gear accented his sculpted and tanned body. Masculine approval blazed in his eyes. "Never figured you as the black lace type, Cleo. Nice."

My ears steamed. "There's a lot you don't know about me, Evan." Appalled, I wished I could rescind those spoken words. Tears brimmed in my eyes.

Oh, dear. Evan. That mound back there was his mother. And he didn't know. I wished I didn't know. I couldn't look at him again for fear of what else might rocket out of my mouth. Clamping my jaw shut, I trudged onward.

Hammers pounded in my head. My torn shorts flapped in a sudden gust of wind. I counted ten pairs of sandals, six sets of sneakers, two pairs of pumps, and four wing-tipped Oxfords on my march of shame.

Officer Wagner halted beyond the crowd and unlocked both sets of cuffs. "Scram."

He didn't have to tell me twice. Ignoring the pins-and-needles sensation in my arms, I clamped one hand over my torn shorts and caught Jonette's eye. "Let's get out of here."

"Roger that," she said.

Flashes of pain radiated from the skin abrasions on my knees with every forward step. If a sidewalk crack opened up, I would gladly slither right down into another universe. Britt had made his point. I'd never fall into another crime scene.

I snuck a glance at Jonette. Did she see the gold sandal? Did she know that Mama's archrival was under that tarp in the parking lot?

Could I tell her what I'd seen, or would that make everything worse? Jonette shared no love for Erica, but would she blame Mama? I hated that I had doubts about Mama. If only she hadn't been acting so odd lately. What a mess.

Jonette's car sputtered to life, and she executed a hasty U-turn on Main Street. "You know something." She punched me in the arm. "What is it? What do you know?"

I shoved my fingers through my tangled hair. I decided to keep my suspicions to myself. "The whole world saw me in black underwear and handcuffs."

My friend smirked. "You swore you'd never be caught dead in that black lingerie. Now I know you're all talk."

"I had an underwear emergency this morning." My nose twitched. "These were the only clean pair in my drawer."

The pounding in my head intensified. That gold sandal tap-danced into my thoughts. I shuddered. "I don't feel right."

"Me, neither. And that rat-faced weasel got in my face and implied bad things about me."

In the past, Britt gave me the benefit of the doubt. For him to act otherwise was out of character. Even though I was still angry with Britt, I wouldn't let Jonette disparage him. "Britt was doing his job."

"Britt's Mister Straight-Arrow all right, but I wasn't talking about him. He's not a rat-faced weasel. Darnell is. And I'm going to get him back. He's had it in for me since day one, and I'm sick and tired of his snide remarks."

Relief warred with bewilderment in my head. "Darnell is a total jerk."

When Jonette's car slowed to pull into my gravel driveway, I breathed easier. I was home. I would get a cup of hot tea and relax and figure everything out. But before I could gather my purse to hop out of the car, Charlie's sleek black BMW edged in right beside us in Mama's empty spot.

I closed my eyes and groaned. I needed peace and quiet, not an ex-husband asking questions. "Wonderful. Just wonderful. Why don't I take a sharp stick and poke myself in the eye?"

"Because it would hurt like hell," Jonette said. "We'll get rid of him."

Woodenly, I stumbled from the car. The shortest distance between two points is a straight line, so I glued my gaze to the front door and marched forward. The only silver lining in this was that the girls weren't home. Today was the first day of school, so I had the afternoon to come up with a plausible explanation for my behavior.

I swallowed hard. I could explain my black underwear. I could even explain being cuffed. But I couldn't explain what had happened to Erica Hodges.

"Clee, you're hurt," Charlie said, his voice softening as he followed me inside the house.

Traitorous tears welled up in my eyes.

Not now.

Sampson women were strong. They did not run from trouble. Mama had drummed that into me from the cradle. Those words haunted me, and I shivered. Was Mama in trouble? Had she stared it down the throat? Why was she being so secretive?

I couldn't fix Mama's troubles until I got myself right. "Nothing that antiseptic and a few bandages won't fix." I busied myself filling the tea kettle with water. My hands steadied, but my insides quivered like pudding. Charlie's familiar masculine scent wafted over, bringing with it a confusing glut of memories. I steeled myself against them.

Charlie was just my size, the same five-foot-six height, same slight build. I knew exactly how blue his eyes went when we made love. I'd traced the freckles on his face and arms so often I could map them in my sleep.

After he cheated on me, I put our closeness in the trash where it belonged. No matter how much I wanted comfort, I didn't want his version of it.

He headed for the cabinet that served as our household first-aid cupboard, but Jonette beat him to it. "I get to be the nurse," she said, snagging the Inspector Gadget lunch box of supplies.

Charlie's voice cracked with intensity. "Give me that. She's my wife."

"No, she's not." Jonette cradled the blue box and motioned me to the kitchen table. "She's my best friend, and I'm taking care of her."

His face contorted. His hands fisted at his sides. "Dammit, Cleo. I want to help."

"I don't need your help." I flinched as Jonette dabbed antiseptic on my cuts and scratches.

Charlie hovered over me. "What happened? Did Britt do this to you?"

His closeness irritated me more than the stinging antiseptic. "Leave Britt out of this," I grumped. "I fell through a bush."

"Are you sure you're all right? Should I take the girls this afternoon so you can rest?"

"Go back to work. I'm fine. I can handle the girls." Charlie would seize control in a heartbeat. The only way to win was to freeze him out of my private life. Easy in concept, harder to do in person.

Charlie's gaze snagged on my ripped shorts. His gaze heated. "Since when did you start wearing black underwear?"

The pounding in my head intensified. "I will not discuss my underwear choices with you."

He drew closer, and I resisted the urge to tug my shorts back together. He'd seen it all before. The only thing new was the underpants.

His fingers stroked the top of the ladder-back chair next to me. "Very nice. Buck didn't mention black panties when he called me at the bank."

I'd wondered how Charlie had gotten here so quickly. "Buck called you?"

The kettle whistled, and Jonette tossed in the tea. She took down three mugs, even though Charlie never drank hot tea.

Charlie's fingers tightened on the chair. "He wasn't the only one. I swear it's getting so that as soon as I hear there's trouble,

I know you're in the middle of it. It's not safe to have you living here in town, Clee. I want you and the girls to move back home with me."

We'd had this discussion before. Charlie was quite intelligent about banking practices, but he was absolutely dense when it came to his chances of winning me back. In his mixed-up mind, it was a matter of time until I caved. I waved off his concern. "Forget it. I will never move back into that house."

"Yeah." Jonette stepped between the two of us. "Forget it."

Charlie glared at me over the top of Jonette's head. "Call off your pit bull, Cleo."

Jonette's interference had riled him. Too bad. The volatile moods of Charlie Jones were no longer my concern. My priorities consisted of my children, my mother, Jonette, and my house. My business came next. Then Rafe. And my dog. Charlie was no longer in my top five. He wasn't even in my top ten.

I laid my palms flat on the table. "I'm okay. My skinned knees will heal. So will my pride. You've got to step back, Charlie. You've got to move on. I have."

Something in my expression must have told him not to push his luck any further. If nothing else, our divorce had caused Charlie to master the strategic retreat. "You're overwrought. We'll continue this conversation later." He ducked around Jonette to kiss me. I turned my cheek just in time.

After Charlie left, I swapped my ruined shorts for a pair of elastic-waist gym shorts in the laundry room. Jonette and I carried our tea to the living room. I sat long-ways on the couch with my feet up and contemplated her pristine appearance. "How come you aren't scratched up?"

Jonette's foot tapped rapidly on the Oriental carpet beneath her wingback chair. "Because I didn't dive through the thicket or slide my face across a rock bed. I didn't mean to give us away. I only wanted a better view. Are you sure you're okay?"

The steam from my tea infiltrated the chaos in my head. I inhaled deeply of the soothing moisture. "I'm fine."

Jonette gulped her tea. She crossed and uncrossed her legs. Finally she said, "I'm with Charlie on this one. You don't look so good."

A golden sandal the size of a two-story building winged through my thoughts. Dread tangoed through my pores. This is what came of keeping secrets. Problems assumed astronomical proportions. "I can't get that image out of my mind."

"Me, neither," Jonette said. "And I'm going to do something about it right now." She tore out of the house as if the hounds of hell were nipping at her heels.

CHAPTER 3

I scraped my jaw up off the floor as my front door slammed behind Jonette. How bizarre. I'd been concealing my worries. Now it appeared that Jonette had secrets, too. What was so private that she couldn't tell her best friend?

Had she driven like a lunatic over to the church this morning and then pushed me into the crime scene on purpose? Did she have a death wish? Had I offended her in some way? What?

This whole day seemed fun house carnival weird, without the fun. Everything felt distorted. Unreal. Like I'd been stretched thin and then squashed flat. No matter which way I turned, the view was skewed.

Why was this happening? My life had finally settled into a decent routine. I loved the normalcy of knowing what happened next. But I hated this nerve-jangling, skin-crawling, upset-stomach, tension-headache feeling I was having right now.

Jonette's jarring behavior added another discordant note in a symphony of strangeness. I couldn't explain her irrational actions anymore than I could fathom Erica's death.

Where was Mama?

She wasn't here, where she was supposed to be. She wasn't with Muriel and Francine, or I would have seen her at Trinity Episcopal. Her car should've been parked in our driveway, and she should've been sitting in our office out back. But she wasn't.

Mama was unaccounted for, and Erica was dead.

Were the two events related?

I smelled the fear on my breath, felt the fright diffuse through my body like carbon monoxide, stupefying my brain. It wasn't a stretch for me to imagine Mama had been reckless enough to mow Erica down with her Olds. Their decades-long antagonism had reached a critical point with Monday's confrontation. Why?

I needed to know.

All I had in the way of data was a series of unrelated events. No Mama. Crazy Jonette. Dead Erica. Handcuffed me. Lousy golf. And that was just the morning.

I'd planned to work this afternoon, but my frazzled brain couldn't do simple arithmetic much less accounting. Neither my thoughts nor my trembling hands would settle. But restless energy wouldn't allow me to mope around all day.

So I cleaned house. The kitchen floor gleamed. I cooked, too. Simmered down a pot of fresh tomatoes into a thick, rich spaghetti sauce.

After I finished with the downstairs bathroom, I stood listening to the sighs and creaks in this old house. I couldn't remember the last time this place had been so quiet. This house usually brimmed with four females and a large dog.

The dog.

A tremor of unease flickered down my spine. Where the heck was the dog? Normally she shadowed my every move. Was she ill? Or even worse, in the throes of early labor? Jonette and Lexy were supposed to oversee the whelping. Not me.

I peeled off my yellow latex gloves and dashed up the carpeted stairs, praying there wouldn't be a litter of puppies in my bedroom. My prayers were answered. Only, I didn't like the answer.

I opened my mouth to yell and squeaked instead. The carnage stopped me cold, shot my pulse through the roof. Never in my life could I have imagined such a mess. My hand covered my gaping mouth. I couldn't bring myself to step across the threshold.

Snowy white feathers from my lightweight goose-down comforter spilled off the bed, littering my dresser, my closet. In the current from the ceiling fan, eddies of weightless feathers swirled along the wooden floor. My good sheets, four-hundred-thread-count satiny-soft deluxe sheets, were ripped to shreds. Trails of dried dog drool adorned my beautiful maple headboard.

If I were a cartoon character, the top of my head would have popped off, my eyes would have bulged out, and twin jets of steam would have blasted out of my ears. Rage boiled up out of a dark place deep inside me. "Bad dog!"

Madonna opened one eye, but she didn't move from atop my bed. Her paws curled down in the pillow-soft mattress top. I was so mad I could spit nails. My fingers flexed in anticipation of lifting the jumbo pooch and shaking her. "Get off my bed, Madonna. You're in big trouble."

No response. Feathers took flight as I stomped into my bedroom. I tugged on Madonna's leather collar. "Get. I mean it. Get off my bed."

Madonna didn't budge. She looked mortally wounded that I would raise my voice at her. My gaze strayed to her very large stomach, and I tamped down a wave of guilt. I tugged on her collar again. "Pregnant or not, you're a bad dog. You're sleeping in the laundry room from now on, you hear me? Get up. Get out!"

Madonna exhaled heavily, sending another flurry of snowy feathers into flight. My fists balled at my side in impotent fury. I wanted her out of my bed right now. But she outweighed me, and her center of gravity was low. And she seemed to understand that possession was nine-tenths of the law.

Feathers whirled around my face. I batted them away ineffectively. In frustration, I picked up a mangled corner of my pillow and swatted the mattress next to Madonna. "Dammit. Get up! Get off my bed. I'm taking you to the pound right this instant."

Footfalls pounded up the stairs. "Mom! Don't swear at the dog." Lexy rushed in and hurled herself on the bed, wrapping her arms protectively around the short-haired Saint Bernard. Like that would keep me from removing the dog.

"That dog is in serious trouble." I gestured at the feather-filled room. "Do you see what she did?"

"It's okay, Mom," Lexy said in a soothing tone. "Really. It's okay."

I unclenched my jaw. "This is a monumental disaster. I gave this dog food and shelter. See how she repays me?"

"Mom, get a grip," Lexy said. "If you'd read any of the whelping stuff, you'd know Madonna did exactly what she was supposed to do."

I'd been meaning to read those slick pamphlets and the stack of Internet articles on doggie childbirth that Jonette and Lexy were studying, but I hadn't gotten around to it. I'd been through childbirth myself. I knew firsthand what labor and delivery felt like.

I glared at Lexy.

Lexy cooed at the dog and petted her. Madonna sniffed copiously and stirred herself to lick Lexy's hand. The effort exhausted her. Madonna immediately lay her head back down in the tangle of ruined bedding and moaned.

In a twinge of sympathy, I remembered how the last month of my pregnancies seemed to go on forever. "Is she in labor right now?"

Lexy gently massaged Madonna's bulging stomach. "I can't tell. Did you take her temperature? It hadn't dropped as of last night."

My hands clenched into tight fists. "No, I did not take her temperature. I came up here to check on her and found my bed destroyed. Taking the dog's temperature never crossed my mind."

Lexy hopped off the bed, a trail of feathers floating in her wake. "I'll be right back. Don't do anything, Mom."

As if I could do anything. The dog wouldn't budge. My bed was in shreds, and my mother was missing. My head pounded fiercely.

"Holy crap!" Charla dashed into the room, feathers swirling and catching in her thick red hair. "What's going on?"

"Mom wants to get rid of Madonna." Lexy returned with the thermometer and tended to business.

"No way. She's our dog, Mom." Charla wedged herself between me and the dog. "You said we could keep her. You can't get rid of her because of a little mess."

"She destroyed my bed." My voice squeaked again. If I didn't calm down, I would have a heart attack. Not good.

This was a power struggle. Power was all about control, and right now, Madonna controlled the bed. She wasn't giving it up, either.

My bed.

Not hers.

I never should have let her sleep with me in the first place. The dog thought she owned the bed, but it was mine. I had only been sharing my bed with her. It wasn't hers. Not by a long shot.

"Well, Lexy?" Feathers flew as I drifted closer. "Is she in labor?"

"No," Lexy said. "Her temperature hasn't dropped."

"Why did she do this?"

"I already told you, Mom. She's nesting. She needs an area to have her puppies."

I pointed over to the inflatable kiddy pool we'd installed in the corner of my bedroom. "Why isn't she nesting over there in the waterproof area? I bought everything on the list. Are you telling me I wasted my hard-earned money?"

"Maybe she wanted to nest here because it smelled like her. Or," Lexy brightened, "because it smelled like you."

I grabbed my hair and yanked on it. "Why would she need her puppy box to smell like me?"

"Dogs are particular about scents," Lexy said. "Madonna chose you over Charla or me or Grammy. She likes your scent the best."

I didn't ask for preferential doggie treatment. "She has a funny way of showing it. Couldn't she like me without shredding my comforter and ripping up my sheets?"

"I'll clean it up, Mom," Lexy offered.

"No. I'll clean it up." Charla jerked her thumb toward her chest. "I'm the oldest. I take complete responsibility. I'll pay for your new sheets, too."

"Madonna destroyed hundreds of dollars' worth of bedding." To my horror, my voice shrilled to wicked-witch level. "It will be years before you save up that much allowance. This is a disaster."

"Lexy can bunk with me, and you can have her room." Charla crossed the room to hug her sister.

Lexy clung to Charla. "Please, Mom. I'll help Charla raise the money. Madonna didn't mean to be destructive. She's a victim of her instincts."

The only victim in this room was me. I took a deep breath, then another. My head cleared a little, and I realized something special had happened. Charla and Lexy had united for a common goal, an unprecedented event. They were willing to bunk together so that I had a bed with sheets on it.

My anger faded. I had no spare set of sheets. If I stuck to a tight budget this month, I could afford clearance-sale sheets. A look of resignation must have passed across my face.

Charla declared victory by hurling herself into my arms. Feathers twirled around us. "Thanks, Mom. You won't regret this. Everything will work out. You'll see."

"Yeah, thanks, Mom." Lexy stayed by Madonna's side just in case I still thought to get rid of the dog.

This was a battle I couldn't win. Not without removing the dog. And, with Erica's death weighing on my thoughts, there had been enough loss for one day. "I want this mess cleaned up before dinner."

I left them to it.

My stomach growled as I stirred the mouth-watering spaghetti sauce. I started the noodles for dinner. Upstairs, the vacuum cleaner roared to life. A minor victory, but a victory all the same. The girls felt responsible enough for the dog to clean up her mess. Good info to file away for when the puppies came.

I shuddered. I wasn't ready for puppies. This afternoon had shown me that. I'd never had the urge to chew up sheets at any time prior to the onset of labor. Clearly I was ignorant of the doggie version of birth. I'd better get with the program. I pulled an article on whelping out of the stack on the kitchen table and sat down to read it while the noodles cooked.

I'd barely started reading about loss of doggie appetite and excessive licking of personal areas when Mama staggered in. Not even the shoulder pads of her double-breasted mauve blazer could disguise the droop of her frame. With her heavy step, glassy eyes, and pale skin, I worried she was having a heart attack.

My own heart nearly stopped. I leapt to my feet and raced to her side. "Mama! Come sit down. Let me fix you a glass of water. Where's your nitroglycerin?"

"My heart's fine. Forget the water. Gimme a shot of Jack Daniels."

It wasn't her heart. I exhaled a little easier. But why the booze? Mama didn't drink. We had a bottle of Jack Daniels left over from when Daddy was alive. The bottle hadn't been opened in the three years since he'd passed.

The wires of the universe must have crossed. What else would explain the strange events of today? "What happened?" I asked as I seated her at the table. "Where have you been all day?"

Mama sat soldier straight in a kitchen chair and waved off my questions. "I don't want to talk about it."

"Mama, you were gone for hours. I've been worried sick." I reached behind the cookbooks over the microwave and found the dusty liquor bottle.

"I've been looking after myself for years. You can't shoehorn me into a nursing home."

Clever of her to try to distract me, but I was onto her tricks. And I had guilt in my arsenal. "I thought you were home keeping an eye on the dog while I golfed this morning."

"That dog's got better sense than any of us. She can look after herself. I had an errand."

I poured out a straight shot of Jack Daniels and set it before her. Mama belted it back like water. She shoved the shot glass over to me for a refill.

I sat down beside her and stared her straight in the eye. I wanted answers. "Where have you been, Mama?"

She eyed her empty shot glass. "Minding my own business, that's what."

Her color was coming back. The liquor must have helped. Perhaps another shot of Jack would loosen her tongue the rest of the way. I handed her a refill and tried again. "Tell me what's going on."

Mama glared at me. "It's none of your beeswax, that's what."

She was hiding something. "Mama, the police responded to a call at Trinity Episcopal Church today. There was a fatal accident in the parking lot."

I watched her closely, hoping against hope that her secret wasn't related to the gruesome incident. To my relief, Mama's rigid posture never waivered. She seemed to be braced for bad news. "Erica Hodges is dead," I said as gently as possible.

Mama's shoulders shook with emotion. Her eyes brimmed with tears. Great gulping sobs wracked her slender frame.

I wrung my hands. God, I'd done it now. I'd made Mama cry. She never cried.

Well, almost never. She'd cried when Daddy died. I remembered feeling helpless then, too.

Her depth of feeling shook me. While I thought she'd have a reaction to the news, I hadn't expected this outpouring of grief for a woman she despised. But she wasn't faking this. I'd never seen her so distraught, so vulnerable.

My heart ached for her. Sympathetic tears brimmed in my eyes. I had to do something. I rose, grabbed several tissues, and put them in her hand. I patted her cushioned shoulder, wishing I could do more.

Mama smashed the tissues into a tight wad in her fisted hand stared out the window. Tears ran down her rouged cheeks and dripped off her quivering chin.

"I'm so sorry." I blinked back my tears, wishing I knew what was wrong. Were her tears a guilty sign? I didn't believe it. I couldn't believe such a thing of my mother, could I?

I heaved in a tremulous breath. "It's okay, Mama. Everything will be all right. I'm so sorry to have been the bearer of bad news."

Mama stirred to blot her face with the tissues. Her icy gaze chilled me to my core. "Erica Hodges was a miserable excuse for a human being. I'm glad that bitch is dead."

My head recoiled as if I'd been struck. The stark pain in Mama's voice knocked me off-balance. I hardly knew what would come out of her mouth next. Britt's advice to talk some sense into Mama rang in my ears. "Mama, you don't mean that."

"Yes, I do." Mama knocked back the second shot of whiskey and set the shot glass down with a sharp crack. I looked twice to make sure the glass was intact. "I don't care for any supper tonight," Mama said. "I want to go to bed now."

I leaned toward her. "Mama, we need to talk."

"I don't want to talk about that vile woman." Mama banged her fist on the table, scattering my reading material. "I hope I never hear her name again."

I glanced at the digital clock on the microwave. It was barely five o'clock. Way too early for bed. "I made spaghetti."

Mama arched a perfectly drawn eyebrow. "Boring, normal spaghetti?"

"Thick, homemade, stick to your ribs spaghetti," I countered, straightening the stack of whelping literature that was on the table.

"No, thanks, I'm not hungry."

Mama wobbled as she stood. Could be nerves. Could be the booze. Whatever the reason, she wasn't falling on my watch. I took her elbow and guided her upstairs to her bedroom.

She halted just over the threshold, blocking my way. "I can take it from here." With that, Mama closed her door firmly in my face.

Her secretive attitude irked me, but Mama had her own way of doing things. I cruised down to my room to check on the cleanup. The feathers were gone for the most part, and my ruined sheets lined the inflatable kiddy pool we'd set up for the birth event. Two garbage bags bulged with the remains of my down comforter and pillows.

Charla walked in with a pillow. "Here, Mom. Take my extra pillow."

I'd tried to get her to throw out that rock hard lump last year, but she refused to part with the pillow because it smelled just right. "Thanks. Where's the dog?"

Charla tossed the pillow on the bed, then posed with her hand on her hip. "Lexy took Madonna for a walk. Lexy doesn't get it, Mom. I'm oldest. I get first dibs on the dog."

The girls were acting normal again. The universe was on track after all. I managed a tight smile. "I hear you, dear. She'll get it right someday. Meanwhile, I could use your help setting the table."

Charla rolled her eyes. "How about if I make blue garlic toast to go with the spaghetti?"

Mama had been teaching the girls to cook. Adventurously, I might add. After the day I'd had, blue garlic toast sounded like just the thing. "Sure."

Charla beat me to the kitchen, not that it was a race, but that was her way. I set the table and captured Lexy when she returned. "Feed the dog and wash up for dinner, Lex."

We sat down to eat. Charla noticed the empty place. "Where's Grammy?"

Unless I missed my guess, Grammy was sleeping off two straight shots of whiskey. I cleared my throat. "She's resting in her room. She doesn't want dinner."

"It's because you cooked, isn't it?" Charla asked.

I wasn't so calm that flip remarks about my cooking would just run off my back. "My homemade spaghetti sauce isn't boring. Skipping dinner was her choice."

A car door slammed. Madonna woofed. *What now?* I wondered as I answered the crisp rap at the back door.

My reluctance turned into a broad smile as I recognized my visitor. Six feet of athletic perfection with lady-killer brown eyes, strawberry-blond hair, and a smile that could charm the pants off any woman. I sighed dreamily. Here was my reward for all the strangeness of today. "Rafe!"

I stepped outside to greet him, pulling the door shut behind me. Rafe Golden swept me into a wondrous kiss that had me wishing we were alone and that the night was young.

"Hey, Red. You taste very Italian," Rafe murmured against my lips. "My favorite."

With sincere regret, I broke off the kiss. "Come on in and have some spaghetti."

He frowned as if he suddenly remembered another engagement. "You left your car at the club today. Is anything wrong?"

"Well—" I stopped as soon as I started. How much could I tell him without sounding like a crazy woman? Madonna scratched at the door and whimpered piteously. "It's a long story. Why don't we eat first?"

"Lead on." Rafe squared his shoulders.

Was he bracing for the odd food that normally graced our table? Or did my whacky family have him worried? Madonna quivered all over when I opened the door. She nearly licked the skin off my hand. "It's okay, Madonna. I'm not leaving you."

Rafe and the girls exchanged stilted greetings as I fixed Rafe a plate. I kept hoping the girls would warm up to Rafe, but they barely tolerated him. To Rafe's credit, he didn't blanch at blue garlic toast or my girls' frosty welcome.

"Madonna's traumatized from you yelling at her earlier," Charla said when I rejoined them at the table.

"Is not." Lexy twirled sauce-free noodles around her fork. "She's got separation anxiety. That's what the whelping literature says about bitches. They attach to one person and become out of sorts if that person isn't available."

"Mama, Lexy said the b-word," Charla said.

" 'Bitch' isn't a bad word." Lexy's pert nose went up in the air. "Breeders use the term to indicate female dogs."

I wasn't crazy about my thirteen-year-old daughter getting in the habit of using the word "bitch." Bad enough that Mama used it to describe Erica. "As an accountant, I'm a fan of both precision and accuracy. But I agree with Charla. Let's avoid using that term."

Rafe's plate was empty. "Would you like some more?" I asked.

He nodded wearily. "Sure. I didn't eat all day."

"Whyever not?" Charla asked, forgetting for a moment she'd been ignoring him. "Are you on a diet?"

"I don't eat breakfast, and the shop was slammed at lunchtime," Rafe said.

"You had that charitable tournament this afternoon, didn't you?" I spooned out another generous helping of spaghetti.

"It was a zoo," Rafe said between mouthfuls. "In addition to getting the carts out, we had to do the pairings at the last minute. The organizer was a no-show."

"Who left you hanging like that?" I asked. With the blue crusts from my garlic toast, I sopped up the last bit of red sauce from my plate.

Rafe paused with another forkful of spaghetti in midair. "Bud Flook. I thought for sure he wouldn't miss this event. He's been planning this tournament for six months."

How odd. Bud was an avid golfer, a contemporary of my father's. We'd golfed with Bud many times over the years. I couldn't imagine Bud missing a golf tournament for any reason.

Rafe lounged back in his chair after emptying his plate for the second time. He shot me a pointed glance. "What happened today?"

I glanced over to see girls were hanging on our every word. "Didn't you hear already?"

"Nothing like getting it straight from the horse's mouth." He flushed. "Not that you're a horse, I didn't mean that. I meant

53

that you were there so I can get an eyewitness accounting."

"It was an accident! I swear." My hands waved in the air. "No one would have even known we were there if Jonette hadn't pushed me. We didn't mean to fall into the crime scene."

Three sets of eyes latched on to me. Rafe's mild amusement vanished. Too late, I realized he'd been asking me about my lousy golf score. He'd probably been insulted that my score was so high when he'd given me so many free lessons.

"What crime scene?" Lexy stared at me with doglike fixation.

I swallowed thickly. I might as well tell them the truth. God knows what they would hear at school tomorrow. "There was an accident in the church parking lot. The police roped off the entrance to Trinity Episcopal, so Jonette and I scooted around back to see what had happened. It wasn't our fault. In fact, it was downright embarrassing."

"What have you done, Mama?" Charla put down her fork.

I started laughing in spite of my red face. I couldn't help myself. If anyone was going to be embarrassed by my behavior, it should be me, not my kids. "Jonette and I were forcibly removed from an off-limits area in handcuffs. And my black underwear showed through my ripped shorts. I couldn't hold my shorts together because of the handcuffs. Then little Eddie Wagner, I used to babysit him before he grew up to be a cop, paraded us through the assembled crowd with cuffs on."

Charla groaned and clapped a hand to her cheek. "How could you do this to me?"

"You went to jail?" Lexy asked.

I shook my head. "No jail. Only a few minutes of handcuff time on Main Street."

Rafe's narrowed gaze didn't offer much hope that he approved of my clandestine activity. Not that I thought he would approve, but still. How could he blame me for what happened?

"It was an accident," I reiterated. "We didn't mean to cause any trouble."

"I am never leaving this house again," Charla said, her wavy red hair forming a thick curtain over her woeful brown eyes.

CHAPTER 4

We rode with the top down. Honeysuckle-scented wind whipped my shoulder-length hair around my face. The cooler air of twilight had me burrowing deeper into the sumptuous leather seats. Usually a ride in Rafe's luxurious convertible had me purring with delight. But each rotation of the tires added to my unease.

Rafe drove his high-performance car with single-minded precision. Trouble was, that's all he was doing. His eyes stayed on the road, his hands on his side of the wood-grained console. He hadn't touched me once.

He had every right to be mad at me. I had behaved like someone half my age. But he'd known I wasn't suave and sophisticated from the start. I hadn't misled him. I stared straight ahead at the headlight beams, but I was too conscious of the man beside me. What was he thinking? Why didn't he say something?

His brooding silence got to me. "I shot a sixty-two today," I blurted out. "I lost strokes around the green. Those bunkers were brutal, and me with no sand wedge. The greens kept getting faster and faster. I couldn't read a putt to save my life. Good thing I know an excellent golf teacher."

Rafe shot me a stern look. "Don't think you can distract me with flowery golf talk. How did you end up in handcuffs?"

I squirmed in my seat. His crazy meter would peg off-scale if I told him I'd been acting on a feeling. Accountants like me went on hard facts, and that was how I operated, for the most part. "I'm not a criminal. I was curious. I acted on that curiosity and got caught. That's the whole story."

Rafe stopped behind my Volvo sedan in the empty golf course parking lot. "Curious people do not have nine lives. You can't claim ignorance. You purposefully put yourself in harm's way. Why were you anywhere near a crime scene?"

I shivered at the frosty disapproval in his voice. Had my impulsive actions opened his eyes to the real me? "Believe me, I have had my fill of crime scenes. At the risk of repeating myself, today's incident was an accident."

Rafe released his seat belt and leaned against the interior of his door. Though I could reach over and physically touch him, the emotional gap between us yawned like a fathomless bunker.

Was he breaking up with me? I waited in agony.

"I don't want you to get hurt, Red." His deep voice rumbled through me.

Was that catch in his voice concern, pity, or control? My Sampson pride sparked. "I can take care of myself."

"Touchy little thing, aren't you?"

What kind of a sexist remark was that? A warning voice in my head whispered to tread cautiously, but I'd already used up today's patience and tomorrow's too. "What's your point?"

Rafe absently fingered the steering wheel. "Your safety. It's important to me. It tears me up inside to think of something bad happening to you."

Oh.

I inhaled slowly and got a thick dose of male and expensive leather. The potent combination fogged my thoughts. I'd nearly blown it because I thought he was pulling a Charlie on me. Rafe wasn't Charlie. He didn't want to control me. He valued my safety.

Honeyed warmth spread through me. "Thanks. I care about

your safety, too."

There. We'd declared an interest in each other's safety. Not exactly a declaration of undying love, but close. Or at least, I hoped it was. My feelings for Rafe ran deep these days.

Those feelings brought joy and uncertainty, giddiness and despair. Rafe seemed comfortable in this middle place between dating and commitment, but I wasn't so sanguine. I wanted more.

Rafe didn't talk about his feelings. He talked about golf and cars. He tolerated my family's lukewarm reception of him. His hobby was women, and for all intents and purposes, I was his current hobby. Not exactly the stuff of lasting commitment.

His gaze warmed. "I know how you can reassure me that you're okay."

The pheromone level in the car spiked abruptly. I fingered my shirt collar, allowing the sudden heat of my body to escape before it gave me away. Don't get me wrong. Spontaneity has its place. But the girls knew what time I left.

"Rain check?" I asked.

He stroked the side of my face, practically igniting my skin. "Come home with me. It's early yet."

The sharp edge of desire jabbed at my sense of duty. "For you, maybe. I've got two kids and a pregnant dog counting the minutes until I return."

Need and something much more primitive flashed across his face. "Kiss me goodnight?"

I slid across the leather seat and into his open arms. I'd never done it in the front seat of a car, but his sensual kiss had me thinking there had to be a way.

He blazed a trail of fevered kisses down the column of my neck. Entranced, I strained upward to meet his touch. Rafe's passion stirred needs buried deep within me, needs I'd thought to never again have filled after my divorce. I ran my hands through his hair and held his precious head close. My heart fluttered wildly.

"You're driving me crazy," Rafe murmured against my tingling skin. "You know that, don't you?"

My senses spiked at the vibration of lips on skin. I wanted this man. Wanted him in my bed. In my life. For better or worse. In sickness and in health.

I was vaguely aware he'd spoken. "What?" My voice sounded husky and full of longing.

"I want more of you," he said. "We never have enough time together."

Time.

We needed it.

I didn't have it.

With that realization, the fizzle went out of my sizzle. Adrenaline still pounded through my bloodstream, urging me on. Where, I didn't know.

The steady pressure from the center console on my hip bone dictated a shift in my position. I eased back slightly and banged my elbow on the steering wheel. The sharp pain lent clarity to my jumbled thoughts.

"There are limits to what I can give, Rafe," I said with resignation. "I have responsibilities. My family depends on me."

His expression hardened.

My voice sounded cold and exact. I winced inwardly. Why couldn't I throw caution to the wind? Why couldn't I say, yes, let's take a cruise together and leave Mama and Charlie to deal with the girls?

The answer to my questions came to me with startling rapidity. I was trapped in my small-town world, hampered by my view of what everyone might say, but more importantly, afraid to step out on that plank all alone and take a chance.

Bottom line, I was a coward.

But I had really good excuses. The best in the world. Saint Cleo would do anything for her family, but she wouldn't grab something she very much wanted because of paralyzing fear.

Wait.

That was the old Cleo.

The new Cleo wasn't afraid of living. The new Cleo had a plan, a cool sophisticated plan. Have the hottest, sexiest affair on record. No emotional entanglements, unless that was what he wanted as well. And there was the rub. The new Cleo was hardwired to be the old Cleo, the woman who gave love and expected commitment.

Until Rafe shared more of his feelings with me, I had to keep my emotional distance from him. Otherwise, I'd lose everything. My self-respect, my honor, and my heart.

Why didn't he say something?

I rushed to fill the void. "You think I don't want more time with you? You think I don't want to run off and have wild sex with you whenever the need strikes? I do. You're a fever that complicates my life."

Oh, God, my hands were waving in the air like a crazy person's. I sat on them.

He stilled. "I'm a fever? Like the flu?"

Crap. I'd shocked him. Better fix it quick. "Not literally. I don't think of you and vomiting in the same breath. Not by a long shot. Look, I don't want to screw this up. And I am feeling pressured tonight, like I'm on the clock because my family is waiting. Can we continue this later?"

He hesitated for an eternity of seconds. I held my breath in the awful silence, wanting the world from him. Was it a false hope?

"How about Friday night?" he asked.

I exhaled slowly, allowing hope to sparkle and twirl and dance. This was Wednesday. I could hold my lust for him in check for two more days. "Friday works for me."

His dark eyes gleamed. On Friday he would fill all of the sensual promises his kiss had implied. Of that I had no doubt.

"I'll pick you up at six. And Cleo?"

"Yes?" I collected my purse and fumbled for the door handle.

"Wear the black lace underwear."

Heat returned to my cheeks instantly. I wasn't that easy. The black panties were supposed to be held in reserve for special occasions. "We'll see. Thanks for the ride."

I fanned myself all the way home. Rafe's kiss lingered on my mind. He wanted me. For some magical, logic-defying reason, he wanted me, Cleopatra Jones.

The thought made me long for a whole drawer full of black lingerie. Not practical, especially when I was living on such a tight budget. I had household items I desperately needed. Like new sheets because the dog ate mine.

I pulled up in my gravel driveway, wishing we were on even footing. I pushed Rafe out of my mind, and my thoughts slid around to Mama's peculiar behavior. Something more was going on in her life, something she'd chosen to keep secret from me.

The events of the day returned in a rush as I locked my car. I ticked them off on my fingers.

One, there had been a vehicular accident at the church. Two, Erica Hodges was dead. Three, Mama had a history of run-ins with Erica Hodges. Four, on Monday I listened to Mama and Erica Hodges exchange insults in public. Five, Mama's whereabouts today were a mystery and her over-the-top behavior even more of a mystery.

I don't know what made me look at her Oldsmobile. Honestly, I don't know why I looked at all. But I did. And then I wished I'd gone straight inside the house and minded my own business.

The motion-detector light on the corner of the house had activated when I pulled into the driveway. The parking pad was now brightly illuminated.

I touched the jagged safety glass of Mama's shattered headlight cover. A suffocating sensation tightened my throat at the large indentation in her not-so-shiny bumper. The hood of her car mounded in the middle, pushed back from the leading edge. This car had hit something.

Or someone.

Dread charged through my veins, taking my breath away. Fear clawed at my heart, dragging me down to a place where I didn't want to go. Dazed and bewildered, I staggered over to my Volvo for support. The hood warmed my cold fingers.

This was very, very bad.

Unthinkable.

The pieces of the puzzle resolved in my head. With each connected piece, the picture became clearer. Mama and Erica. Rivals and combatants. Mama alive. Erica dead. Mama's car damaged. Erica dead.

Even to a rank amateur like me, the evidence pointed to a devastating conclusion. I shook my head in disbelief. This was Mama I was talking about. She was stubborn, opinionated, and bossy, and those were her finer qualities.

Stars twinkled in the night sky overhead. Crickets chirped in the darkness. A light went on in my next-door neighbor's kitchen. A diesel pickup truck rumbled past on Main Street. And I stood beside my mother's damaged car in my driveway.

Ordinary things. Trivial things

But my life wasn't ordinary or trivial any longer.

A cold-blooded killer lived under my roof.

CHAPTER 5

When the door to the outer office of Sampson Accounting finally opened on Thursday, I startled and tipped over the mug of pens on my desk. Annoyed at my clumsiness, I brushed the mess off my ledger and tucked today's newspaper under my arm. "There you are. I was getting worried about you." Madonna followed me to the connecting doorway.

Mama didn't have her usual glow. Her lipstick was crooked, and her moss-green jacket was one button off from top to bottom. Her triple-stranded pearls tangled on her pale neck. Even her helmet of white hair seemed flatter than usual.

"Some days it takes longer to pull body and soul together," Mama said. "But I'm here now. Is there an accounting emergency?"

Judging by her haphazard grooming and tardiness, the news of Erica's death had hit her hard, not that she'd admit it. I could make sure she didn't see our paper, but that wouldn't stop others from telling her about the article.

"Business is slow, the same as yesterday and the day before," I said. "I was concerned about you. The news yesterday shocked and upset me. I thought you might want to take the day off."

Mama squared her notepads and fiddled with her pens. "I can work."

"But you don't have to. I can manage on my own for a few days."

"No way. I skip work and the next thing you know I'll be

shipped off to an old folk's home. There's no law that says you have to retire at sixty-five. I'm still rocking along on all eight cylinders."

"That you are, but one of your acquaintances died yesterday. Even if you didn't like her, it's okay to take time to process your feelings."

"I'm fine."

"Are you?"

"Cut that out, Cleo. I hate it when you do that thing with your eyebrows."

My hands crept up to my face. Nothing seemed amiss. But Mama's fleeting smile gave her away. She'd almost deflected the conversation from herself to me. Almost.

Though I hated to deliver bad news, Mama needed to know what was in this paper. She needed to know before one of her friends called to discuss it. Showing her the paper was the right thing to do. So why did I feel so lousy?

"Take a look at today's paper." I unfolded it on her desk. She paled at the screaming headline, jumped up, and fixed a cup of coffee. Was she running from the news or the truth?

"You have to face this, Mama," I said.

"Maybe I don't want to. Whose side are you on, anyway?"

"Yours, Mama. If you don't want to see it, I can read it aloud."

Mama sniffled. "Suit yourself."

Determined to see this through, I picked up the paper and read the top story aloud to her. "Prominent Civic Leader and Beloved Philanthropist Dead. A vehicular incident behind Trinity Episcopal Church resulted in the death of a fifty-eight-year-old Hogan's Glen woman. Erica Crandall Hodges was pronounced dead at the scene by the county coroner, according to an official spokesperson. Detective Britt Radcliffe is investigating the incident and had no comment at press time.

"Mayor Darnell Reynolds is saddened by our loss. 'I will

personally monitor the investigation,' Reynolds said. 'Erica Hodges was a well-respected member of our community and she will be sorely missed. Erica's unexpected demise leaves a large hole in many of our charitable organizations. Her death will be thoroughly investigated and appropriate measures will be taken to see that justice is served.'

"Erica Crandall Hodges was a direct descendant of Hogan's Glen founder Lucian Crandall. Ms. Hodges was the driving force behind the Crandall Reading Room in the Hogan's Glen Public Library. Anyone who has information about the incident is encouraged to step forward."

Mama circled around me with her steaming coffee. The pungent aroma of strong coffee mixed with her heavy-handed floral perfume to form a cloying yet familiar vapor.

"So?" she asked.

Couldn't she see that a kindergartener could connect the obvious dots from Erica to Mama? Couldn't she see how serious this was? "Britt will ask you questions about Erica's death. What will you tell him?"

Mama set her cup down so fast that black coffee slopped over the rim onto a stack of yellow sticky notes. Her shoulders sagged. "I'll tell him the same thing I told you. Erica Hodges got what she deserved."

I died a little inside. *Please God, let her have an alibi. Let there be a reasonable explanation for the damage to her car.* "That kind of attitude will get you arrested."

"When it comes to Erica Hodges, all I have is attitude. That woman rode on my coattails for nearly forty years. She was a miserable excuse for a human being, and the only reason people tolerated her at all was because of her revered ancestors."

I circled Mama's desk, Madonna at my heels. I'd gotten nowhere with the kid-glove approach. Time to get serious. I didn't want so much as a desk coming between us. "Be that as it may, Erica Hodges had family and friends who cared about her. Britt knows you two quarreled recently. You have to be prepared for his questions. What were you doing when she was killed?"

Mama mopped up the spilled coffee with a handful of paper towels. "Seeing as how I don't know what time she was killed, I can't answer your question."

Can't or wouldn't? She couldn't dissuade me that easily. "I was there for your fight with Erica on Monday. The whole room heard you two go at it." I cleared my throat. "And there's the little matter of your car."

"What about my car?" Mama barred her arms across her formidable chest. The pale green fabric of her suit coat strained at the shoulder seams.

I returned Mama's unblinking stare. "Your bumper and headlight are smashed."

Color flooded Mama's face. "You're making that up. Don't tease me like that." The triple-stranded pearls at Mama's neckline dug into her neck as she swallowed thickly.

I waved her toward the door. "Go look if you don't believe me."

Mama swept past me so fast I got caught in her draft. Madonna and I shadowed her to the driveway. Mama stood with her hands on her hips in the dappled sunlight and studied the damage. Anger then fear flashed across her face.

Her changeable expression reminded me of shock and awe, the military term for a powerful weapons demonstration. Only, Mama looked as if she'd been at the detonation end of the missiles.

"This isn't right," she whispered.

Her shoulders trembled, and her hand clutched at her breast. The color drained from her face. A fresh wave of alarm shot through me as I realized how stressed she was. "Let's get you inside out of this bright sun, Mama." And closer to your heart medication.

I steered her to the rocker in the living room, Madonna padding silently beside us, her belly waddling as she walked. I brought Mama a glass of water and her pills, then sat across from her and waited. Her color slowly returned to normal as she sat motionless in the rocking chair.

Madonna thrust her head in my lap, and I stroked her broad head. Poor Madonna. Her world had been turned upside down twice, once with her owner's death and then again with her pregnancy. Her life would never return to its old familiar routine. Events were sweeping her along in a new direction, one she'd never before envisioned.

I understood completely. I'd finally found a new normal, and now this. I wasn't mentally prepared to deal with Mama killing anyone. Taking a life went against everything she'd ever taught me. I couldn't reconcile her damaged car with what was in my heart. But she could. Or at least, I hoped she could.

I brushed a clump of dog hair off my fingers onto the Oriental carpet. Time for some answers. "How did that happen?" I asked, nodding toward the driveway.

Mama's knuckles gleamed on the padded handles of her rocker. "I have no idea."

Her lips pursed so tight that deep lines ran from her mouth clear back to her ears. I blinked in astonishment at how old and tired she looked. Mama never wrinkled her face like that. She made a point of living a wrinkle-free existence. This was really bad.

"You don't remember hitting anything?" I asked.

"I didn't hit anything."

"You hit something."

"My car hit something."

"Did you loan your car to anyone recently?"

"No."

"Did you notice it was unlocked or parked in a different place?"

"No." Mama regarded me with unblinking brown eyes. "Why are you giving me the third degree over this?"

"Because I can't get a straight answer out of you."

Mama sipped her water. "Erica got me good this time. Even in death she one-upped me."

I shook my head in disbelief. "Are you smoking crack? Do you think she staged her own death? It's not possible."

"Erica hated me."

"I know that, and everyone in this town knows it, too. Let's start over. Where were you Tuesday night?"

"Out."

We were back to that, were we? I stared at Mama, and she stared right back. "Out where?"

Mama's head drooped, and her chin quivered. Whatever she was hiding, it greatly troubled her. Did she run over Erica? The question flashed in my head like a possessed computer cursor.

Another thought occurred to me. Mama had been forgetful and disoriented before Erica died. Was her medication to blame? Could her recent behavior be a side effect of the pills she was taking?

Nah. I picked up her prescriptions from the pharmacy. Her pills and dosage hadn't changed in the last six months. What else would make her behavior change?

An undiagnosed medical condition could explain her odd behavior. What if she was blacking out? That would explain why she didn't know what happened to her car.

If I was right, Mama needed a doctor's attention. I could fix that. I stood abruptly. Madonna whimpered at being dislodged off my leg. "I'm going to get you in to see Doctor Cannon this afternoon."

"I'm not sick." Mama shook her head in defiance. "I don't need a doctor. I won't keep the appointment."

I sank back down on the sofa and recalculated. Just because she wouldn't go see her favorite doctor didn't mean she was healthy. "Don't shut me out, Mama. I want to help."

Nothing. No response. What was she afraid of? I approached the problem from a different direction. "I'm not going to stick you in a nursing home."

Anger flashed across her face with the intensity of a summer thunderstorm. "Damn right you're not. This is my home."

"Why can't you tell me what's wrong?"

Mama seemed fascinated by the whirls in the carpet.

Frustration had me shoving my fists into the sofa cushions. The damage to her car and her unexplained absence were big problems. It irked me that she didn't understand. "Mama, did anyone see you when you were 'out' Tuesday evening?"

She shot me another tight-lipped stare.

My heart sank. Daddy used to say that if it looked like a duck and quacked like a duck, it was probably a duck. Using that logic, Mama might be guilty. My back teeth ground together.

A good daughter wouldn't let her Mama go to jail.

Although I didn't wish ill health on Mama, a medical problem would be a convenient excuse. An illness would provide her with extenuating circumstances and possibly absolve her from any wrongdoing.

Like inadvertently running over Erica Hodges.

How could I work this medical angle?

I'd need a doctor.

I didn't need Mama's permission to talk to Doctor Cannon. Once he heard about her cagey behavior and possible blackout, he'd demand Mama come in for an evaluation. If he changed Mama's medicine, it might be all the ammunition a good lawyer would need to get her off a murder conviction.

"Are we done here?" she asked.

Mama's voice sounded suspiciously fine. My wishful thinking about a medical defense faded. Mama was nobody's fool. She was one sharp cookie, and she'd played on my sympathy.

She'd probably counted on me overreacting and dragging her in for a battery of medical tests. At her age, they were bound to find something wrong if they looked long enough. I had to be strong here. I needed tough love to deal with a slippery Mama.

"No, we aren't done." I sprang to my feet and paced the room. Madonna followed my progress with sad eyes. But I couldn't worry about the dog right now. I had to keep Mama out of jail. "Who ran over Erica Hodges?" I asked.

Mama studied the carpet. "I don't know."

"Don't know or won't tell?" My shoe banged into the back of the sofa and startled the dog. Madonna scurried behind Mama's chair.

"You're scaring the dog, and frankly, you're scaring me too. Are you going to kick me next?" Mama asked.

Her defensive reaction verified her mental fitness. I leaned on the sofa. My tense fingers dug into padding along the sofa back. "Of course not. Have I ever been violent with you or the girls? These questions are for your own good. Can't you see that?"

"No."

I covered my eyes with my hand. Mama was stonewalling me and the only reason that made any sense was that she was guilty. I didn't want that to be true. God, I didn't want that to be true. But I didn't have any other answers. The chilling realization turned my stomach and I knew an awful sense of loss.

This situation was beyond my control. The only way I could help her was to delay the inevitable. That wasn't lying. Not really. "Until we get a handle on things, leave your car parked in the driveway. We don't want to advertise your accident."

"The car had an accident," Mama asserted. "I didn't."

"Right. The car. It drove itself into someone."

We glared at each other again like steely-eyed gunfighters.

Why wouldn't she tell me what happened?

"Hey, anybody home?" Jonette called from the kitchen.

Madonna thumped her tail on the hardwood floor at the familiar sound of Jonette's voice. The dog crept out from behind the rocking chair to greet Jonette.

I blinked away my confusion and turned to greet my friend.

"Am I interrupting?" Jonette knelt to hug the dog. A sliver of tanned back winked at me as her snug blue top stayed put and her sunny shorts stretched to accommodate her new position. "I knocked. When nobody answered, I let myself in."

"You're always welcome here, Jonette. You know that." How much of our conversation had she overheard? I clenched my hands together at my waist, hoping for the conversation fairy to help me out.

"I'm sorry I'm a few minutes late," she said.

"Late?" I blinked some more.

"Don't tell me you forgot."

At my blank look, Jonette said, "The vet appointment. Madonna has a prenatal checkup in ten minutes. Doctor Murphy at the animal clinic. Ringing any bells now?"

"Oh." Air leaked rapidly out of my lungs. Worry about Mama had scrambled my circuits. Maybe I needed a doctor's appointment. "I forgot."

"I'll grab Madonna's leash and wait with her outside while you get your purse." Jonette petted Madonna again and made kissing sounds. "Come on, sugar. We're going for a walk."

Madonna padded off with Jonette. I turned to tell Mama we'd finish this later and her rocker was empty. Didn't she know that her furtive behavior made her appear guiltier? My hand went to my mouth. The room spun a little off its axis. I had the sensation of tumbling through a rabbit hole into another universe.

I wanted to help Mama, to protect her. How could I cover for her when she wasn't being honest with me?

Jonette poked me with her elbow. "Do you have any questions, Cleo?"

I shook the wool from my head. I had plenty of questions. But the stocky veterinarian in baby-blue scrubs didn't have the answers I needed. Only Mama had the answers, and Mama wasn't talking. "No questions."

I had caught the gist of what the vet said, but a doggie prenatal visit couldn't hold my attention today. On the other hand, Jonette appeared to be hanging onto young Dr. Murphy's every word.

The vet folded his paw-print-decorated stethoscope around his neck and caught my eye. "I urge you to minimize this dog's distress."

His patronizing tone cut right through my fugue. Did he believe I stayed up nights plotting ways to upset the dog? Frustration spiked through my bloodstream. "I'm already cutting her a lot of slack. You want me to spend every minute of the day with her?"

"I realize that's unlikely, even from the most devoted pet owners." The vet managed a little half smile that didn't reach his slate-gray eyes. "Madonna's anxiety is real. Relieve her distress as much as possible. A healthy, happy mom makes a great mother."

I'd experienced that firsthand. When my marriage failed, I'd been less attentive to my daughters. I'd been lucky they hadn't acted out. For a time it seemed all of us walked on eggshells.

Dr. Murphy was charging me eighty-five dollars for this advice. If I didn't respond appropriately, he'd repeat himself until I got it. No sense running up extra charges on my bill. I mentally reviewed his speaking points and recited them for him. "Got it. Keep the dog calm. Let her pee as much as she wants. No problem."

The vet nodded. "The important thing is to stay calm. Madonna has enough anxiety. She doesn't need to mirror your stress."

Stress? At my house? "Sure. Calm. Piece of cake."

Jonette hit me with her elbow again. "Don't kid about this. We don't want to mess this up." She turned her reverent gaze on the vet again. "How will we know when the big moment arrives?"

"Based on the timeline we've established, I believe you have another two weeks to go, and then you'll have your puppies."

Two weeks?

Yikes.

That was soon.

Would Mama be home to witness the birthing? Or would she be locked in jail for making a speed bump out of Erica Hodges?

Birth and death. Opposite ends of the spectrum, forever linked through the process of living. You couldn't have birth without death following. Or office visits without bills.

After paying Madonna's vet bill, I waited in the parking lot while Jonette used the restroom. Madonna peed on every bush we passed. If she started peeing more than this, she wouldn't be able to walk without hosing down the sidewalk. Sympathy welled within me. I'd been this huge with Charla, waddling around, peeing every chance I could. It wasn't much fun. "You're almost to the finish line, Madonna." She licked my hand.

Poor baby. I squatted down and hugged her neck.

Orphaned. Pregnant as a whale. Living with four females. We weren't complete strangers, but we weren't what she was used to, either.

"You didn't do anything wrong, sweetie. It's going to be all right."

Madonna leaned into my embrace, soaking up that physical contact and assurance. It floored me that I'd been so oblivious to her distress. It hurt more to think I'd added to her anxiety. This gentle giant deserved better. I rubbed behind her ears, and she made a happy dog sound.

"We'll get through this, I promise. Those puppies will be here, and you'll be dreaming of peace and quiet and doggie naps."

Jonette joined us with a laugh. "You were paying attention. Atta girl."

Her words were for me, but she'd cooed them in the special voice she used for the dog. Madonna thumped her tail.

I scrambled to my feet and allowed Jonette to take the leash. We strolled through the park, heading home. "Sorry, I've been a bit out of it today."

"I noticed. The vet noticed. Even the dog noticed. How do you do that? No one notices when I'm upset."

I glanced her way, studying her profile. Had I missed something with Jonette, too? "Don't sell yourself short. I'd know. Mama and the girls would know. Dean would know."

"But it isn't the same. My life has always been chaos. You are the stable one. Or you were. Charlie's betrayal changed more than your marital status. You're different now."

Leaves crunched underfoot on the sidewalk. School buses passed on the road bounding the park. "Not so different, really. Just a bit more likely to view the world without rose-colored glasses. Believing the best of everyone led to heartache and desolation. I won't be that stupid again."

"You weren't stupid. Charlie was. He knows it now. But that's not what I'm talking about." Jonette watched the darting flight of a yellow butterfly. "You used to be happy."

I grinned. "I'm getting happy again. Sometimes twice a week."

Jonette let out more leash. "I'm not talking about sex. I'm talking about you. I was so worried about you, then you pulled yourself together and I thought you would be okay. But now I'm not so sure."

My heart raced. I didn't know where she was going with this, but it couldn't be good. Did she share my suspicions about Mama? I inhaled a shaky breath. "What are you getting at?"

"You're keeping secrets from me."

I blinked a few times. Denial formed in my mouth. But this was my best friend. My lifelong confidante. "I am."

Jonette flashed me a look of triumph. Then her expression sobered. "I saw the car."

My step faltered. I nodded toward the wooden park bench. "Want to sit?"

"Sure."

We sat. Madonna circled and sat a couple of times before she got it right. I remembered that part about pregnancy, too. "I heard you talking about her car as I came in," Jonette said. "When Madonna and I went outside, I saw the broken headlight and bent bumper."

From her factual tone, Jonette didn't appear to be judging Mama by the evidence, or me for withholding said evidence from a police investigation. "You've got to promise not to tell a soul," I said. "This is the biggest mess ever."

Jonette nodded, her chin-length hair cupping her intent pixie face. "Promise."

After glancing around to make sure no one could overhear us, I leaned in close to Jonette. "Mama is thrilled Erica is dead. Put that with the person-sized dent in Mama's car, and it doesn't look good. Add in that Mama won't account for her whereabouts the night of Erica's death, and the final picture is absolutely grim. I'm no police detective, but Mama's in big trouble here."

Jonette didn't hesitate. "Then we have to find out who killed Erica. Plain and simple."

My gaze swept the park again, sure that the entire Frederick County police force would jump out from behind the slides, swing sets, and seesaws, and arrest us both for withholding information. "But what if Mama was involved with Erica's death? I don't want to be the one who seals her fate. I want to protect her."

"By letting her go to jail?"

The air swooshed out of me like a spiked tire. "That's the flaw in my plan. How do I help her without hurting her? It can't be done."

"If you do nothing, she'll go to jail anyway. Once Britt focuses on a suspect, he gets tunnel vision. That's what he did with me, anyway. You don't have a choice. You have to look into Erica's murder."

If only life were so black and white. "I have nothing to go on. It's a miracle Britt hasn't already questioned Mama on the basis of Mama and Erica's past antagonism."

"You figured out who killed Dudley," Jonette reminded me. "Finding Erica's killer can't be any harder than that."

"Rafe read me the riot act on self-endangerment."

"You letting all that butter-soft leather in his expensive car go to your head? The new Cleo doesn't take orders from any man, remember?"

I snorted. "The new Cleo is making up the rules as she goes along."

Jonette blinked slyly. "Doesn't everyone?"

We shared a laugh. My feeling of gloom and doom lifted, and I felt pounds lighter. It was unrealistic for me to believe I could control everything. But that didn't mean I would sit back and leave things to chance.

Jonette rubbed my tense shoulder. "That's the spirit. Laughter is the glue gun of life. You laugh enough and the important stuff falls into place."

My expression froze as the true weight of my problem settled on my shoulders again. "Joking aside, there are serious consequences here. If you help me, you may become an accessory to Mama's crime."

"Do you believe your mother did it?"

I flinched. Madonna whimpered. It was one thing to think it, quite another to voice my fears. Good thing I didn't shy away from difficult tasks. "I don't think it was premeditated murder, but, yes, given her recent mental state, she could've killed Erica. Car accidents happen all the time. What if Mama didn't mean to kill her, and Erica inadvertently got between Mama's car and the pavement?"

"Then it was an accident. We'll prove it wasn't Delilah's fault, and everything will go back to normal. Piece of cake."

"Not hardly. Mama's not talking. She doesn't want my help."

Jonette shrugged. "So, we help her anyway. What's the big deal?"

The big deal was that Mama was hiding something. Whatever it was, it was tearing her apart. If I looked into Erica's death, chances were I would find what was turning Mama into a cranky old woman.

Secrets were kept for a reason. Odds were this was no featherweight problem. This was surely the heavyweight champion secret of the world. No stress there. None at all.

"This is Mama we're talking about." I looked around furtively to see if anyone noticed my voice had gone shrill again. Madonna whimpered and placed her head in Jonette's lap. I took a deep breath. My anxiety upset the dog, just as the vet said it would.

Dang.

If the people police didn't get me, the dog police surely would.

A few deep breaths, and I felt calmer. "She won't tell me what happened. When I brought the subject up today, she stonewalled me. Then her face went pale and she clutched her heart. Face it, I'm putty in her hands."

"We don't need her cooperation. We'll grill her friends, and they'll give us the scoop."

I wasn't buying that logic. "I'm not convinced they'll tell us anything. Their loyalty is to Mama."

"They'll cave if it keeps Delilah out of jail. You work on Muriel and Francine. I'll grill Margie and Edna."

"Why do you get the fun ones?" I asked sourly.

Jonette stood and stretched. So did Madonna. "I get first choice because I'm older than you," Jonette said smugly. "Besides, I should spearhead this investigation. Your detective skills aren't worth a damn."

I hurried after Jonette and Madonna. "What are you talking about now?"

Jonette shot me a thick look. "Gee, Jonette, why did you run out of my house yesterday as if your pants were on fire? Is there something going on in your life?" She looked both ways before we crossed the street. "My best friend in the whole wide world would ask what was happening in my life. My best friend would want to know about the earth-shaking events occurring in my life."

She was right. I owed her a couple of questions. I'd been so concerned about Mama being a killer that I hadn't focused on Jonette's bizarre behavior. "You're right. Inquiring minds want to know. Why did you run out of my house yesterday?"

Jonette shivered with energy. "I've been about to burst with the news. I wanted to tell Dean, but I knew I had to tell you first or you'd kill me. You'll never guess what I decided to do."

With Jonette it could be anything. She'd had more men and

more careers than most. A glance at her animated face showed that whatever it was, she was pumped. "What?"

"This is so awesome. I went down to city hall and found out the requirements for running for public office. And guess what? I meet all the requirements. Aren't you proud of me?"

Public office.

I winced inwardly, though I was careful not to let my personal misgivings show. Doubts and fears congested my thoughts. Public office meant your life was examined under a magnifying glass.

My heart sank.

Jonette was true blue, the best friend anyone could ask for, but there were chapters of her checkered past that might not bear intense scrutiny. Or even casual scrutiny.

On the other hand, she positively bristled with enthusiasm. I couldn't let her down by pointing out the negatives to her idea. I'd manage them behind the scene so that she got what she wanted. Loyal and trustworthy and hardworking, that was me.

The good news was that I was fairly certain it was already too late in the year to file for president of the United States. Perhaps there wouldn't be as much mud-slinging for a lesser election. Whatever it was, Jonette had my unconditional support.

My smile was genuine. "Sure. What are we running for?"

"Mayor." Jonette grinned. "I'm gonna hit that lard-ass Darnell Reynolds right where it hurts."

Chapter 6

After folding church bulletins in the cave-like Trinity Episcopal workroom for an hour on Friday morning, my brain was fried. My arms ached from fatigue, and I desperately needed a nap. How did Mama do this mindless physical labor week after week?

I picked up another lightly creased cream-colored bulletin. Inserted it into the antique homemade press. Pulled the lever arm down. Removed the creased bulletin. Rotated it. Inserted the other side. Pulled the lever arm down again. Removed the finished product.

"How many bulletins are there?" I asked, flexing my aching hands. No matter how fast I went, my to-do pile never got smaller. I was definitely the weakest link in this production process.

"Doesn't matter how many they are," Francine said, hand-creasing the left seam on yet another legal-sized piece of paper. She passed the half-folded bulletin to her sister Muriel and started creasing the next one. "They all have to be folded."

I gestured toward the steel monstrosity I'd been operating. "Why doesn't the church invest in a more modern piece of equipment? This thing looks older than I am."

"You young people have a lot to learn." Muriel folded the second crease in the trifold bulletin before she slid it down to me. Light glinted on her large glasses. "Newer isn't always better. Our generation does things the right way."

I selected another loosely folded bulletin from the pile and put it through the mashing process. "I'm not following you."

"The church tried a new machine about ten years ago," Francine said. "It jammed and hissed and broke and wasted our time. We were lucky to get our money back for that piece of junk."

We worked in silence for a few minutes. I had the routine down cold. Insert. Pull. Remove. Rotate. Insert. Pull. Remove.

If the excess bulletins were made of chocolate, I would've eaten the extras when I fell behind, but my paper-eating days were far behind me. Besides, with such close scrutiny, I couldn't get away with making a single mistake.

Francine and Muriel worked like twin automatons, all the while keeping their hawk-like gazes on my dubious progress. Who knew that their sixty-something gnarled and bent fingers could move with such surprising speed and economy of motion?

"How long have y'all been doing this?" I fed another bulletin into the machine and flattened it.

"As long as the church needed it done, dearie."

Muriel's comment irritated me. There had to be a better way. This medieval process was like trying to fill a hole with steam. "Why don't they hire someone to do this?"

"Money." Francine's lips pressed into thin, disapproving slashes of apricot lipstick. "Hiring people costs money, and then the church would need to take in more money. It's better all the way around if this activity is staffed through volunteers."

"How about recycling? Why don't we reuse the same bulletins each week?"

Francine shot me a caustic look. "The liturgy changes by season and occasion. The readings and the hymns change each week."

Duh. I knew that. I'd been raised Episcopalian. Still. It galled me that so much effort went for a single-use disposable product.

"Does anyone ever notice how flat the bulletins are? Why do they have to be pressed anyway?"

Muriel sighed and tossed another bulletin on my to-do pile. "If you don't want to fill in for your mother, leave. Francine and I can manage."

I couldn't imagine how long it would take the two women to perfectly crease all these bulletins. No way could I just walk out of here. Especially when I hadn't gotten any of the answers I needed.

Silly me.

I had assumed I would breeze in here, dazzle the seniors with my dexterity and youthful energy, and worm their secrets out of them before they knew what hit them. Instead, I felt like I'd been hooked up to an embalming pump and my internal fluids had been replaced with a numbing preservative.

"You say that Dee isn't feeling well." Francine's beady brown eyes surveyed me through the top of her bifocals. "What's wrong with her?"

The pale green walls of the tiny workroom seemed to close in on me. I had planned to say Mama was under the weather and we were worried about the flu. The possibility of contagion would surely cause her friends to shun her for weeks, which would help me to keep Mama safely at home.

Notice I wasn't saying she had the flu, only that we were worried about the flu. Truthfully, who wasn't worried about the flu?

Before I could utter a word, my conscience got the better of me. I was on church property, and I was planning to deceive the faithful? Not a very Christian attitude. I grabbed a bulletin and smashed it into the folding machine. Only I hadn't just grabbed one. Two bulletins went in, two came out folded flat.

Hmm.

Francine and Muriel hadn't mentioned pressing multiple

bulletins during their brief recitation of the machine's operating instructions. I blinked at the implication of what that meant.

They wanted me to fail.

Or at the very least to leave them alone.

My gaze narrowed and my resolve strengthened. Francine and Muriel couldn't run me off that easily. Mama's freedom hung in the balance. I could take whatever heat they dished out. Especially since I'd discovered the secret of the mashing machine.

I cleared my throat. "Mama isn't herself." I flipped the two bulletins over and flattened the remaining fold. "She's moping around and spending a lot of time staring into space."

Muriel's gnarled fingers spasmed and crushed the sheet of paper she was folding. She pushed the crumpled bulletin to the reject side of the table. "Has Delilah seen her heart doctor?"

I nonchalantly stacked both perfectly folded bulletins in the completed box. It took everything I had not to smile in triumph. These wily ladies wouldn't beat me today. "She won't see anyone. But I wouldn't let her stay home if it was her heart. I'd see that she got immediate medical attention."

"Then it must be that young man you're seeing." Francine pushed another bulletin toward my end of the table. "Dee worries you'll put her out in the street."

Outrage boiled out of me before I could close my mouth. "I would never put Mama out in the street, and she knows that. I can't believe you would even suggest such a thing."

Muriel shrugged her hunched shoulders. Her thin neck momentarily disappeared. "It hurt her deeply that you went behind her back to get the deed to her house."

I crammed a handful of bulletins in the mangler thingy and smashed them flat. This accusation was worse than the last. But the bulletin sisters weren't going to break me. "I did no such thing. Daddy expected me to look after Mama's finances. That's why he deeded the house over to me."

"Dee knows how to look out for herself. Why would she suddenly need your help?" Francine asked.

Heat flamed my cheeks. This question had hovered in the back of my mind, too. Mama wasn't senile or demented. She was just Mama. Daddy had trusted her to work in his office. Why hadn't he trusted her with the deed to their house? "I didn't go behind Mama's back. Daddy came to me and told me it was a done deal."

"If you're feeling guilty for cheating your mother out of her inheritance, you could sign the house back over to her. Get one of them, what'cha'macallits." Muriel looked over at Francine. "You know what I mean, Francy. That legal thing that Wanda's daughter did."

Francine snapped her fingers in the air until her memory banks engaged. "Oh yeah. A quit-claim deed. She signed everything back over to her mother."

My chin went up. I crammed a handful of bulletins into the machine. They came out of the pressing machine with a thick wrinkle down the center, obscuring the text in the middle of the page.

Grinding my back teeth together in frustration, I dumped the ruined bulletins into the reject pile with Francine's crumpled efforts. "I'm not doing that. Daddy wanted me to have the house. He knew I would never evict Mama."

"Until you move that new man in," Muriel predicted, shaking a thinly veined finger at me. "Then you'll turn Dee out. I've seen it happen time and time again."

My blood pressure spiked. I grabbed the rounded edge of the table and counted to five. "I am not turning Mama out on the street. I can't believe you'd say such a thing. Please, let's change the subject. What about Wednesday's tragedy? What about Erica Hodges?"

"Why would we talk about her?" Francine asked. "She's gone, and we're glad of it."

Francine and Muriel nodded in tandem. Two sisters with one brain between them.

If they knew how much I wanted answers, they'd clam up to spite me. I had to be smarter than them. "I believe Mama's funk is related to the feud she had with Erica. Do you know why they didn't get along?"

"Sure," Muriel said. "I'm old but I'm not senile."

Much more of this and I'd be senile. "What's the deal?"

Muriel and Francine exchanged a knowing look that made my back teeth grind together. "Why don't you ask Delilah about the argument?" Francine asked.

"I already did, and she wouldn't tell me. Please, if you know anything about what went on, I'd like to know. I'm worried about Mama."

Muriel folded her bony hands together on the scarred table. She leaned forward. "Erica was a terrible thorn in Dee's side for years."

Finally.

I was getting somewhere.

I quit smashing bulletins and sat down across from Francine and Muriel. "You're not telling me anything I don't already know. I can't tell you how many times I heard Mama complain about her. Erica never cleaned out the church coffee pot right, Erica used Mama's assigned parking space at the hospital, Erica took credit for Mama's accomplishments whenever and wherever she could. All of that's water under the bridge. What started this whole mess?"

"Erica wasn't a very nice person. She took pride in hurting others." Muriel spoke so softly I strained to hear her.

"Muriel." Francine's sharp tone sounded a clear warning.

My eyes darted back and forth between the two gray-haired

women. I hadn't come this far to be turned back emptyhanded. "And?"

"And she wasn't above bending facts to suit her purposes," Muriel said in a breathy rush.

I wasn't getting the information I needed. Erica was a nasty user. I already knew that. Muriel and Francine were loyal to Mama, but I sensed Muriel wanted to tell me something. What was it? I replayed the last few minutes of our conversation in my mind.

Erica bent facts. Did she have something on Mama? Something worth killing for? My blood chilled instantly.

If Erica had been blackmailing Mama, that meant Mama had a strong motive to kill Erica. I prayed that wasn't the case. I prayed Erica hadn't pushed Mama over the edge of reason. Regardless, I had to help Mama out of this deep hole. For that I needed more information about the dead woman. What other avenues could I pursue with Francine and Muriel?

Nasty people weren't just nasty to one person. Usually. They were nasty to everyone.

If that were true, there might be other incidents I could uncover. If Francine and Muriel didn't want to talk about Mama, would they talk about their own experiences with Erica? It didn't hurt to ask. "Did either of you have nasty run-ins with Erica?"

Another covert look flashed between the two women. Whatever they knew, it wasn't information they were anxious to reveal. "I promise to keep it to myself," I added.

Francine bowed her head and shook it in mute denial. Whatever Erica had done to her must be too painful to reveal. I felt for Francine, I really did, but her searing silence galvanized my need to know.

What did Erica have on these women?

I turned my attention to Muriel. She barely met my gaze

before she averted her eyes. Bony white knuckles bulged from fisted hands. I was onto something here. Satisfaction hummed through my veins. I waited while she wrestled with her private demons.

"Erica said she had proof my son cheated on his college entrance exams," Muriel whispered, her face ghostly pale, a single teardrop sliding down her rouged cheek. "I didn't believe her, but I couldn't take the chance she would jeopardize Robby's future."

Clanging alarms went off in my head. "What did you do?"

Muriel's gaze darted sideways like a frightened rabbit. "I did what any mother would do. I protected my child."

I saw the raw emotion in her eyes. My heart ached for her, but I had to know how she'd handled the situation. "How?"

Muriel shook her head so fast she looked like a motorized bobble-head doll gone wild. I was afraid she would bolt out of the room, and then where would I be? I wouldn't have the answers I needed to help Mama, and I'd have to finish folding these stupid bulletins by myself. Not good.

I placed my hands palm down on the table and leaned forward. "Please. Tell me what you did."

"I can't," Muriel whispered.

Questions boiled in my throat, but they were silenced by the sudden appearance of Detective Britt Radcliffe. His solid law-enforcing presence filled the doorway. His sharp gaze cased the room. Was that disappointment in his eyes? "Morning, ladies," he said.

I was still mad at Britt for handcuffing me and Jonette on Wednesday. He could have just sent us on our way, but no, he had to be the Cop in Charge. He'd made his point, but in doing so, he'd burned his bridges with me.

But I wasn't a regular here. He'd come expecting to see the bulletin-folding ladies. How did the bulletin sisters feel about having a police detective in their midst? Leaning back in my seat, I pasted a benign smile on my face and studied them. Francine and Muriel had flinched at his deep voice. They knew more than they were telling. Would Britt notice their unease?

Francine recovered first. She reached for another bulletin to fold. "Good morning, detective."

"I see you're keeping the world safe from improperly folded bulletins," he said with a flirty wink.

"We do what we can," Muriel said, accepting the partially folded bulletin Francine handed her.

After what we'd just discussed, I couldn't imagine Muriel calmly going about her business, and yet she was doing just that. A Shakespearean actor couldn't have given a better performance than Muriel.

That last thought had the wheels in my head turning. Was Muriel acting now, or had she been acting when she seemed so distressed a few minutes ago? What was going on with this older crowd? They sure didn't want anyone to find out. Which only made me need to know more than ever.

What were they hiding?

Britt turned his attention to me. His steely gray eyes glittered with intensity. "Cleo, I didn't know you were a member of the folding brigade."

"Just lending a hand where it's needed," I said airily.

Britt wasn't fooled by my altruism. He knew exactly who was missing from this picture. "Where's Delilah today?" he asked.

In a flash of blinding insight, I understood the bulletin sisters' work ethic. A busy person was less vulnerable. I rose to man the folding machine.

Even without Britt stepping foot in the room, his physical presence cast a long, dark shadow in our workspace. His leading questions were like bait in a bear trap. I didn't want to get dismembered when he sprang the trap.

Besides, Britt wasn't asking about Mama for social reasons. This was police business. I inhaled shakily and squashed five more bulletins. "Mama couldn't make it today."

I knew a thing or two about difficult topics. Changing the subject was imperative. Time to apply a little offensive strategy to this situation. "What brings you to church today, Britt?"

"Conducting interviews for the Hodges investigation," Britt said evenly. "I had hoped to talk to Francine, Muriel, and Delilah today. About the Tuesday evening hospitality committee meeting."

So much for my inept attempt to change the subject. Did Britt see my hands tremble as I inserted another wad of bulletins into the folding machine?

Francine didn't miss a beat in her folding routine. "What about the meeting?"

Britt focused on the bulletin sisters. "I wanted to verify the time of your meeting and when everyone went home."

Muriel brushed aside his inquiry. "No need to trouble Dee for that. The meeting started at seven. We discussed the hospitality preparations for the bishop's upcoming visit. At seven-thirty, Dee drove Francy and me home."

"Delilah drove?" Britt flipped his notebook open and scribbled fast.

My heart sank. Would he demand to see Mama's car, now that he knew it had been at the church that evening?

"Yes," Muriel said. "Both Francy and I are night-blind."

"Were there any other cars in the church parking lot that night?"

"Erica drove, so her Caddy was here, but that's all I remember seeing," Francine said. "And Erica left before we did."

Britt scribbled some more. "Did either of you think Mrs. Hodges acted out of character?"

"I didn't notice anything unusual—did you, Francy?" Muriel said.

"Not a thing. It was business as usual around here," Francine said smoothly. The last bulletin passed swiftly between her and Muriel.

"Do you have anything to add, Cleo?" Britt asked.

Color rose to my cheeks. "I wasn't here for the hospitality committee meeting." Praying that he didn't mention the Monday meeting, I ruthlessly shoved the final clump of bulletins into the folding press.

Francine and Muriel were lying about the time they left the church. Either that or Mama went elsewhere after the meeting. It was way past seven-thirty when she returned home that evening. I remembered because the girls and I had gone through their backpacks on the kitchen table to make sure they had everything they needed for the first day of school on Wednesday.

Another piece of damning evidence. Mama's late arrival at home suggested she had a window opportunity to kill Erica. My hopes plummeted. How could I keep Mama out of jail if the evidence pointed to her?

"I need to talk to Delilah, Cleo," Britt said.

"You know where to find her," I said with false lightness. At this rate Mama would be behind bars by nightfall.

Francine rose. "Will you be needing us for anything else, Detective?"

"Not right now. Don't leave town, ladies."

Francine and Muriel collected the boxes of neatly pressed bulletins and scurried out of the small workroom. I tried to make myself appear as inconspicuous as possible, hoping Britt would follow them out and leave me alone. No such luck. He blocked the doorway again.

"They're lying," Britt said, his arms barred across his chest. Thick muscles stretched his shirt sleeves to their maximum endurance. "Why? Do you have any idea why they'd lie to a police officer?"

"They lied to me, too," I admitted.

Britt leaned heavily in the doorway. "I'm going to have to arrest every gray-haired lady in town for obstructing justice. The mayor will flip out."

I remembered Darnell's quote in the paper. He'd promised a swift but thorough investigation of Erica's death. The mayor thought it was bad for tourism to have killers running loose on the streets of Hogan's Glen. I agreed with him on that point.

Britt's detective gaze settled heavily on me. "You know something. What is it, Cleo? Do I have to arrest you too?"

The things I knew were only exceeded by the things I didn't know. I needed to toss Britt a bone, or he'd figure out I was investigating Erica's death. "This isn't public knowledge yet, but Jonette has decided to run for mayor."

Britt cracked a smile. "That's something to look forward to."

"She'll give Darnell a run for his money, that's for sure."

Britt steeled his face. "Be careful, Cleo. Something ugly is afoot in this town. I don't want you mixed up in it."

I raised my hands in mock surrender. "Hey, me neither."

"Seriously, go home. Stay away from Trinity Episcopal until I get this mess straightened out."

"You think someone on staff here killed Erica?"

He scowled at me. "You're not going to trick me into revealing how Erica Hodges was killed."

Of all the nerve. "I'm not trying to trick you into anything. I don't understand what's going on. What happened to our sleepy little town?"

Britt ignored my question. "I thought your recent stint in handcuffs would have kept you from snooping around, and yet here you are back at the church."

His accusation heated my blood. "If you notice, I'm not

outside poking around the church parking lot. I'm volunteering in the church office. Big difference."

"Not in my book. I know you, Cleopatra Jones. You won't let good enough alone. I've got enough to do without worrying about your safety."

I resented his implication. "I don't need a bodyguard. If you recall, I got myself out of trouble last time."

"Exactly my point. You put yourself in a very dangerous situation. Let me handle this hunt for Erica's murderer."

"Murder?" That two-syllable word clanked in my empty stomach. I searched his face for something more to go on. His rugged features were as inscrutable as ever. "I thought Erica's death was an accident."

"I shouldn't tell you this, but I'm going to. Maybe it'll shock some sense into you. Preliminary autopsy reports indicate that Erica Hodges was struck by a vehicle, run over repeatedly, and left for dead."

I grimaced. Erica hadn't been a nice person, but no one deserved to die slowly, painfully, and alone. "She didn't die right away?"

"Not at the slow speed of impact a vehicle could muster in the church parking lot."

I grabbed my middle to corral my jittery stomach. Thank God I hadn't actually seen Erica's body the other day when I'd trespassed in the parking lot. My active imagination brought up a visual of Erica, cartoon-character thin with limbs bent at impossible angles. As flat as if she'd been passed through the bulletin-folding machine. I shuddered. "That's terrible. I had no idea."

Britt handed me my purse and clamped a beefy hand on my shoulder. He ushered me out the nearest door. "Get out of here and don't come back."

I didn't like being manhandled or shoved around, but Britt

meant well. Trouble was, I needed to be in that church. I needed to know the dark secrets surrounding the life of Erica Hodges. Otherwise, how would I have a chance at saving Mama from herself?

Since the fall weather was so mild, I'd walked the eight blocks down to the church this morning. While I'd been inside working on the bulletins, a stiff breeze had sprung up and it went straight through my thin, summer-weight clothing. I shivered and headed home.

"Need a ride, Cleo?"

My head whipped around. A dark Beemer pulled out of the traffic lane on Main Street and idled next to me. Through the open window a slug of familiar cologne wafted out to me, confirming what I already knew. Charlie Jones had stopped to give me a lift. Ordinarily, I wouldn't consider getting in the car with my ex-husband, but this wasn't ordinary times.

I was filled with an urgency to get home and talk to Mama. "Thanks." I stepped toward his Beemer as he opened the door from inside.

"I'm headed out for lunch." Charlie's grin stretched from ear to ear. "You interested?"

Lunch with my ex-husband would give him hope he could win me back. A ride was one thing. Sharing food took our level of intimacy to a whole other level. "No, thanks, I've got to get home."

"No problem there. I love your cooking." Charlie masterfully steered through a series of lefts as we reversed direction. Already I regretted the impulse that led me to accept this ride. I had to be very firm about the boundaries I set for Charlie, or he would insert himself in the picture.

"You're not invited to lunch, Charlie."

"Don't be cruel, Cleo. I've apologized for my mistake. I'm a new man. Promise. A man who wants you back. What's the harm in a lunch?"

He had my complete attention. Purple cows could have fallen from the sky, and I wouldn't have noticed. "It's not about harm. It's about trust. I don't trust you anymore. Why can't you accept that and move on?"

"You want to talk to me about trust? How come every time I turn around, Britt Radcliffe has his hands on you? He's a married man, Cleo."

My blood raced at the insult. I couldn't believe how quickly Charlie could get me riled up. This was exactly why I stayed away from him. "I am not interested in Britt Radcliffe. He's not interested in me. I don't know where you get these bizarre ideas, Charlie."

Charlie slowed the car. "Then what did I just see?"

"You saw me being ushered out of a crime scene by a police officer."

My driveway was full since both my car and Mama's were there. Charlie parked on the street next to the curb. "Crime scene? Are you in trouble with the law?"

"Don't be ridiculous. Britt took exception to my helping fold the Sunday bulletins."

Charlie rubbed his chin. "I don't buy that. Not for a minute. Erica's death wasn't an accident?"

I chose my words with care. "Britt thinks there was more to it."

A frown flickered across Charlie's face. "I thought he got all the sinister folks rounded up a few months ago."

"Apparently not." I opened the car door. "Thanks for the lift. I appreciate the favor."

"I know how you can make it up to me." His eyebrows rose suggestively. "Lunch?"

"No lunch."

"I'm not giving up, Cleo. You need me."

I slammed the car door. "Goodbye, Charlie."

I mounted the porch stairs searching through my purse for my keys.

Mama opened the door before I could get my key in the lock. She grabbed my arm and pulled me in the house. After working the bulletin mashing machine all morning, I wasn't surprised at her grip strength.

Static electricity crackled in the air. "Are you satisfied?" Mama snapped.

I was satisfied I wasn't eating lunch with Charlie. I was satisfied Mama wasn't going to jail right this minute. I was satisfied Francine and Muriel didn't beat me at the folding game. I bent down to pet Madonna, who had waddled forward to greet me. "What do you mean, Mama?"

"Muriel called. She said you grilled her and Francine about Erica. I should have known you would spy on me. Only, why did you have to damage my car and make me hide in the house for two days? Why not just ask me?"

Talking to Charlie about lunch reminded me of how empty my stomach was. I started toward the kitchen. "I did ask you about Tuesday night, and you didn't tell me a darn thing. Furthermore, I did not damage your car. You did."

Mama circled around and blocked my way. "I told you I didn't run down Erica Hodges. Why don't you believe me?"

"Because the evidence points to you, Mama." I ticked off the facts on my fingers. "You and Erica had a public blowout on Monday. She turns up dead at church after being at another church meeting with you. You won't account for your time Tuesday night. And finally, your car looks like it hit someone. Britt said Erica's death was murder. Murder, Mama. Serious stuff. You could go to prison for life."

Mama's face darkened. She hammered one fist into the palm of her other hand. Flesh smacked against flesh. "This is

America. I'm innocent until proven guilty."

"I want to help you, Mama. Don't shut me out."

"This isn't fair. Erica Hodges was a rotten person. I'm not the only person in this town who hated her guts."

My stomach growled. I identified with its emptiness. Despair ate at me. Mama's future seemed bleak, and I couldn't do a darned thing about it. Britt would never believe it was accidental that Mama ran over Erica a bunch of times. Mama's chances of convincing him of her innocence were slim to none.

I did my best imitation of Britt's steely gaze. "Britt is interviewing the clergy and the church office staff right now. It's only a matter of time until he interviews you. He knows your friends are lying. He told me so. When he sees your car, he'll lock you up and throw away the key."

Mama's chin jutted out. "Let him come," she growled. "I didn't murder anyone."

Her nostrils flared pure dragon fire. "And another thing. I'm sick and tired of you bossing me around. This is my house. I can come and go as I please. Stick that in a boring sandwich and eat it."

CHAPTER 7

Water pulsed out of the showerhead, kneading the knotted muscles in my back. I rolled my shoulders every which way to relieve tension. Between the murder investigation, Mama's secrets, and my hot date tonight, I couldn't relax. The kids weren't helping either.

"Mom, I have to have that new camera," Lexy shouted through the bathroom door. "Did you even read that spec sheet I brought home?"

"I'll check into it, Lex. But not right now. Later," I promised. I ducked back under the stream to rinse conditioner from my hair.

Blessed silence followed. Then Charla burst into the bathroom. "Mom, I desperately need a new wardrobe. Misty Rogerson has the cutest jean skirt ever invented. When can we go shopping, Mom? Can we go this weekend?"

After three days of school she already wanted new clothes? I gave up on the water massage. At this rate I'd be wrinkled as a prune if I didn't finish up in here. I lathered up with the expensive soap Jonette had given me. The kind that matched the perfume I planned to wear. The kind I had never used before.

The fragrance was heavenly. I inhaled a lungful and hummed inside. "You're in charge of your clothing allowance, dear. You know if you have money left."

She wiped the steam off the mirror and studied her face. "That's another thing, Mom. My clothing allowance isn't nearly enough. You can't expect me to wear the same things day in and day out. Plus, my clothes are lame."

"Charla, you selected every item in your closet. Don't blame me if you don't like them." I had clothing worries of my own for tonight. The selections in my closet weren't exciting. I'd bought conservative clothes because the old Cleo didn't like drawing unwanted attention to herself. But the new Cleo had the opposite goal.

My daughter stomped her foot and whirled, red hair flying like a wind-tossed veil. "All the guys couldn't keep their eyes off of Devon today, Mom. I'll bet she doesn't have a clothing budget."

I shut the water off and reached for a towel. "I'm an accountant. Your grandfather was an accountant. Even if we became wealthy overnight, we'd live on a budget. That's how Sampsons are."

"That's like so unfair. I'm not a Sampson. I'm a Jones. I'm talking to Daddy about this."

I hoped Mama didn't hear Charla denying her Sampson heritage. Her flip dismissal of all that my parents and I had worked for wouldn't set well with Mama. We owned this house free and clear, the business, too. Sampsons were long-term planners. And my plan for tonight was to enjoy time away from my responsibilities.

Wrapped in a damp towel, I darted to my bedroom, expecting both girls and the dog to be camped out at the bathroom door, but I only had to navigate around the dog. Ah, peace and quiet at last.

Madonna lumbered up with a groan and followed me to my bedroom. She padded over to the inflatable whelping box, grabbed a huge mouthful of ruined sheets, then headed for my bed. Only she was too heavy to get more than her front legs up on the mattress. She cried pitifully.

Sympathy welled. The vet said I was supposed to relieve her anxiety, not add to it. The dog sensed something was different about tonight. The least I could do was to help her get what she wanted. I was probably confusing the dog by allowing her back on my bed, but I needed her to be content. I lifted her rear end, and she licked my face appreciatively.

With that done, I headed over to my closet. I needed to focus if I wanted to look like a woman Rafe dated. Sophisticated and polished didn't come naturally to me.

Too bad my wardrobe lacked zip. Jonette had threatened to toss everything out and start over, but I wouldn't let her. Conservative is my middle name, although tonight, I wanted something fun to wear.

I flipped through the outfits hanging in my closet. Too old. Too frumpy. Too ten years ago. I settled on a taupe blouse and a pair of slacks that were a shade darker. Not exactly a hot outfit, but tasteful. Tasteful was important.

"Mom, whatcha' doing?" Charla entered the room and joined Madonna on my bed. Madonna's tail thumped happily against my rock-hard pillow and scratchy bargain-basement sheets. The dog rested her jumbo head in Charla's lap.

"Getting dressed for my dinner date," I answered, removing the taupe shirt and slacks from my closet. I wished for privacy, but I'd always had an open-door policy with my girls. One man wouldn't change that.

"About that new camera, Mom," Lexy stated as she entered the bedroom and climbed up on the bed, flopping across the pillows. "When can I get it?"

The taupe blouse was just light enough that the black bra might be visible through it. Darn. I wouldn't dream of going out in public like that. With a sigh, I settled for an institutional white bra and cotton panties. Too bad for Rafe. Too bad for me, too. I needed a black blouse. Looks like I'd be frequenting the clearance sales.

"Mom, are you listening to me?" Lexy asked.

Under cover of my damp towel, I shimmied into my panties. "Sorry, Lexy. I didn't promise you a new digital camera. Those things cost a fortune. I promised we would price them out, borrow one, or see if we could buy a used one."

"Mom, that won't work," Lexy insisted. "I need the latest technology if I want a shot at staff photographer. The photos from the old digitals are too pixilated for the yearbook. I need a brand new camera."

I blotted my damp hair on the towel before I donned the rest of my clothes. The mirror on my dresser reflected three pairs of eyes avidly watching my every move. The girls hadn't been this fascinated with my clothing since potty-training days.

I slipped into my bra. "I can't believe the yearbook staff is required to own state-of-the-art technology. You're going to a public high school, for Pete's sake. What's wrong with our old thirty-five millimeter? It takes excellent photos."

"But in order to use them for the yearbook, we'd have to pay to convert the images to electronic files. I have to have this digital camera, Mom. My whole life depends on it."

"Let's talk about me now," Charla said. She flipped her curly red hair over her shoulder. "We should start shopping for my fancy white dress tomorrow. Barbie Sperry and Marissa McGregor already found their dresses at a bridal shop. They say the good ones go first, and I definitely want a good one."

I slid into my slacks and blouse. I was not taking my fifteen-year-old daughter to a bridal shop to try on wedding gowns. "What about the stores that sell prom dresses? Don't they have white ones left over from last spring?"

"No one gets their Snow Ball gowns from a department store, Mom." Charla's expressive hands punctuated her every word. "Don't you know anything? Besides, look at it this way. It will be a two-for-one deal. Once we have the gown for the Snow Ball, I'll be all set for my wedding."

Madonna moaned as Charla's movements shook the bed. "Careful with the dog, dear. She shouldn't be jostled around."

Charla cooed and kissed Madonna on the nose. "I'm sorry."

Madonna thumped her tail again, whacking Lexy on the butt. "Hey. Watch it," Lexy said.

"About the dress," Charla continued, "We could start at Wedding Central tomorrow and work our way down the wedding food chain."

"No way," Lexy said. "I need that camera for school next week. I get Mom tomorrow."

Ignoring them, I opened my jewelry box. Pearls reminded me too much of Mama. My heart-shaped locket had been an anniversary gift from Charlie. I chose a delicate gold chain with an emerald pendant. Daddy had given me that necklace for my thirtieth birthday.

A splash of cologne, a pair of gold hoops, taupe heels, and I was ready to go. "How do I look?"

"Isn't that shirt see-through?" Charla said.

I glanced in the mirror. Was the shirt too sheer? I would be mortified if everyone in the Boar's Head could see my bra. Even if my bra was white. "Do you think so?"

"Don't worry, Mom," Lexy said. "It isn't like anyone would actually look at your shirt."

Her comment sent me scurrying back to my closet. What good was going out on a date if no one saw the clothes I wore? I didn't want Rafe to be bored.

Ten minutes later, every outfit I owned had been rejected by my fashion critics. Tufts of white dog hair dotted my clothes, and the wild look in my eyes was exceeded only by my pounding headache.

"Cleo?" Rafe called from the foot of the stairs. "You ready?"

Panic flashed through my veins. Not only was I not ready, but I literally had nothing to wear. I made an executive decision. "Out." I pointed to the door. "Both of you. Out."

As they filed out, I hollered down to Rafe. "Just a minute."

I hurried to the phone and called Jonette at the Tavern. "Emergency. No clothes. Hot date. What to do?"

Loud music and raucous laughter filled my ear. "Where are you going?" Jonette asked.

"Boar's Head."

"No problem. Your taupe slacks and blouse are perfect."

In dismay, I glanced at the discarded clothing strewn all over my bedroom. From the disarray, it appeared a tornado had whirled through my belongings, scattering and destroying everything in its path.

I had no idea where my taupe outfit was. But it had to be in here somewhere. "Charla said the shirt was too see-through."

Jonette snorted her disapproval. "Charla wants you to get back together with Charlie. She can't be objective about your date clothing. Trust me. The taupe outfit is fine. But we need to work more on the see-through angle."

I stopped rifling through my discarded clothes. Anxiety knotted my stomach. "My taupe blouse is see-through? I've worn it all over town. For years. I've even worn it to church."

"Would you stop with that? Your taupe outfit isn't see-through. Just the opposite. What I meant is you need to buy sheer blouses. I can help you with that."

I pawed through the clothes, left shoulder pressed up high to keep the phone in place. Taupe slacks. Where were they? "Okay. Thanks, Jonette. I can handle this from here."

"Wait. Did you find out anything from the church ladies?"

The cuff of my taupe slacks protruded from a prim hunter-green suit I'd tried on and hated. "Maybe. Muriel was starting to tell me something Erica did to her when Britt showed up.

Erica had run-ins with people besides Mama. The trouble is that Mama was Erica's most vocal opponent. How about you? Did you have any luck?"

"I heard that Erica visited her lawyer's office a lot lately. Plus, she hadn't paid her weekly bill at the beauty shop in over three months."

Triumphantly I snatched the clothes I'd been searching for from the discard pile. I shook the dog hair and wrinkles out of my slacks and shirt. "Why do some people think they don't have to pay for things? I would no more get a haircut I couldn't pay for than fly to the moon."

"Me, neither."

"I've got to go. Rafe is waiting."

Jonette laughed, deep and throaty. "Waiting is good for men. Puts them in their place and heightens anticipation. Don't worry about the delay. Your date will be fine."

I hoped she was right. I didn't want to send Rafe the wrong signal. But I'd feel much more comfortable if I knew what the right signal was.

Rafe's eyes lit up as I descended the staircase. "You look great." His possessive kiss curled my toes. "You smell even better."

My tingling skin had me wishing dinner was done, and we were alone at his place. I kissed him back. "You, too."

"Watch that. There are impressionable young children in this house," Charla said, using her cheerleading voice that carried across two football fields.

I shared a conspiratorial look with Rafe that I hoped said "we'll finish this later" loud and clear, then I reached for my purse. Madonna, who had been watching me like a hawk, started whimpering.

Her neediness reminded me of Charla at two. I patted the dog on the head. "I'll be back soon, Madonna. Until then,

Charla and Lexy will take good care of you."

"She wouldn't cry if you didn't leave her," Lexy pointed out. "Mom, did you see the 'For Rent' sign on Ed Monday's house?"

The house next door had been empty ever since my next-door neighbor, Ed Monday, was arrested and incarcerated. I'd gotten used to it being quiet around here these last few months. Guess the kids had, too. I squeezed Lexy's shoulder and managed a smile. "I'm sure it will work out fine, dear."

A timer buzzed. "Dinner's ready," Mama announced from the kitchen. She'd spent the better part of the afternoon working on one of her creations.

The rich aroma of homemade pizza filled the air as Mama opened the oven. For a moment, I wished I was eating here. Then I remembered she'd made Christmas pizza, and I was glad for Rafe's invitation to eat out.

Charla hustled us out the door. "You kids have fun."

I wasn't ready to go yet. I hadn't given them the standard warnings about locking the door behind us and looking out for each other while I was gone. I hadn't kissed either of them good night. My heels drug.

Sensing my reluctance, Rafe halted on the porch. "We can stay here tonight if you like."

His acceptance and understanding cleared the doubts from my head. The girls knew the drill. I had to let go of the reins if I was going to enjoy myself. I needed that time off, and so did my girls. Besides, Mama was here with them.

"No way," I said. "We are eating out and spending the evening together. No kids. I require grownup food and grownup entertainment, if you catch my drift."

His gaze warmed. "I like a woman who knows what she wants."

If he kept looking at me like that, I'd jump him on the porch. Not a good idea. I needed to put things back on a less intimate footing for my own peace of mind, so I spoke the first thing that popped in my head. "You don't think I'm a ball-busting, snooping Amazon with control issues in the bedroom?"

I held my breath in horror.

Those were the very words my ex-husband flung in my face when I'd uncovered the evidence of his affair. Jonette was the only person I had ever told, and she'd said not to believe a word from a man who couldn't keep his pants zipped. How would Rafe take my unfortunate remark?

Maybe there are no accidents in life. Part of me feared Rafe would agree with Charlie. That part had taken over my brain and acted stupid. Blood roared through my ears.

Would I eat Christmas pizza after all? Visions of pepperoni snowmen dancing on a field of gooey mozzarella cheese bounded by a lake of Christmas green tomato sauce and thick ropes of red dough flitted through my head. My empty stomach rumbled.

Rafe laughed heartily, tucked his hand under my arm and steered me down the gravel driveway toward his fire-engine red convertible. His lips nuzzled my ear, sending feverish chills down my spine. "Red, you can control me in the bedroom anytime you like."

I grinned. If Rafe thought I was hell-on-wheels in the bedroom, who was I to correct him? "Count on it. But it'll cost you a candlelight dinner."

His powerful car growled beneath me as we drove up the mountain. The smell of oiled leather and virile man filled my senses. Anticipation pulsed through my veins. I could get used to this. Oh yeah, very used to this.

As I sailed into the Boar's Head on Rafe's arm, I felt like a million dollars. But on the way to our table, I spotted Evan and Eleanor Hodges, and my heart went out to them.

Years of Mama drilling manners in my head wouldn't allow

me to pass them without a brief word. I inclined my head towards the siblings. "Hello, Evan. Eleanor. Have you met Rafe Golden?"

"I've seen you out at the club," Rafe said easily to Evan, shaking his hand. Rafe smiled brightly at Eleanor. "How do you do, ma'am?"

Jealousy screeched in my head as bright flags of red appeared on Eleanor's pale cheeks. She wasn't lushly sensual, but she looked attractive in her ice-blue suit and stylishly coiffed short blond hair. Her innate royal bearing was no doubt due to the pure, undiluted blue blood flowing through her veins. I couldn't compete with Eleanor academically, socially, or even superficially.

I'm sure her brain ticked off my failings in crisp text bullets like a lecturing professor's overhead slide. Poor lineage. Unpolished appearance. Inferior brain. Sure enough, Eleanor dismissed me in a single glance.

On the other hand, Rafe held her undivided attention. Her gaze widened as she gave him the same analytical assessment she had given me. Her thoughts about him probably ran along the lines of excellent conformation, well dressed, and well spoken.

I cleared my throat delicately. "You have my deepest sympathy."

Eleanor's gaze shuttered. "Mother's death will be deeply felt throughout the community. She was tireless in her devotion to Hogan's Glen."

She said the words to Rafe, as if this was their private conversation. Enough of that. I stepped between them. "How long will you be in town, Eleanor?"

Annoyance flashed through her perfect blue eyes as I blocked her view. "As long as it takes to settle Mother's affairs."

Those unpaid bills at the beauty shop came to my mind.

Eleanor could be stuck here longer than she realized. "What about your practice? Won't your patients need you?"

"Due to the circumstances, I transferred my immediate surgeries to a colleague."

"Eleanor founded Crandall Brain Clinic," I explained to Rafe. "She's a brain surgeon down in D.C."

"Not just any brain surgeon," Evan piped in, his voice full of brotherly pride. "Eleanor won the prestigious LeClair Award for three years running. She's the best there is."

Eleanor glowed under his praise.

My hands curled into tight fists.

I had accomplishments, too.

Two healthy children.

My accounting business.

Friends.

I'd bet Eleanor didn't have a single friend. And since she was pushing forty, her window of opportunity for having children had probably passed.

So there. I didn't have to feel inferior next to Eleanor Hodges. I had kids. She didn't.

"I'll keep that in mind if I ever need brain surgery," Rafe said, applying gentle pressure to my lower back with his hand.

"If you'll follow me," the hostess said mercifully.

I'd forgotten about the hostess and everyone else in the restaurant who was listening to our conversation. Good thing I'd kept my reproductive bragging to myself. "Sure."

Rafe ordered a bottle of wine when were seated in a private alcove. Classical music flowed softly around our little island. Once the wine had been opened, tasted, and we were alone again, he asked, "You want to tell me what that was all about?"

"What?" I sipped my wine slowly, savoring the excellent vintage.

"You can't fool me, Cleo. I saw the claws come out. What is

it with you and that woman?"

Years of slights and insults simmered beneath my surface. Every female of my generation had stood in Eleanor's long shadow. I didn't know how everyone else felt, but her achievements had always stuck in my craw. I thought I'd gotten over it.

I was wrong.

I would be irritated with perfect Eleanor until my dying day. "You can't fully appreciate the problem of Eleanor Hodges if you didn't grow up here."

Rafe leaned back in his chair. "Try me."

I knew better, but ancient wrongs tumbled out of my mouth. "Eleanor was the Virgin Mary in the church Christmas pageant four years in a row."

"So?"

"Mary was a highly coveted role. I wanted to be Mary, so did the other girls at Trinity Episcopal, but none of us radiated serenity and distinction like Eleanor did. She hogged the limelight."

Rafe arched an eyebrow. "This happened how many years ago?"

I downed a gulp of wine. "It's not something you forget." More stuff from the past percolated up and I let it out. "Eleanor never missed a day of school or Sunday school. Perfect attendance for twelve years. Who does that? No one. She even got a special commendation from the governor."

"I can see how that might be annoying."

"No kidding." I leaned forward in my chair. "Those straight teeth of hers? A product of her flawless bloodlines. I wore braces and so did most the kids in this town. Not Eleanor. And she was never sick. Not once. Can you believe that?"

Rafe grinned.

"Where was I? Perfect attendance. Perfect health." I ticked the accolades off on my fingers. "Perfect grades." I rolled my eyes. "Every teacher I ever had rhapsodized about Eleanor the Wonder Student. I can't tell you how annoying that was."

I went to take another sip of my wine and realized the glass was empty. Rafe moved to refill my glass, but I stilled his hand and drank water instead. Eleanor's supremacy wouldn't ruin my evening.

I buttered a slice of warm sourdough bread and munched on that. "I'm sure you noticed how pretty she is. That flawless complexion. Not one zit, ever. How fair is that?"

"Not fair at all." Rafe reached for the warm bread. "Your complaints against this woman are that she's pretty, smart, and healthy?"

"And she hogged the Virgin Mary role for years."

Rafe's eyes twinkled again. "How could I forget that? She's pretty, smart, healthy, and saintly?"

I sighed. "It sounds small-minded when you put it that way. God knows I've tried to rise above the smallness of it all, but Eleanor isn't easy to like. She looked down her nose at the rest of us mere mortals for years. Seeing her tonight brought those buried memories to the surface."

"You hate her?"

Classical music swelled through the candlelight room. I had a belly full of wine and bread. And my date was hanging on my every word. Life was good. "I don't hate her. I don't hate anybody. I'm much more comfortable being far out of Eleanor's orbit."

I felt so good about all this honesty that I went one step further. "And for the record, I didn't like the way she was sizing you up."

"Ah." Rafe stroked his chin. Without warning, he stretched, his long legs invading the space on my side of the table, his feet tangling with mine. "For the record, I like my women to have fire in them. I'm not the Ice Maiden type."

Warmth flooded my face. I didn't much like being one of his women. I wanted to be the only woman in his life. But there was a silver lining here. He didn't want Eleanor. I leaned forward conspiratorially. "You think she's frigid?"

Rafe's eyes sparkled in the low light. "Definitely."

"Interesting. I would have thought she'd be perfect in that way, too."

"Not hardly."

"How do you know?"

Rafe shrugged. "A man knows these things."

Our salads arrived, and the waiter refilled our wine glasses. This wasn't turning out to be the romantic dinner I had envisioned. Time to get my seduction back on track. I raised my glass to the center of the table. "To us."

Rafe clinked his glass against mine. His dark eyes held enough stored heat to charbroil the entire room. "To us."

I took a small sip of wine and put the glass down. Awkwardly I cast around for a topic. We always seemed to talk about me and my problems. I didn't want to talk about Erica's murder or Mama's smushed headlight. There must be another, less controversial, topic.

Both of us were attracted to each other, but talking about sex was tacky. Besides, who wanted to talk about sex? Better just to do it.

"Tell me about your family." There. A new conversational gambit. I was polished and suave. I smiled encouragingly.

Rafe's wary expression alarmed me. He put down his fork and sat up straight. His voice iced. "What do you want to know about them?"

Mental quicksand edged up around my neck; I didn't have long before it would suck me under. "We never talk about your family. If you want to keep it that way, that's okay."

"I keep my family separate from my day-to-day activities."

That was weird.

I couldn't imagine relegating Mama offstage. She wouldn't hover on the outskirts of my life for any reason. Front and center, that was Mama. I frowned. That was me, too. I couldn't imagine my girls keeping me at arm's length.

I had a sudden inspiration and went with it. "Separate worlds. Like George on the *Seinfeld* TV show. He didn't want his sets of friends to meet because worlds would collide. I get it."

Rafe looked like he'd eaten a lemon slice instead of an elegant plate of mixed greens lightly brushed with raspberry vinaigrette. "I am not a television character. I am a real person."

Dang. Every time I opened my mouth I offended him. "Gotcha." I smiled with false radiance.

He muttered something unintelligible. "You don't give a man much wiggle room, do you?"

He'd turned the topic back to me. At least this was a subject we were both familiar with. "With good reason. Once burned, twice shy."

Color climbed up his neck. "I am not your ex-husband."

"Thank God for that."

"How am I supposed to take that?"

"Like a real person?"

Rafe glared at me.

I was saved from his reply by the arrival of dinner. I had ordered the stuffed pork chops, Rafe the prime rib. Neither of us wanted to continue this scary conversation. How could I convey my longing for a person to share my life with to Rafe if we couldn't get through the salad course without quarreling? Not a good sign for the long haul.

Dinner melted in my mouth. The succulent pork chops and the rosemary-seasoned stuffing were the best things I had ever eaten. I plowed through half my meal before I ventured into conversation again. "You never told me how you got interested in golf," I said between bites.

Rafe signaled the waiter to refill our water goblets. "Golf has been a passion for as long as I can remember."

At last. Something we were both interested in. "My dad used to take me golfing with him. That's how I learned the game. Is that way you started?"

He took his time answering. "My mother golfed, and our family belonged to a golf club. Once I realized my aptitude for the sport, I spent more and more time golfing."

"Your parents must be so proud of you. My dad was absolutely thrilled when I got my CPA and went to work with him. He bragged about me to his friends."

Rafe slathered butter on the heel of bread in precise strokes. As much as I wanted to discover what made this man tick, I realized my mistake. I'd blundered again into forbidden family territory.

My lips compressed. Brick walls irritate me. I'm a big fan of windows and open doors. My life is an open book. Open is good.

He ate the heel of bread, one small bite at a time. I put down my fork and waited. If he didn't reply, our relationship was doomed to be superficial and shallow. The whole focus of the evening narrowed down to this one critical moment.

I couldn't live with a man who was a brick wall. I needed a man who would trust me with his secrets. His gaze met mine. I was surprised at how flat and expressionless his eyes were. Not his usual hot-enough-to-melt-chocolate gaze. Not by a long shot. His pain tore at me.

"My family doesn't approve of my career choice," he said.

With those words, my emotions veered sharply. I couldn't believe his relatives could be so blind. Poor Rafe. No wonder he was sensitive about his family.

Golf came to him as naturally as breathing, but he had to go against his family to do it? I couldn't imagine my parents being unsupportive of any career choice I made. If I'd wanted to be an astronaut or a ditch digger, it wouldn't have mattered as long as I was happy and I could pay my bills.

All those thoughts flashed lightning quick through my head. I sensed an undercurrent of tension in the brittle silence. My response mattered to him.

I wanted honesty from him. He should expect it from me. I covered his hand with mine. "That must be rough. I'm sorry I reminded you of a painful situation."

His face remained impassive, but he rotated his hand to hold mine. Warmth flowed between us, not just the comfortable friends kind of warmth. A deeper current that pulled at the underpinnings of my heart.

I had misjudged his brick wall. I understood blocking off a painful area of your life. God knows, I would have built a brick wall between myself and Charlie two years ago if I could.

He drew my hand toward his face, brushing his lips against my knuckles. "Thanks for understanding."

He needed me.

Lord, I needed him too. I needed his physical strength, his radiant vitality, his exquisite gentleness, and his driving passion. Heat flooded my body, filling me with an intense urgency for things yet to come. Soon. We'd be alone soon.

I had a feeling tonight would be the best yet between us. When he looked at me like this, rakish and tender, I felt young again. Attractive and desirable. Alive.

A faint ringing sound penetrated my sensual haze. Bells? Was I hearing bells? Not wedding bells, surely?

"Your phone is ringing," Rafe said, releasing my hand.

I fumbled for my purse. "Right. My phone."

If this wasn't an emergency, I would kill whomever was on the other end of the call. "Hello."

"Mom?"

At the sound of that tiny, tremulous voice, my desire-fogged brain cleared. Dread stilled my lungs. The soft classical music receded in the distance. Every ounce of my attention went to the voice in my ear. "Charla, honey. What's wrong?"

"The most awful thing happened. The police have Grammy. They just took her. Right off the street. And they towed her car. This is so horrible, I can hardly think straight. Grammy turned white as a ghost. Then she started cussing and telling Detective Radcliffe he was a damned fool. He stuffed her in a police car like she was a criminal. Mom, what are we going to do?"

Charla's rendition of events stole my breath away. I closed my eyes against the onslaught of failure. I hadn't protected Mama or my children.

An icy claw of fear gripped my heart and wouldn't let go.

I hovered in that breathless void of agony.

Why did I leave them alone tonight?

CHAPTER 8

Despair filled the void in my lungs. Thoughts burned through my skull, a boiling torrent of misgivings. My girls were in trouble. Mama was in trouble. I was miles from home. For an awful moment, I poised on the brink of meltdown. But I wasn't a Sampson for nothing.

I shuddered in a shaky breath and opened my eyes to the shadowed alcove in the Boar's Head. I couldn't fall apart now, even if my blood was icy hot and brain combustion was likely. Immediate, decisive action was needed. "Charla, where are you?"

"At the police station. I don't like it here, Mom. The people are sketchy. No one will tell us a thing."

"I'm on my way. Is Lexy with you?"

"Yes, but she's no help because the dog is freaking out. Madonna keeps trying to hide behind Lexy because she's scared, too."

There was so much noise on Charla's end of the phone that I covered my other ear and jammed the phone against my ear to hear. Adrenaline surged through my blood like a blazing comet.

I had enough energy to run the twenty miles to the police station without once touching the ground. "I'm coming, sweetheart. Stay with your sister. One quick question. Did Mama call Bud Flook?"

"Who knows? We haven't seen her since they took her. She went all pale like she does when she needs her heart medicine.

I'm scared, Mom."

"Stay together. I'm on my way." I clicked off the phone and stood up. "I have to go."

Rafe stood with me, concern ringing his eyes. "What happened?"

The urgent messages boiling through my brain found their way out. "Family emergency. I have to go. Right now."

"Then we'll go." Rafe tossed a couple of large bills on the table and signaled the waiter.

We hurtled down the winding mountain road, my seat belt cinching on the turns. Pork chops and stuffing sloshed in my tummy. White knuckles bulged from my hand as I gripped the leather arm rest. "Slow down. You're going to kill us both."

"Don't worry. This car handles like a dream. You want to tell me where we're going once we get down the mountain?"

"The police station."

Rafe glanced over at me. With only the glow of the instrument panel lighting his face, I couldn't gauge his reaction. "Charla said the police stopped Mama's car," I said. "Britt took Mama and impounded her Olds. My children and my dog, who were with her, are stranded at the police station."

His silence unnerved me. Charlie would've been yelling by now. But Rafe wasn't Charlie. He wasn't criticizing Mama or outwardly judging us. He was helping by getting me to my family. Relief whooshed out of my lungs, loosened my tongue. "I've been dreading something like this for days. But I never thought the girls would get tangled up in Mama's mess."

"I see."

Did he? We rocketed down the dark road, in a tiny car, and all I saw was the road before us. I wished we were there already. But what was I going to do to help? Think, Cleo. Your family is depending on you. Make a plan. Analyze the data. I could do that. The police had Mama. She needed more than a hug and a ride home. She needed a lawyer. With trembling fingers, I dialed her lawyer, Bud Flook. No answer.

Where was he?

Hogan's Glen was small enough that I knew Bud Flook played poker every Friday night. Some of his poker buddies were my clients and listed in my cell phone contacts. Two calls later, I found him.

I cut right to the chase. "Bud. This is Cleopatra Jones. Mama needs you at the police station."

"Now?" he grumbled.

Bud's gruff tone hit a raw nerve. Did he object to being told what to do? Tough. I couldn't pander to male egos right now. "Yes. Now." I ended the call.

"Is Bud a good lawyer?" Rafe navigated a tight curve with the skill of an Indy 500 driver.

I tunneled my fingers through my hair. "Criminal matters aren't his forte, but I've known Bud for years. He's solid. He'll get Mama out of jail."

"Was Delilah arrested?" he asked.

"I don't know." I tried to inject an optimistic tone in my voice. "Earlier this week Britt mentioned he needed to talk to her."

In the back of my mind a little voice warned that Rafe didn't sign up for family high drama. His interest in me was physical. Chances were good none of his previous dates had ended up at jail. Given that, chances were very good this was our last date. My spirits sank even lower.

"From your earlier comment, it sounded like you expected this to happen," he said.

I stared at the blur of dark trees and faintly illuminated houses rushing past my window. The swiftly changing landscape held no easy answers. Rafe wasn't family. He wasn't involved. Except for driving me to the police station.

Our relationship had boundaries. Dirty laundry fell outside the arena of great sex and fine dining. I wanted to confide in him because shutting him out seemed wrong. Except I was vulnerable. My whole family was vulnerable. What a house of cards I'd built.

But the new Cleo didn't sit back and let life happen to her. The new Cleo took calculated risks. The new Cleo wanted a future with Rafe. I sighed out a long, shaky breath and crossed my fingers. "It has to do with Erica Hodges." His sidelong glance had me balling my fingers into tight fists.

"I thought Erica was a hit by a car," he said.

"She was."

"Your mother's car?"

"Probably," I whispered. Hot tears stung my eyes, and my expensive dinner clotted into a solid lump in my queasy stomach. I squeezed my eyes shut to keep the tears from falling. Mama wouldn't crumble in the face of adversity and neither would I. But taking risks was harder than I thought.

"You knew about her car?"

My stomach slid around in my throat as Rafe wheeled through another series of sharp turns. "I knew her car had been in an accident."

"I see."

I sighed. Poor deluded man. He couldn't know what it was like to live with a stubborn, opinionated woman like Mama. Daddy had looked after Mama for years, and he'd passed the baton of caretaking to me. I couldn't let Daddy down.

Even though Rafe had every right to walk away from this situation, I hoped otherwise. "I need another favor. Would you take the girls home and stay with them until I spring Mama from jail?"

"I'm being sent home with the children?"

His incredulous tone snapped the thin rein on my patience.

"You're being entrusted with the two most precious things in my life. If you screw this up, I will hunt you down like a dog and tear you limb from limb."

"Got it."

I massaged my pounding temples.

I didn't want to fight with Rafe. I wanted him on my side. "If it's not convenient, I can call Jonette at the Tavern. She'll come get them."

"I'll do it. But I want a full explanation of what's going on."

"You and me both."

Fluorescent lights starkly illuminated the no-nonsense white walls of the county police station. The heels of my taupe pumps clicked on the tile floor as I strode inside. A central wooden information kiosk blocked direct access to the reception desk.

I adjusted my course to navigate around it. This place wasn't old, but it felt like the end of the road. Panic nipped at my nerves. My kids were in here somewhere, and I had to get them out.

Immediately.

The uniformed desk sergeant behind the thick glass barrier glared at me in stony-faced grimness, but I quickly forgot about him at the excited shouts of my girls.

"Mom!" Charla and Lexy darted out of a seating area on the side of the room. They flew into my arms and held on tight. Madonna barked her relief at being rescued. Thick threads of doggie drool splattered against the center island, on the tile floor, and on my taupe pants. Lord, what a mess.

I held my daughters close and took strength from the fact that they were unharmed. Charla burst into tears. Lexy let go of me to calm the dog. Madonna usurped Lexy's place at my side and licked my slacks.

After sending up a prayer of thankfulness, I took a deep

breath and made eye contact with my girls. "What happened? I thought you were having a quiet evening at home."

"We were," Lexy said. "Then we wanted Italian ice to wash down our Christmas pizza. Only we never made it to the place by the park. A policeman stopped us on the way because of Grammy's headlight being out. The cop made us stand on the side of the road until Detective Radcliffe got there. When he looked at Grammy's car, his face got hard and mean."

Charla swiped at the tears on her cheeks and choked back her heartrending sobs. "Detective Radcliffe hustled Grammy into a police car. Then he didn't know what to do with us. Another cop car came, and we ended up here. The officer tried to give us stuffed animals like we were little kids. I've never been so humiliated in my entire life."

She didn't look humiliated. Her eyes glittered with excitement. I'm sure she would recover from this trauma. I knew exactly where to place the blame for this disaster, and I would deal with Mama next.

Mama had no business driving that car. The keys for my Volvo were on the hutch. None of this would have happened if she'd stayed home tonight or used my car. I intended to give her a piece of my mind.

I stroked Lexy and Charla's youthful faces. "You girls had quite a shock tonight."

"And Madonna. She had quite a shock, too," Lexy said, sounding ten years older than her thirteen.

I petted my dog, and her tail thumped against the center island of the room. Tufts of white dog hair swirled on the floor. "We all had a shock tonight."

Lexy tugged on my blouse. "Mama, what about Grammy? Why can't we see her? Is she coming home tonight?"

I ruffled Lexy's dark hair. "I'll find out. I want you girls and Madonna to go home with Rafe. He'll stay with you until I come home."

"I don't want to go, Mama," Charla said. "I'm not a child."

My back teeth ground together. Regardless of what she thought, Charla was a child, and I wanted her safe at home. A little reverse psychology was needed to finesse her compliance. "No problem. You can wait with me. The thing is, it may take hours until we know something. I thought you might be more comfortable waiting at home."

"I'll be more comfortable at home," Lexy said. "Madonna and I want to go home. This place stinks."

Emotions flashed across Charla's face in rapid-fire succession. I could see that she wanted to go home with her sister and she wanted to stay with me. "It does stink here. I have to shampoo the nasty smell out of my hair before I can go to sleep."

"I don't know how long I'll be," I said.

Charla wrinkled her nose. "I'd rather wait at home then."

"It's your choice," I said, as if her decision didn't matter to me. My eyes met Rafe's above the top of Charla's curly red hair. He'd listened to the exchange with rapt attention. Did he think I was shamelessly manipulative?

"Call us if you hear anything," Charla said.

"Are we ready?" Rafe asked.

"Shotgun," Lexy called, jostling past her sister toward the door.

"No way." Charla stood her ground. "You had shotgun last time. Mom! It's not fair. She can't call it all the time. I'm the oldest. I get shotgun. Tell her, Mom."

I threw my hands up in the air. "It's not my car, not my rules. Rafe will decide who sits in the passenger seat."

Rafe brushed his lips across mine. "Thanks a lot, Red."

"No reason why I have to make all the hard decisions." Chills ran down my spine at his touch.

The grumpy desk clerk and Charla watched us in stern

disapproval. Madonna and Lexy stood poised in front of the glass doors, Madonna looking mournfully sad as if she didn't want to leave me here.

"Stay out of trouble," Rafe directed before he left.

I approached the window and leaned down to speak into the intercom. "I'm here to see my mother, Delilah Sampson."

The desk clerk glared at me. "Who was the arresting officer?"

I swallowed harshly. Arresting officer sounded so negative. But here in the police station, one had to speak their language. "Detective Britt Radcliffe."

"And your name is?"

"Cleopatra Jones."

He gestured to the plastic orange chairs lining the side of the room. "Have a seat. I'll let Detective Radcliffe know you're here."

I didn't budge. "Can I see my mother?"

"That will be up to Detective Radcliffe. Take a seat."

As if I could sit calmly when Mama was being grilled or fingerprinted. I paced the room until Mama's lawyer showed up. Bud Flook wasn't tall for a man. He was exactly my height, five-foot-six. He wore his salt-and-pepper hair closely cropped. Light glinted off his rounded frameless glasses. The sleeves of his blue Oxford shirt were rolled up, and his tan trousers were wrinkled from sitting. The haze of cigar smoke enveloped him.

"What's the deal, Bud?" I blushed, realizing how ungrateful I sounded. "I mean, thank you for coming."

"No problem." Bud set his battered briefcase down on the center island kiosk. "What are the charges against Delilah?"

I swiped my hair back from the side of my face. "I have no new information. I can't get past the guard at the door."

His voice broke. "I can."

I blinked at the unusual sound. Bud had always been in control of his emotions. He was lethal on the golf course because you never suspected someone who was so quiet to be such a good scorer. I studied his face and realized his color was off. Tension radiated from him in unrelenting waves. "You okay, Bud?"

"I'm fine," he grumbled, picking up his briefcase. "I'll let you know what I find out."

"Can I come with you?" I asked, following him to the front desk.

"No," the desk clerk said, motioning me back to the seating area. "You wait here."

Bud Flook vanished into the building. I sat. I paced. I waited. And I waited some more. The wet spot on my blouse from Charla's tearful outburst dried. I went to the bathroom. And still nothing.

I walked up to the front desk again. "Are you sure I can't go back there?"

"I'm sure, lady." He gestured toward the orange chairs. "Take a seat."

I didn't want to sit. I wanted action. I wanted the sinking feeling in the pit of my stomach to go away. I wanted my skin to stop crawling.

Pairs of officers passed through the room and entered the sacred inner sanctum. Their cop eyes studied me and dismissed me. The contrary part of me wanted to stand up and say, "I can be a threat. I'm trouble." But I stopped short of making a spectacle of myself.

One spectacle in the family was enough.

I crossed and recrossed my legs. I brushed the dog hair off my slacks. I counted the tiles on the floor, then the ones in the ceiling. I thought about calling Jonette to come keep me company when her shift at the Tavern ended.

Then the door opened. My least favorite cop in the whole world stepped forward. He motioned me over. I leapt to my feet and followed. My heart raced as I was ushered down a side corridor and into a sterile-looking room. My thoughts about the décor came in crisp bullets. Pale blue walls. Classier furniture than the lobby. Beige-colored padded chairs with chrome frames and plastic-covered armrests.

I took the seat he indicated on the far side of the room. Questions burst out of me with machine-gun rapidity as I perched on the edge of my chair. "Where's Mama? Why did you arrest her? Can I take her home tonight? Can I see her?"

Britt sat down across from me, pen and notebook in hand. Oh, Lord. Was I under suspicion too? My palms dampened. Fear clawed at me, but I held tough. I was innocent. "Well?"

"There is a broken headlight on Delilah's car."

Britt's dark eyes drilled into me. The chords in his thick fireplug neck bulged. I gave it right back to him. "Headlights get broken all the time."

A muscle in his tanned cheek twitched. "You should have stepped forward."

Why would I volunteer incriminating evidence? He had the power here, and that didn't sit well with me. Britt claimed he was my friend. He wasn't treating me like a friend. "You should have told me Mama was being investigated."

"You should have realized Delilah was a suspect based on her relationship with the deceased."

His unyielding tone worried me. Had he already tried and convicted Mama in his head? Was he forgetting that the deceased wasn't little Miss Sunshine? "Erica had run-ins with other people. Mama wasn't the only person she didn't get along with."

He studied me intently. "Delilah is the only person she didn't get along with who has a damaged car."

I swear I didn't squirm in my seat, but I mentally flinched. Poor Mama. One misstep on my part and she would wear a prison jumpsuit the rest of her days. She hated the color orange.

"Mama says she didn't kill anyone," I said.

He tugged at his shirt collar. "I have a team of forensic experts going over her car. We will know soon if that car was the murder weapon."

I paled. "You think Mama intentionally killed Erica Hodges?"

"Delilah had the motive and the means. Whether she had the opportunity remains to be seen."

I'd thought the same thing, but I didn't like hearing it from a police detective. I could buy that there had been a car accident. Not murder. "Mama didn't murder anyone."

Britt glared at me.

"What did she tell you?" I asked.

"Nothing helpful. She called me every name in the book. The only thing that shut her up was the arrival of her lawyer. Bud got her calmed down, but now she won't tell me anything."

I shook my head in disbelief. Mama's behavior made no sense. "I don't understand."

Britt ignored my comment and flipped his notebook open. "I need to ask you a few questions, Cleo. What can you tell me about that night?"

My heart sank. Britt would know the times didn't match up, and that would be all he needed to lock Mama up for good. God help us all. I swallowed thickly. "The night Erica died?"

"Yes. Where was Delilah?"

"She was home all afternoon." I thought about the events of that night for a few seconds. I would state things in the most favorable light. If Britt drew the wrong conclusion, that wasn't my fault. "After supper she drove Francine and Muriel to the Hospitality Committee meeting. Mama went straight to bed when she got home."

"What time did she go out?"

"A little before seven. You asked me these questions this

morning at church."

Britt scribbled something else. "What time did she return?"

I stared at my hands on the table. "I was busy with the girls when she came in. We were getting their new bookbags ready for school the next day. The thing that stuck in my mind was that Mama went to bed earlier than the girls. Sorry. I didn't note the exact time."

With any luck that would be good enough.

Britt pressed on. "What time did the girls go to bed?"

He wouldn't let this go. I exhaled half a breath of air. "Sometime between nine and ten."

"If you estimated the time of Delilah's return, it would be?"

"I wasn't paying attention. I don't recall." Britt jotted more notes. I would have given anything to see what he was writing.

"What level of physical activity can she reasonably perform with her heart condition?"

Fear for Mama washed over me. "Is Mama all right? Does she need her heart medicine?"

"Delilah is fine. I brought her in myself."

My stomach clenched. "You took her off the side of the road. In front of my children."

"I had no choice. Not once I saw the car." He flipped back through his book until he found what he was looking for. "What would you say her state of mind was prior to going out Tuesday evening?"

I chewed on the inside of my mouth. I didn't want to answer this question.

Britt leaned forward. "Her state of mind, Cleo. What was her state of mind that night?"

My lungs burned for air. I took a shallow breath. I loved my mother. I did not want to do any harm here. The room spun a little. I had no choice. The truth was all I had. "Mama seemed off."

Britt's interest level spiked. So did his eyebrows. "Off? How?"

I looked away. I didn't want to do this. Why wouldn't he stop with the questions? "Off." I gestured wildly with my hands. "Preoccupied. Fuzzy. You know. Off."

Britt sat very still. "What did she say when you asked her about her car?"

My clammy skin flushed with heat. "She said nothing was wrong with her car. We went outside, and she was shocked by the damage."

"And?"

"And nothing. She clammed up on me."

"How did you get her to talk?"

"I didn't." I shifted uneasily in my seat. "I've answered your questions. My turn to be the detective. What charges are you holding her on?"

"I brought Delilah here under probable cause. She's a person of interest."

"What's that?"

"The body of evidence points to Delilah."

The room spun faster. I wanted the body of evidence to point to someone else. "Is she under arrest? Do I need to post bail?"

"You were doing good until then. As per police questioning one-oh-one, you only ask one question at a time."

I wanted to snatch him up by the collar of his snug navy-blue polo and shake him. Instead I counted to five and asked again. "Is Mama under arrest?"

"Charges against her are pending."

"Is she free to go?"

Britt frowned. "Yes. But she can't leave town."

I couldn't get her to go twenty miles to visit a retirement community. "Mama isn't going anywhere."

"Just as well. I'd have to come get her if she left. This is very serious, Cleo."

As if I didn't know that. "Can I take her home?"

Britt nodded. "You're both free to go. For now."

For now. Time was running out on Mama's freedom. Fear ruled my heart, hammered through my veins. I needed more time to prove Erica's death was an accident.

Not murder.

It couldn't be murder.

I flicked a quick glance at Britt. His cop eyes didn't miss much. I had the nauseating feeling he knew what I'd been thinking.

I wished that went both ways. All I saw when I looked at him was grim resolve.

I stood up on shaky legs and grabbed the back of the chair to steady myself. "I'm not used to being interrogated."

Britt opened the door with a scowl. "You were interviewed. Big difference."

Easy for him to say. This whole experience had been harrowing. I wanted to get Mama out of here before something else went wrong. I followed him through another door, and there was Mama and Bud Flook. I rushed forward and took her hand.

Mama's face was pale. Too pale. She seemed very surprised to see me. "Time to go home, Mama," I said.

"I can go?" Mama's gaze darted between Britt and Bud as if she thought her release was a cruel trick.

Britt's well-muscled body blocked the doorway. "Charges against you are pending, Delilah. Don't leave town."

"Hmmph," Mama muttered as she stood.

Her legs seemed to be working better than mine. My mind raced ahead to resolve the next obstacle. I didn't have any way to get us home. "Can we catch a ride with you, Bud?"

"No problem," Bud said.

I put Mama in the back seat of Bud's large car and then climbed in after her. I rubbed my face. "God, this has been a long night."

"Don't start in on me," Mama said. "This hasn't been a pleasure cruise for me, either."

"You're in trouble, Mama. Let me help you."

"I made this mess. I'll clean it up."

"It's my mess too, Mama. We'll talk about this later," I replied.

Bud and Mama exchanged a glance via the rearview mirror as Bud eased out of the lighted parking lot. His Lincoln Town Car was older than dirt, but the back seat was spacious and clean, even if it did reek of cigars. I sighed with gratitude. We were finally headed home.

By all rights, I should be playing underwear show-and-tell over at Rafe's house. Not going to happen this evening. *So* not going to happen.

Bud turned on the radio. Big band music blared in my ear the rest of the way home. "Thanks for the lift," I said when he pulled up behind Rafe's red convertible in my driveway.

"Nice wheels," Bud said, nodding towards Rafe's car. "I would have turned pro years ago if I could have bought a ride like that."

Rafe must have been watching for our arrival from the kitchen. He came out and helped me get Mama up the steps and in the house.

"Everything all right?" he asked.

"Peachy." Mama stopped and propped her fists on her hips. "Bud, you go on home. I can walk to my room alone, Cleo. You take care of your fella." She clomped out of the room and up the stairs under her own power. Bud shrugged and left. Then it was just me and Rafe.

I took his hand and led him to the living room. We sat on the sofa. "Thanks for your help, Rafe. I couldn't have done this without you. The girls went to bed without any trouble?"

"They sacked out a few hours ago." Rafe kissed my hand. "Well?"

My fingers itched to smooth his flyaway hair off his brow. "Well, nothing. This rates right up there with the worst evening of my life."

His gaze narrowed dangerously. "I thought you enjoyed dinner."

"I did." I leaned back into the cushy sofa and his arm drew me in close. I needed his warmth. His strength. "It's the other parts of the evening that stink."

"We could go upstairs and I could make everything better for you." A wicked grin lit his face. Hope sparkled in his sexy eyes.

"No. Not here," I said with regret. He knew the rules. I didn't sleep with him in this house.

"Don't shut me out, Red. I want to help. What happened at the police station?"

He deserved to know, even though telling him would destroy any final illusions he had about my wacky family. I gripped my shaking hands in my lap. "Mama's not under arrest. Yet. They are conducting forensic tests on her car."

Rafe whistled softly. "Sounds like you need a criminal defense attorney."

His comment infuriated me, even though my thoughts had been running along the same lines. "Mama didn't murder anyone. You'll see. I'll get to the bottom of this, and then everything will be fine."

His features hardened. "I don't want you getting to the bottom of this. You got lucky last time. You could've been killed."

Frustration sharpened my voice. "I can't sit back and do nothing."

"Your mother is a grown-up," he countered.

"That's what she'd like everyone to believe."

"Dammit, Cleo. Stay out of it."

Patience had never been my strong suit, and tonight's adventure had exceeded my ability to cope. Rafe wanted me to be safe. But I couldn't accommodate his wants and help Mama. I stood and gestured toward the door. "Time for you to go home."

He studied me from the couch. For a moment I thought he wouldn't budge, but he surprised me by taking my hand and rising. "You aren't coming home with me?" he asked.

Perversely, that's exactly what I wanted, to spend the night in his arms and let Mama's problems run their course. I reached deep for the courage to turn him down. "I can't. Not tonight. My family needs me. My family is important to me."

Rafe stopped in the doorway, his fingers skimming the side of my cheek. "You're important to me. I don't want your mother taking advantage of you."

I edged him out the door. The lock snicked in place. "You're about thirty-eight years too late for that."

CHAPTER 9

"Evan isn't here today," the perky blonde said. I leaned forward to read her Mountaintop Gym name tag. Like the other the well-sculpted trainers at the gym, twenty-something Gen could easily drop to the floor and riff fifty pushups without breaking a sweat or a nail. She glowed with health and brimmed with good cheer.

"He's not?" I peered into the gym. Saturday midmorning usually was the time people like me showed up. The fitness junkies cruised through the place before eight. Usually. Today the median age appeared to be much younger, and fitter than me.

Not one of them was sweating profusely or complaining. Drat.

"The poor guy." Gen's radiant smile dimmed a bit. "Death in the family."

I frowned. "I heard, but Evan didn't mention rescheduling when I saw him at dinner last night. Why didn't someone from the gym notify me? I wasted a trip up here."

Gen jabbed both thumbs toward her perky chest. "Because I'm taking Evan's client list today. Let's get started."

"Oh." I wasn't keen on having a kid like Gen tell me what to do. That's why Evan Hodges was my personal trainer.

With my sloppy gray sweats and my ratty workout shirt, I looked like a beached whale standing next to sleek, dolphin-like Gen. I wasn't tanned. I wasn't buff. And I certainly wasn't fit.

Although I was trying.

I'm sure Gen had a different definition than Evan of trying. Machines whirred, rock music blasted, and I dithered. I could go home and bypass certain humiliation. Or I could tough it out. I should have developed some level of fitness by now.

I should have called the gym first. Funny how clear that was now. But I'd been focused on talking to Evan about his mother, hoping he knew the underlying cause of the feud. I'd been focused on my family, not his. At least my mother was still alive.

Gen bounced over to the tall metal file cabinet. There was a spring to her step that came from being new to adulthood. I told myself I wasn't envious of her youthful vitality. I didn't want to reclaim my childhood. That's not why I worked out. I worked out so that I could be strong and flexible.

The trainer pulled my chart and studied it briefly. I had the sick feeling she was laughing to herself over my lack of progress. "Do you need any help warming up?" she asked as a cute guy strolled in.

"I can manage," I said.

Gen dropped me like a steaming sauna towel and bounced back to the front desk. I went through my stretching routine, then hit the treadmill for half an hour. I could have walked a couple of hours on that thing if it had gotten me out of my fitness appointment with Gen.

I'd forgotten my headphones again, and there wasn't much point in watching TV without them. Instead, I listened to the whir of well-oiled machines and the sounds of people using them. I tried reading the lips of the television actors, but no one said, "I love you" or "Hi, Mom."

Before long, Mama's near-arrest hijacked my thoughts. Mama had insisted she didn't kill anyone, but it sure looked like her car killed Erica. Britt believed Mama had murdered Erica. I believed Erica's death could have been an accident. But Britt said Erica had been run over multiple times—

This circular thinking wasn't helping.

Everything was too jumbled up in my head. I needed organization. The facts needed to be sorted like credits and debits.

Mama had no criminal record. That went in the credit column. I thought some more. Mama had held down a job and been an active community volunteer for years. Another item in the credit column. Try as I might, I couldn't come up with anything else for the credit side of the ledger.

Her damaged car. The history of antagonism with Erica. Mama's unaccounted time on Tuesday evening. Her odd behavior before and after Erica's death. The verbal smackdown between the two women on Monday night. All of those things were debits.

More than debits.

They painted a picture I didn't want to see.

A terrible picture that had Mama behind bars for the rest of her life. The thing I kept coming back to was why now? Mama had butted heads with Erica for years. Why would she wait to do something about it?

I needed more information.

There must have been an inciting incident. All I had to do was dig deeper. Only, Mama and her friends were holding out on me. I couldn't very well ask the dead woman, and chances were good her son wouldn't humor me. Heck, he hadn't even let me know he'd cancelled on me.

Mama was in trouble, and nothing I'd done so far had helped. I'd failed to look after her as Daddy had asked. She'd messed up, but so had I. Fatigue hit me right between the eyes. I knew what it felt like to give up. I'd quit on life once before, letting my emotions paralyze me to the point of inertia.

In the back of my mind I heard Mama's voice. *Stop that.*

Sampson women are stronger than this.

She'd been there for me when I was down. Is this how I repaid her? By giving up on her? Where was my faith in the woman who'd given me life and nurtured me?

A spark of hope touched my gloomy thoughts. What if I came at the problem from another angle? Sure, the body of evidence pointed to Mama. But what if that had been engineered?

My pace slowed as the implications sank in. Mama could have been framed. She could be squeaky clean as she'd claimed all along. Well, not squeaky clean. She had a long history of run-ins with the victim.

My blood chilled as the idea took hold. Mama was the perfect patsy. A killer could have taken advantageous of her outrageous, obstinate, and overbearing ways.

Yes. My stride lengthened. That felt right. I was definitely onto something here.

The treadmill timer rang, and Gen bounced over to my side. An hour later, I hobbled out of the gym bathroom and into the parking lot. Every muscle in my body had been stretched to its maximum endurance, every tendon strained.

For what?

So I wouldn't look like a wuss in front of a woman I'd just met. Sad but true. It was barely noon on an overcast Saturday morning, and I needed a nap. I limped toward my car.

I'd started this fitness program to improve my golf swing. At the rate I was seizing up, I'd be lucky if I could even swing my nine wood by the next ladies nine-hole outing on Wednesday.

Home beckoned, as did a long soak in the tub. With Charlie taking the girls this afternoon, I'd have plenty of time to talk to Mama. She might not want to talk, but I'd be firm.

"Cleo. Wait up." Darnell Reynolds huffed over to intercept me. He wore a dark business suit, a blue tie, and a white dress shirt. For our mayor, it was business as usual on a Saturday morning.

"Hey, Darnell. What's going on?" I thanked God for showers and deodorant. Otherwise, I'd be standing here in this herd of brightly colored cars, smelling like the queen of funk. As it was, my jeans and white polo shirt struck just the right note of Saturday casual. Shower-dampened hair cooled my head.

Darnell was my wealthiest accounting client, and he'd steered a lot of business my way over the last five years. I appreciated his efforts, even though I privately thought he was a pompous ass. I hadn't missed a quarterly appointment with him, had I? Or worse, he wasn't going to ask me out, was he? I held my breath.

He glanced around furtively, his odd behavior ramping up my nerves. What was going on in this town? Who was the mayor hiding from?

Did he expect the IRS to be skulking in the gym parking lot? I had it on good authority that the IRS only cared about people's financial fitness. They could care less if I worked out or spoke to my clients about nonbusiness matters.

"I need to talk to you," Darnell said. "Right away."

"Here I am." I shrugged as I spoke. The slight motion had me wincing at the lactic acid built up in my shoulder muscles.

He leaned in a bit closer. "This is a private matter. Follow me to my office?"

Dang. A client request. He had me there. "Okay."

Darnell drove his pickup like a man possessed. I was thankful to be following him in the sturdy Gray Beast instead of inside his very large, swerving vehicle. Every muscle in my body pulled when I got out of my car.

I limped to his office in the stately city hall building. He scurried behind the carved oak desk that had belonged to his grandfather and stopped between the twin oils of the mountain ranges guarding our valley. "What's this about, Darnell?"

"That g.d. housing development, that's what." He closed the door behind us and paced around his office.

There was only one new development in Hogan's Glen. White Rock. Darnell had gone in with the late Dudley Davis and put together an upscale community on the edge of the city limits.

Houses were already under construction when the state issued a building moratorium because of water availability, halting construction. Consequently, White Rock was a ghost town.

"I thought you were working with the state to get the moratorium lifted."

"I am. The town bought the Stewart farm to protect our wellheads. We've got new wells coming online soon. We've got great water reuse ideas in the pipeline. Lots of water plans in the works. It's coming along, but it can't happen tomorrow. Bureaucracies don't move that fast."

I eased into the brown leather chair across from his desk. "How can I help you, Darnell?"

Darnell halted in front of the Maryland flag next to his desk. The redness of his neck and face worried me. His complexion wasn't usually that florid. His neck seemed unusually thick and rigid, too. Not a good sign. Something big was bothering Darnell.

"One of my silent partners wants out. Today. I don't have the money until I sell the lots and build the houses. What am I going to do?"

"Why don't you sit down with your partner and explain the situation to him or her?" Was it Dudley's ex-wife who wanted to sell? I'd known Bitsy Davis for years, and if she was the problem, I could see how Darnell thought I could persuade her to wait.

I'd drawn up the original financial information for the investors in the development. There had been another key investor, only I couldn't remember who it was.

Darnell rubbed the back of his neck. "Did that. Didn't help."

My brain slid into accounting mode. "Show your silent partner the balance in the bank account." Money always talked. So did the lack of money.

"This person is unreasonable. I explained how the corporation assets aren't liquid and got nowhere. What the hell am I going to do? If I sell enough of the land to buy this person out, I'll cripple the development and lose my shirt."

"How about a gradual payoff?"

"Nope. This person wants the entire chunk of change up front. And they want it yesterday."

"Who are we talking about here?"

Darnell grimaced. "You don't remember?"

I shook my head. My stiff neck strained at the movement.

Darnell looked me straight in the eye. "Erica Hodges."

Erica Hodges.

I was beginning to hate the sound of her name. Every time it cropped up, something bad happened to my family. I stated the obvious. "She's dead."

"But her heirs aren't. I had a phone call from her daughter, Eleanor, last night, demanding Erica's share immediately." Darnell wiped his brow. "It makes no sense to liquidate White Rock now."

"Are there liquid funds in your other investments that you could move around to cover Erica's share in White Rock?"

"No. I'm completely leveraged. I never should have tied up so much of my personal money in this development."

Another idea occurred to me. Maybe I could help Darnell. "What about Bitsy Davis? Why don't you ask her if she'll purchase Erica's share?"

A faint glimmer of hope appeared on Darnell's face. "Would she do it?"

"I don't know, but it won't hurt to ask." I rose to leave.

Darnell reached for the phone, hope flaring in his eyes. "Thanks, Cleo."

I limped out of there, satisfied I'd helped him. If only I could fix Mama's troubles so easily. I checked my watch. The girls were getting ready to spend the afternoon with their dad. Mama wasn't going anywhere without a car, but I dreaded the conversation we would surely have.

The wind stirred my damp hair. Here I was in downtown Hogan's Glen on a Saturday morning. I wasn't normally down here this time of day. But Jonette was. She'd whip me into fighting shape in short order.

The Tavern was around the corner from city hall. As I hurried there, the breeze picked up and blew right through my thin white shirt. A glance at the darkening sky alerted me of an approaching storm.

The thing about living in a valley was that you couldn't accurately predict how far away a weather system was. Once you saw clouds over the mountain range, you might have a few hours or a few minutes, depending on the height and speed of the front. With any luck, the shower would come and go while I was at the Tavern.

I hugged my arms close to my body and walked as fast as my aching muscles would allow. I stepped inside the Tavern, entering a world where time stood still. It was permanently 1970s in here, from the rock-n-roll paraphernalia dotting the walls to the raucous music filling the cozy room. Due to the dark-red ceiling and the hunter-green walls, the dim lighting seemed barely adequate.

The wonder of it was that Jonette wasn't blinded by sunshine after being in such a murky environment most of the time. I headed for her section in the back of the room.

"Cleo!" Jonette took one look at me and handed off the tray of food she carried to a solid pony-tailed man behind the bar.

"Dean, I'm going on break," Jonette said. "Take this to table five." Jonette untied her black cocktail apron and fixed us two cups of coffee. She slid in the booth across from me.

I wasn't surprised she told her boss what to do. Jonette had a way of twisting men around her finger without even trying. What surprised me was the look of alarm in Dean's eye until he realized Jonette was sitting with me.

"What's wrong, Clee?" Jonette asked.

"You haven't heard?"

Jonette's eyes lit up. "Oh goody. News. It's been slow in here this morning."

"It may be news to you, but it's a nightmare to me." I leaned forward to sip my coffee. The moist steam rising off the coffee opened my senses, the jolt from the caffeine revved up my flagging energy. "Mama was taken in for questioning last night."

Jonette grimaced. "Why didn't you call me?"

"I couldn't." I shook my head sadly. "I just couldn't talk about it."

"Wait." She met my level gaze. "Last night as in hot date last night?"

"Only half of a hot date. We were dining when I got the call."

"Frustration on top of frustration, right?"

I rubbed my eyes. "It's such a mess. Britt believes Mama murdered Erica."

"Murder? I thought it was hit and run. An accident."

"Britt says it wasn't an accident. He's convinced Mama was behind the wheel."

"Dang." Jonette sipped her coffee. Around us, Lynyrd Skynyrd sang of coming home to Alabama. Conversations at the bar counter ebbed and flowed. I caught Dean glancing at us as we put our heads closer together.

Smart man.

He had to know Jonette and I were scheming and anything

could happen.

"Where is she? Did Detective Dumb-as-Dirt keep her locked up overnight?"

"No. He said she wasn't a flight risk. She hasn't been officially charged with murder. They're checking her car against the other evidence."

"What have they got?"

"Nothing good. All the evidence indicates Mama's car ran over Erica. More than once. Intentional acts of violence. Britt says it's murder. Mama says she didn't kill anyone. I want to believe her."

"You know you do. Me, too. What's next?"

I sighed. "That's the trouble. I'm exhausted, and I can't think straight. Mama's not talking, Rafe's mad at me for ruining our night of wild sex, and Britt's breathing down my neck. Top that off with a morning with Atilla the Grinning Gorilla at the gym, and my life sucks."

Jonette laughed. "No wonder you're hiding out in here."

I bristled. "I am not hiding out. I came here for sympathy."

"Forget it." Jonette waved off my remark. "You don't need sympathy. You need a swift kick in the pants. We're good at figuring out stuff, so we'll find out what your mother is hiding. That will take care of Britt, too. Rafe will be fine once he gets you in the sack again. What I want to know is, who is Atilla the Grinning Gorilla? Evan the hunky gym dog?"

I waved off Jonette's dancing eyebrows. "Don't go looking at me like that. I am not interested in Evan Hodges. He stood me up. Instead, I had a pint-sized personal trainer named Gen. She was merciless, and she grinned incessantly. I won't be able to walk for days, and I'm sure I've ruined my golf game."

Jonette waved her hand like it was a magic wand. "Your game wasn't good to start with. A few lessons from a certain golf pro will fix what ails you. See. One problem solved."

"If only it were that easy." But I felt better. "How's the election campaign coming along?"

"Been working on a slogan. What do you think about 'Moore for Mayor'?"

"Not bad. Not bad at all." The front door opened and my ex walked in and folded his wet umbrella. I did not want to deal with him right now. "Hide." I ducked under the table.

Jonette joined me. "Who are we hiding from?"

I peeked over the table in time to see Charlie stop at the bar and talk to Dean. He directed Charlie toward our booth in the back corner. "Never mind. Dean ratted us out." I sat up and slid close to the outer edge of my bench seat so that there was no room on my side of the booth.

Undeterred, Charlie slid in next to Jonette. "Hello, gorgeous."

"All my customers say I'm gorgeous," Jonette said, primping her short brown hair, turning his attention from me to her.

"You ladies are too beautiful for words," Charlie said with a broad smile that included both of us. His arm reached casually along the back of the seat.

A glass shattered over at the bar. A spine-tingling shiver shook me from head to toe. "Charlie, what brings you here?" I asked pointedly.

"I heard about Delilah's run-in with the law. I'm here to offer my services. What can I do?"

If I took him up on his offer, he'd think he was making progress toward getting me back. I needed help, but I didn't need it that badly. My spine stiffened. "What makes you think we're doing anything?"

Broken glass screeched on the ceramic tile floor. Behind the bar, Dean muttered something unintelligible. Poor fella. He must be having a hard time collecting the shards of glass.

"Come on," Charlie pleaded. "I know you better than that. You wouldn't sit back and let your mother go to jail."

I anchored my hands firmly on my coffee cup. "You don't want to get mixed up in this, Charlie. Britt's already thinking I'm an accessory to murder."

Charlie leaned forward, his arm slipping off the bench and onto Jonette's shoulder. "Even more reason for me to get involved. I don't want you in Britt's clutches. Besides, I can't let the mother of my children rot in jail as an accessory. What have you got?"

"We've got nothing." Jonette gazed up at Charlie with adoring eyes.

My mouth dropped open. Jonette thought Charlie was the biggest loser on the planet. What was going on here?

"What's the plan?" Charlie asked, his gaze fixed on my face. Jonette might as well have been roadkill for all the notice he took of her adulation.

"The plan is to find out who hated Erica enough to kill her," I said. "Once I know that, I have a chance to clear Mama."

"I'll help," he said.

"No!" Alarm flared from stem to stern. "I mean, no thanks. I don't want a lot of people running around asking questions. If you want to help, keep your eyes and ears open."

"I'd like to do more," Charlie said.

He looked so wistful, so earnest. My heart softened. "How about if I bank your request? I'm sure I'll need help along the way."

Pleasure flared in his blue eyes. "Deal."

Dean approached our booth with a fisted hand. He opened his palm and campaign buttons rained down on the table. "Here. Have a button."

"Moore for Mayor," the bold red print proclaimed. I snatched one up and pinned it on my polo shirt. "Thanks. I'd love to support our candidate."

Charlie stared at the brightly colored buttons like they were a nest of venomous snakes. "What's this?"

Jonette picked up a button and pinned it on Charlie's shirt. "I'm running for mayor. You'll wear this for me, won't you, Chuckie?"

Charlie glanced from Jonette to me and back again. I shrugged. Who knew what the hell was going on here? I certainly didn't. "Uh, sure," he said.

Dean's hand rested heavily on my shoulder. Tension radiated down his arm, infusing me with the sensation of a swarm of buzzing bees. "Break's over, Jonette," he said.

Jonette's lower lip rolled out. "Party pooper."

"I've got to go pick up the girls. Lexy needs a camera for school," Charlie said, sliding out of the booth. "I meant what I said, Cleo. I want to help."

"I won't forget." There were lots of things I wouldn't forget about Charlie Jones. Like the way he had played me for a fool for months. I wouldn't forget that. Neither would Jonette. So why was she acting so strangely around him?

I stood as well. "I owe you for a cup of coffee," I said to Dean. I took a few dollars out of my purse and dropped them on the table.

"Coffee's on the house." He handed me my money back. His sullen gaze riveted on Jonette and Charlie as they walked toward the door.

Dean was ten years older than Jonette. He had the look of an aging biker, with a stocky build, flat belly, silvery ponytail, and arresting gray eyes. The age difference had made Jonette cautious about getting involved with him in the first place. Now I wondered if there was irreparable trouble in paradise.

He seemed like a nice guy and he treated Jonette well, which was more than I could say for Jonette's previous lovers and husbands. A little reassurance might help Dean feel more secure in his affection. "She's not interested in Charlie," I volunteered.

"You don't understand," Dean said. "She's pulling away from me. I feel her withdrawal, and I can't do a damn thing to stop her from leaving me. If I wasn't so dull, she wouldn't look at other men."

The stark pain in his voice ate at me. Dean cared for Jonette. Their personal relationship wasn't casual to him. I'd known Jonette for a long time. She adored masculine attention, which was why the barmaid gig suited her so well. "Jonette's not fickle. She likes to look, but she's never cheated on her partner."

Dean shook his head sadly, reminding me of the gloomy donkey in the Winnie the Pooh movies. "I'm going to come back from my bartender's convention next week, and she'll be moved out of my place. I know it."

"That's not Jonette's style," I said. "She doesn't sneak around. She's very much an in-your-face type of person."

The dimly lit, thinly populated tavern suited Dean's melancholy mood. I couldn't guarantee him she wouldn't leave him. Jonette operated under her own set of rules, in her own time. If she wasn't in love with Dean, she would move on, but not without a fiery showdown.

"She hasn't been in my face lately. That's the problem. You're her best friend. Tell me, what do I need to do to get her back?"

Lord, how was I going to talk my way out of this? "I want Jonette to be happy, but I don't know what to suggest."

Dean mopped his brow. "I've spent every waking moment with her, giving her my complete attention, doing chores for her, but it's not enough. I'm blowing it and I wished to God I wasn't."

He was smothering her. A little time apart would do them a world of good. Poor Dean. He really was gone on Jonette. "My best advice is to be yourself."

"Be myself?"

"Yeah. Don't try to impress Jonette. Relax. Enjoy your trip

next week."

He looked skeptical.

"Hey, life is short," I said. "Don't worry. Be happy."

Dean nodded. "I know that song."

"I thought you might." I summoned a fleeting smile.

I walked back to city hall to collect my car. Some of my workout stiffness had abated, but I was physically drained. The day was half over, and I had yet to learn a single thing to keep Mama out of jail. I'd better make progress soon, or it would be too late.

Mama was drinking coffee in the kitchen when I walked in. I'd had enough coffee, so I poured myself a glass of water and sat down beside her at the scarred kitchen table. As a child I'd done my homework at this table, and now my kids did their homework here. Funny how life circled around.

"About last night," I began conversationally. "I know you are holding something back. I need to know what you know so I can help you."

Mama stared into her coffee as if the dark beverage contained the secrets of the universe. She hadn't bothered to dress this morning, and her pale neck looked naked without her usual triple strand of pearls. Her short white hair was snarled and matted. I made a mental note to replace her faded baby-blue bathrobe with a new one at Christmas. If she wasn't in jail.

Would Mama tell me her secret? I'd expected her to tell me I was nuts, but her silence told me more than any protest she might have mounted. I had no choice but to keep dancing around the topic.

"You're not the only one that had run-ins with Erica," I said. "I believe she extorted money from Muriel. Erica was three months behind in her beauty shop bill. Given those circumstances, I assume she needed money. From there it's no stretch to assume she was blackmailing you as well as Muriel. What did she have on you?"

Mama's eyes flared in alarm. Her lips tightened to a thin colorless line. Deep creases lined her washed-out face. Bingo. I'd hit pay dirt. Erica was blackmailing her. For Mama to be wrinkling her face like a sun-dried tomato meant she was too upset to care about her appearance. A rare moment.

I'd gotten used to Mama running the world whenever she took the notion. Seeing her as frail and fragile was like splashing cold water in my face. Sobering. Shocking, even.

Another realization set in. Though she was broken and hurting, Mama wouldn't easily yield up her secret. I'd have to push her, hard. Could I be that ruthless? With Mama's heart condition, I'd be taking a big risk. What if I caused more harm than good? Could I live with the outcome?

Despair welled up inside of me. Her stubbornness might condemn her to a life behind bars. She needed to trust me. Frustration warred with anger, and anger won. "Dammit, Mama, what is this all about? Why did Erica make your life hell on earth?"

A fat tear inched down her cheek. Another tear followed. Mama closed her eyes to stem the tide. She uttered a one-syllable word. Her voice was too soft for me to make out what she'd said.

I leaned forward, cupping my ear. "What's that? What did you say?"

Mama's bleak face filled with sorrow. The spark of life that characterized her gaze was missing. In its place was a glazed look of sorrow. Her head bowed, and her shoulders slumped.

The bereft woman before me seemed a stranger. A stranger wearing my mother's ratty bathrobe. When was the last time I'd looked at Mama and really seen her? I couldn't remember.

She'd always been there for me, a pillar of feminine strength, with boundless reserves of energy. Now it seemed she'd aged twenty years in the space of ten minutes.

Guilt stabbed my heart. Mama didn't get like this overnight. Why hadn't I noticed the heavy load she carried? I should have noticed her torment before it broke her. I bit my lip in dismay.

"What is it, Mama?" I asked, my heart in my mouth. "What could be so terrible?"

I hung there, suspended in that miserable, aching silence. Mama's anguish and longing crowded out my thoughts, overwhelming all but my autonomic body functions. Warmth drained from my core.

"Joe." Mama's breath caught on a sob. "She wanted my Joe." She burst into heart-wrenching sobs, cradling her head in her hands.

I recoiled. I'd done it now. I'd opened Pandora's box. Predictably, furies poured out and wreaked havoc. "Daddy? She wanted Daddy?"

CHAPTER 10

My world reeled. I clung to the kitchen table because if I didn't, I would surely slide into the darkest hole of my life and never see daylight again. Everything I valued about honesty and reputation and integrity, it all came from Daddy.

I had his green eyes, his fiery red hair. I had his uncanny aptitude for accounting and his dogged determination to endure in the face of trouble. He'd been a rock through every storm of my life. We'd worked and played together. He'd devoted his life to me, to Mama. Erica Hodges had no place in that world. No way. I'd have known.

Mama's pathos drew me out of my reflections. This wasn't about me or my childhood. This was very much about my mother. "It's okay, Mama. It's okay." I went to her, wrapping her in my arms, holding her tight. We huddled together, mother and daughter, and I cried with her.

I smoothed her curly white hair away from her face and patted her back until she quieted.

"I am so ashamed." Mama's ragged voice held no hope. "I'm so ashamed."

Snapshots of the past swirled through my mind like a video montage on fast forward. Mama and Daddy. Mama and Erica. Daddy's funeral. Daddy's willing the house to me. Everyone, including me, thinking that was odd. Why had he done that? Did he know something was amiss in Mama's life back then?

What else was Mama concealing?

I needed to know.

I dreaded knowing.

Terror weighed heavily on my chest, pushing the air from my lungs, making me fight for every breath. I couldn't do this standing in the kitchen, not after the gym workout I'd endured. "Come on, Mama. Let's go sit in the living room."

Mama sank onto the sofa, and I joined her with a sigh of relief. I wiped the tears from my cheeks with the back of my hand. Sunshine streamed through the side window, creating a pool of light on the wood floor. I was glad for the light and the warmth. Just what I needed to combat the cold hard truth of life.

It was time for secrets to be revealed. "Whatever it is, we can deal with it," I said. "Tell me what's wrong."

"I can't. You're going to hate me."

"You're my mother. I won't hate you."

Mama found a tissue in her robe pocket and used it. She plucked a stray dog hair off her sleeve. Her lower lip trembled.

"Tell me, Mama. Please."

She groaned in misery. The inner corners of her eyebrows lowered, while her nose wrinkled. Her hand went to her throat. She glanced everywhere but at me. Finally she whispered, "I had an affair. I cheated on your father."

I blinked. Then I blinked some more as the foundations of my world tilted. I didn't believe it. I couldn't believe it. "Someone else is my father?"

Her head snapped back into the sofa cushions. "Don't be absurd. Joe's your father. You're the spitting image of him and everyone knows it. Thank God for that thick red hair of yours."

My red mop was nearly unmanageable, which is why I clipped it up and out of the way. I'd never once thought of it as an asset. Now I was thrilled to share this physical trait with my father.

"This is so hard." Mama sighed. "You'd think it would be

easy to confess and get it over with, but the truth is, my behavior sounds so callous. First, you have to understand that I loved your father with all my heart. I loved him from the first moment I laid eyes on him until his dying day. I love him and miss him and wish he was still a part of my daily life."

Madonna lumbered into the living room. She rested her head in my lap and drooled on me. I patted her head absently, my attention one hundred percent focused on my mother. I was afraid of what came next, and I hated how much I needed to know.

"I don't understand, Mama. How could you love Daddy and cheat on him?"

Mama drew in a shaky, deep breath. "You remember I had an older sister?" At my nod, she continued. "Ruth died when we were in high school."

"I've gone with you to put flowers on Aunt Ruth's grave."

A faraway look came into Mama's eyes. "Ruthie and I were as different as night and day. While I craved respectability, Ruthie walked on the wild side. We grew up across the mountain, over in Metter, but we were bused to Hogan's Glen for school. We had nothing, Ruthie and I. Both of us wanted out of poverty, but we took different roads. She used her body to attract attention, and she ended up pregnant."

"Pregnant? Aunt Ruth had a baby?"

"Ruthie died during childbirth. My mama said the baby died, too."

"What does Aunt Ruth have to do with your affair?" Horrible thoughts raced through my head. Had Aunt Ruth been pregnant by Daddy? "Don't stop now."

"Ruthie was a high school senior, and I was a junior when she died," Mama said. "I missed her so much that I couldn't stand going to school. When my math teacher arranged for another student to tutor me to bring my grades up, I came this close to not doing it." She pinched her fingers close together.

"The only reason I followed through was that I'd always had a crush on this particular boy."

I stroked Madonna's broad head and tried to imagine Mama in high school. We had no pictures of her at that time. Her pictorial history began when she married Daddy. There were no photos of her mother or of Aunt Ruth, either.

Personalities didn't change. Mama would have been outspoken and obstinate back then. Petite and loaded with vitality and sass. Dark curly hair with arresting brown eyes and a wicked sense of humor. Daddy would have latched on to her and held on tight.

"Joe was Erica's beau back then. He was smart and hardworking and had endless patience with me. Those tutoring sessions were the only bright spot in my life. Whenever I wasn't being tutored or at school, I helped Mama with the wash she took in. Erica knew about Ruthie and her wild ways. They'd been classmates, you see. Erica was furious with Joe for tutoring me. White trash she called me, and she was right. But the more she ragged Joe about his tutoring, the more he turned from her to me.

"Honestly, I didn't try to lure him away from her, but I didn't chase him away. Joe was old Hogan's Glen. He came from a good, decent family. I knew he could give me the life I wanted."

"So you married Daddy," I added, hoping to move this story along and get to the affair.

"We got married. His parents supported us while Joe went to college. I kept house and learned how to be Joe's wife. Joe was very attentive. Loving. Constant. And I was scared to death of having marital relations with him. Every time Joe wanted to, you know, I froze up inside."

I did not want to hear about my parent's sex life. But I couldn't help myself. "What did you do?"

Mama buried her face in her hands. "This is the part I'm

ashamed of. I assumed since I wasn't interested in sex, it was because Joe wasn't exciting in that way. I found someone else, a friend of Joe's. He was happy to pay me that kind of attention."

Ice chilled my blood. "You betrayed Daddy with his friend?"

"I never thought of it as a betrayal. It was like trying on a new dress. For years Ruthie had been the wild one. I'd never even kissed another man besides Joe. Your father was the only reference point I had. So I found time to be with his friend."

My stomach lurched, and I grabbed my middle with both arms. "I don't want to know intimate details about your love life."

"Good. I have no intention of telling you. Here's the deal. I didn't sleep with Joe's friend. We shared several meals, saw a movie, and kissed exactly once. That's all it took, you see. I found out the problem wasn't Joe. It was me."

"You?"

"Me. Ruthie died from childbirth. I realized I was terrified of becoming pregnant. Sex led to pregnancy, and in my mind, pregnancy to death. That's why I didn't light up the sheets."

"You figured that out by yourself?"

"No. I went home to Mama after I kissed Joe's friend. I told her I couldn't go back to Joe because of what I'd done. Mama was incredibly nosy—you take after her by the way—and she dragged the whole story out of me. Then she took me home to my husband. I never told Joe about the kiss, but I broke it off with his friend. However, the horse was out of the barn. Someone had seen us together. Someone who knew what my betrayal would do to Joe."

My heart sank as the picture clarified. "Oh, Lord. Erica knew? Erica attended the same college?"

Mama nodded, her expression sad. "Erica was there, and she'd taken a leaf from Ruthie's book. She assumed the best way to land a husband was through his fly. When Joe wouldn't accommodate her, Erica slept with William Hodges until she got herself good and pregnant. They had a quickie marriage and ended up back in Hogan's Glen. Erica had William but she always wanted Joe."

"Was William the man who kissed you?"

"No. Thank God for that. William and your father knew each other, but they were never friends. Your father preferred friends who drank less, who played golf, and who shared his passion for truth."

Daddy had had one lifelong friend. The horrible truth dawned on me. "Bud? Bud Flook? He was the man you kissed?"

Mama nodded, her hands clutched tightly in her lap. "You have to understand. I was so deeply in love with Joe, I didn't realize what that kiss and those few dinners meant to Bud. Not once. Over the years, Joe ribbed Bud about his permanent bachelorhood, and Bud said some guys weren't meant to find happiness. Believe me, I was stunned when I learned Bud loved me."

The walls of the room pressed in on me. My head pounded. "Your lawyer, the person whose sole responsibility is to keep you out of jail, is the man you passed over all those years ago?"

Mama's face crumpled. "I never meant to wreck Bud's life, but I did. Now I have to make it up to him."

I glanced over at the doorway, wishing I could bolt out of this room. Mama had been in a love triangle? My mouth soured. "Rafe was right. You need a new lawyer."

"Bud's the only lawyer I want."

"That doesn't make any sense."

"I almost died after I had you. Bud stood by Joe through my hysterectomy. Joe wanted more children, and I couldn't give them to him. I was a failure as a woman."

Mama stopped to heave in a breath. She exhaled slowly as if it ached to part with a single molecule of oxygen. "That's when

Erica made another huge play for Joe. Her husband was dead, and she'd already borne two healthy children. She'd flounce over here in the flimsiest outfits, swimming in perfume, pretending to have accounting emergencies. Her overt sexuality scared the snot out of me. I thought I would lose everything. How could Joe resist that much temptation?"

My eyes widened and nausea threatened. The foundations of my life shivered and shook. "Please tell me he did. Tell me that he didn't sleep with Erica Hodges."

"Not once. Although I worried over it so much, I had a few lunches with my best friend and discussed it."

Madonna nudged me to pet her again. I tried to guess what came next in this story. "Francine and Muriel? They know about this drama?"

"Good heavens, no. Why would I tell them about my sex life?"

"Who did you tell?"

"Bud, of course."

My jaw dropped. "You used him a second time?"

Mama's face flushed bright red. Sparks flashed through her eyes. "You don't understand. I can talk to Bud about anything. Always could. Still do. He loves me."

"Bud is your best friend?"

"We've kept it real quiet." She gazed at the Oriental rug, rasped in a breath, and grabbed my arm. "Bud proposed. He wants to marry me."

Omigod! Too much information. I shook off her hand. "You want to get married?" That unspoken look Mama and Bud had shared in his car the other night made sense. It had been warm and knowing, intimate even. How could I have missed that at the time? "You're sleeping with him? You cheated on Daddy after all?"

Mama's spine stiffened. "Watch your mouth, missy, or I'll

wash it out with soap. I never slept with Bud until this summer. The man waited thirty-nine years for me. That's devotion."

My cheeks heated at the thought of Mama sneaking around and having sex with Bud Flook. Had they done it in the back seat of his car? I squeezed my eyes tight to ward off the image of Mama and Bud being intimate. There had been a point to this conversation. I needed to find it. "How does this tie into Erica's death?"

Mama curled into herself. "Erica took pictures of Bud and me eating lunch in Frederick about ten years ago. She's been blackmailing us ever since."

Now we were getting somewhere. Ignoring my pangs of sympathy for her, I pushed forward, determined to get to the bottom of this. "Why would you pay her a dime?"

"Because I didn't want Joe to see those pictures and get the wrong idea. I love your father. Always have. Always will."

I replayed the key facts. Mama loved Daddy. He loved her. Bud loved Mama. She liked him as a friend. Erica wanted Daddy but didn't get him. It was starting to make sense. "Why would Erica blackmail anyone? She was loaded."

"She spent money like it was water. She went through her fortune and her husband's."

Once again, Mama's logic made sense, to a point. "But the blackmail ended when Daddy died?"

"No. It never ended. I paid her a thousand dollars last Tuesday."

My heart skipped a beat. This wasn't ancient history. This was present-day blackmail. Worse, it spelled motive for murder. "Where'd you get a thousand dollars?"

"I sold my car to Bud. He's been letting me drive it, but technically he owns my Olds."

"Why did you keep paying her?"

"Because the truth could hurt you and the girls. You were so fragile after your father died. I had to be strong for you. And then Charlie took up with someone else, and you came to live with me. There never was a good time to end Erica's chokehold on me. I didn't want you to think poorly of me. I never wanted my granddaughters to know what I'd done."

I felt sick to my stomach. I was thirty-eight years old. Mama and Erica had been enemies for my entire life. And she'd paid blackmail for ten years. "How did you pay her? Didn't Daddy notice the expense?"

"Grocery money. You think I came up with cheese doodle croutons for fun? I bought sale items in bulk and gave her my grocery money. Why do you think I shopped four places before I bought a pair of shoes? Because I had to have money for Erica."

I couldn't comprehend the scope of what Mama was saying. I had reached my saturation point and needed time to process the information. But while she was handing out secrets, I had one more to probe. "Where did you go on Tuesday night after the hospitality committee meeting?"

Mama flushed. Bright red flags appeared on her thin cheeks. "Bud's house. We had a drink. One thing led to another, and I fell asleep in his arms. A phone call woke us up. I rushed home and hurried up to my bedroom so you wouldn't smell Bud's cigar on my clothes."

I believed her. "You didn't kill Erica?"

"Nope. Though I wish I'd thought of it."

A blizzard of relief showered through me. Mama had an alibi. "Bud will corroborate your story?"

"Of course."

I tried to put this together in a logical format, but it wouldn't go. A huge piece of the picture was missing. "Did anyone else know you went over to Bud's after the meeting?"

"No. Francine and Muriel don't know about our affair. No one does."

"You're wrong there. Erica knew. So did her killer. Was this the first time you went to Bud's after a church meeting?"

"No. I've been going there after every hospitality meeting this summer. You didn't think those church meetings ran for several hours, did you?"

Truthfully, I hadn't paid any attention to Mama's comings and goings. I'd had my hands full of teenaged angst and a hot boyfriend all summer. But someone else had plenty of free time. Someone had been skulking around Hogan's Glen. "It was your routine to sneak over to Bud's whenever you could?"

"Only after your father died." Mama drew cross over her heart. "I swear I didn't sleep with Bud before Joe's aneurysm."

It was hard to set aside Mama's secret romance and focus on the murder, but I did it. "Someone went to a lot of trouble to set you up. They knew where you were going to be, they knew how long you would be there. They stole your car, ran over Erica, and returned your car without you noticing it was gone. Who called Bud's house that night?"

Mama shrugged. "It was a wrong number."

"Man or woman?"

"I don't know. Bud answered the phone."

The phone call worried me. Especially the timing of it. Someone had planned this to the nth degree. Someone wanted Mama to take the blame. "Chances are the murderer made that call so you would be on the road near the time of Erica's death."

Mama slumped into the sofa, defeated. "Who is doing this to me?"

"Someone who wants you and Erica out of the way. My guess is the killer is someone you know. Someone who knows your crowd and your personal routine."

"Good Lord. You think Francine or Muriel did this?"

I rubbed my face with my hands. It had been a long day. My muscles were stiff, my brain was numb, and a nap still sounded like a great idea. I stood and stretched. "It wouldn't have taken brute strength to run someone over. Though they are frail, Francine and Muriel are prime suspects in my book."

"They would never do this to me," Mama asserted loyally. "They are my friends."

"They didn't stick up for you in the meeting last Monday. Everyone has a breaking point. Maybe they got tired of your constant bickering with Erica. Maybe they got tired of you bossing everyone around. Who knows? We have to be careful not to tip the killer off while I figure out who it is."

"How are you going to question Muriel and Francine without their knowing it?"

"The hospitality committee is a good place to start. They will be busy arranging the food for Erica's funeral. I'll step into your role for the reception, and they won't even realize I'm questioning them."

Mama drew herself up to her full five-feet-four inches. A determined gleam glittered in her eyes. "Oh, no you don't. You're not leaving me out of this. Not when my butt is on the line. I'm manning the church kitchen for the funeral reception. That's my final answer."

CHAPTER 11

As I dressed in my black sheath dress and strappy sandals for Erica's funeral Monday afternoon, the notion of Mama and Bud Flook as lovers danced through my head. She'd blindsided me with that news. Not that she didn't deserve happiness.

Heat rose to my face. Gracious, who was I to judge anyone in that regard? I was enjoying being "happy" again. What would sex be like when I was in my sixties? Would it still be the blood-racing, earth-shattering, thrilling event of age thirty-eight?

I hoped so.

Madonna whimpered as I buckled the slender straps at my ankles. "You'll be fine, Madonna. Take a short nap, and I'll be home before you know it."

I applied a hint of blush, dark brown mascara, and neutral lip balm, then splashed on a dab of new cologne. Slightly lemony with a hint of musk and sandalwood. Understated. Elegant. It suited the new me.

The new me came with old responsibilities—namely, saving Mama from the slammer. Unless I came up with proof she'd been framed, she would take the fall. I'd dreaded answering the door and the phone on Sunday, sure that the police would be there. But the phone hadn't rung, and we'd had no uninvited visitors.

My suspect pool was as broad as Erica's circle of acquaintances: basically everyone in a ten-mile radius, which was way too many to investigate. The people who spent the most time with her were those senior ladies, which was where I would focus my snooping. My gut insisted they knew more than they were telling.

Erica had been raised in historic Crandall House in Hogan's Glen, the town her ancestor founded. She'd come from money, and she'd married money. She'd received two million in life insurance money when her husband died twenty years ago. Hard to believe she'd run through that much money in Hogan's Glen.

I already knew she'd been short on money. She'd stiffed her hairdresser and extorted money from her peers. Every ounce of my accounting blood insisted Erica's death was about money. One thing about money. It left a trail. All I had to do was find it.

Erica's heirs, Evan and Eleanor, would be at the funeral. I'd read newspaper accounts of kids killing their parents for money. Hunky Evan and Perfect Eleanor didn't appear to be cold-blooded killers, but, hey, I was desperate. If I didn't find a credible suspect, Mama would go to prison.

I shifted a few items into my black purse and hit the stairs. The funeral started in half an hour. I planned to hang out in the church kitchen and ask everyone plenty of loaded questions. And keep Mama out of trouble. Couldn't forget that important task.

Mama waited on the bench by the front door in her funeral attire of black crepe jacket dress, triple-stranded pearls, sheer stockings, and black pumps. Next to her were glass trays of deviled eggs and sliced banana nut bread. Both looked suspiciously normal.

"What took you so long?" she asked. "I don't like to be late."

I put on a good face. "You ready to kick some funeral butt?"

Mama rose. Her dark eyes sparkled. "I was born to kick funeral butt. Let's go."

As I drove us to the church in the Gray Beast, Mama fingered the dusty console. "Charla's going to be driving soon. She needs a new car," Mama said.

Yep. Mama was back in fighting form again. I'd missed sparring with her. I grinned. "Charla's not getting a new car. If I buy a second car, she'll get this one."

"This car's older than dirt. She wants something peppy."

Alarms clanged in my head. "Peppy will get her killed. She needs a safe car to drive."

"You sound just like your father. I tried to get him to buy you a little convertible, and he wouldn't do it. Said he'd rather have his daughter alive."

His caring filled me with righteous fervor. "I'm still alive, so he must have been right."

"You accountants are a boring, dull lot," Mama said, but there was an undercurrent of praise in her voice.

It felt good to talk about Daddy. I'd missed him so much these last few years. I couldn't remember the last time I'd really thought about him. Maybe that was the key. Thinking about him would remind me of the things he used to do and say.

What would he do in my shoes? He'd go into this funeral reception loaded for bear. He'd grill everyone there, from the kitchen help, to the clergy, to the mourners. He wouldn't leave a stone unturned until he found out who killed Erica Hodges. I wouldn't, either. Not when Mama's freedom was at stake.

"Let me out here," Mama said as I drove under the portico at the parish hall entrance.

"Forget it." I frowned and kept driving until I found a parking space in the back. "I'm not letting you out of my sight. We're doing this together or we're going home."

"I thought you trusted me."

"I do trust you. It's everyone else I don't trust. Sending you in there alone is like sending Charla off in a peppy car. It's not going to happen."

Mama couldn't quite hold her smile in as we walked into the parish hall together. I couldn't remember when I'd felt this in sync with her. We were a team. I wouldn't let her down.

"You're late, Dee," Francine said as we walked into the large industrial-sized kitchen bearing our containers of food. She shook an arthritic finger at Mama, the motion sending the tiny polka dots of her dress into a frenzied flight.

"Yeah, well, we can't all be early birds like you," Mama snapped back. "Muriel, get your head out of the fridge before you freeze your boobs off."

Muriel peeked around the refrigerator. Her soft white hair clouded around a cherubic face and an impish smile. She'd matched her lipstick to her dusty rose-colored cardigan. "You all right, Delilah? No more house arrest?"

"Put those down over there," Mama said, pointing me toward the center island. "Did anyone start the coffee?"

"We wouldn't start the coffee without you," Muriel said, containers of orange juice and ginger ale in her thin arms.

I set down the trays of deviled eggs on the stainless-steel counter. "Shouldn't these go in the refrigerator?"

"Fine. Fine. Everyone's a critic these days," Mama said. She stowed our purses under the counter and pulled out red cotton vests for us to wear. The word "Hospitality" was embroidered in black thread in the upper left side of each vest.

I donned a vest, cinching the sides so that it fit me. Then I put the deviled eggs in the fridge. "What should I do?"

"All the serving dishes need to be wiped off," Francine said.

I opened cabinets until I found the good stuff. The sterling silver dishes had been a gift to the church from Erica's grandmother. "They look clean to me," I observed as I pulled them down.

"Wipe them down," Mama said, wrestling the top off the

large coffee urn.

I had visions of coffee grounds flying everywhere. I placed the gleaming platters on the counter and rushed to Mama's side. "Let me help you with that, Mama."

She brushed me aside. "I can do it."

I took the urn from her and tried the lid. It stuck fast until I twisted with all my might. "Good heavens. Why don't y'all replace this monster? Get something that's more manageable."

Francine cackled as she poured mixed nuts into small crystal bowls. "Can we keep her, Dee? I like hearing her sass you."

"Cleo's not here for your entertainment." Mama filled the coffee pot with water. "She's here to find a murderer."

I stopped in my tracks. This wasn't how we had agreed to proceed. "Mama!"

She fussed with the coffee urn as if she hadn't seriously deviated from our game plan. "I don't care what you think, Cleopatra Jones. Francine and Muriel didn't kill Erica."

Mama's statements clanked around the tile floor of the industrial-sized kitchen. Francine's hand fluttered to her apricot-colored lips. "You suspected us?"

With a harsh stare at Mama, I picked up a clean dish cloth and wiped off the spotless sterling silver trays. "I suspect everyone. Muriel, last Friday you mentioned your grandson and his college entrance exams. How did you handle that?"

Muriel's pale skin went a tone lighter than her white hair. She gripped her clutched hands to her breast. Her watery blue eyes went wide behind her large glasses.

"Cleo, you don't need to know that," Mama said, standing next to Muriel.

"Yes, I do, Mama. We have to eliminate suspects or we'll never get anywhere."

Francine turned to her sister. "She's going to eliminate us, Muriel. I should have had Joan color my hair this morning. I always wanted to be a blonde."

I couldn't believe Francine was cracking jokes. Anger hummed through my veins. "This is serious. Erica is dead, and someone went to a lot of trouble to make it look like Mama killed her. Was it one of you?"

Muriel laughed shakily. "You don't know us very well, do you, Little Dee?"

I shook my cleaning cloth at her. "I'm not little. And I want to know what happened with your grandson, Muriel. What did you do?"

"I paid Erica off, of course. What choice did I have?"

She said it so matter-of-factly that her admission floored me. Erica had her fingers in the same pies as these women, the hospital auxiliary, the church, the library board. "How could you work beside a woman who extorted money from you for years?"

"I didn't like her. None of us did. But we wouldn't kill her. We made a pact years ago."

"A pact? What kind of pact?"

"One where we would stick together. Don't you see? Erica was into all of us."

"You, too, Francine?"

Francine nodded.

"What did she have on you?"

Francine chewed her lip and stole a glance at Mama. "Do I have to tell her?"

Mama nodded.

"She knew about my gambling problem. She made me sign over the deed of my house to her to cover a gambling debt."

"Your house? The house where you and Muriel live?"

"Yes. We pay her a thousand dollars a month to rent our own house. It was either that or be put out on the street."

"Where do you get that kind of money?"

"We pool our Social. We work part-time at the drugstore. We manage."

"What happens with your house now?"

"We don't know." Worry lines etched across Muriel's powdered forehead.

"One last question," I said. "Where did you two go on Tuesday night after the hospitality meeting?"

"We didn't go anywhere," Francine said. "We were in for the night. The night-blind thing, remember?"

"Are we in the clear?" Light glinted off Muriel's oversized glasses.

"I suppose so," I said, glumly heading back to my stack of sterling silver platters.

More food trays came in, and we didn't get another chance to talk about Erica's blackmailing ways again. Between making the coffee, mixing up the punch, pressing the linens, setting up the serving tables, and handling the donated food, we couldn't catch our breath.

But the new information churned in my head. Francine had deeded her house to Erica. That meant Erica's heirs now owned Francine's charming little two-bedroom Victorian cottage. Would the bulletin sisters soon be homeless?

Jonette brought in a bag of fancy chocolate mints after the reception started. She was a vibrant study in royal blue. She leaned close so she wouldn't be overheard. "Did you see the 'For Sale' sign?"

"What sign?" I poured the mints into a crystal dish and prayed she wasn't talking about Francine's house. If Mama's friends were put out on the street, she'd insist we take them in. I'd have to move Lexy in with Charla to make everyone fit. And, if I remembered correctly, Muriel had two large cats. Between the cats, the soon-to-arrive puppies, and the people, my house would become a zoo overnight. I didn't want that.

Jonette munched on a handful of cashews. She leaned in and whispered, "The sign in front of Crandall House. It's on the market."

My jaw dropped. Thoughts tumbled out of my mouth in a breathy rush. "My God. That house has been in the Crandall family for generations. I can't believe they'd sell it. Erica isn't even in the ground yet."

"No kidding."

Didn't they value their family heritage? I peeked out the kitchen door at Evan and Eleanor. The dark knight and the ice maiden. Who knew they were so greedy? What was it with this family and money? Where did their money go?

To follow Erica's money, I needed a credit report. My heart sank at the obvious answer. Charlie could get it for me. All I had to do was ask. There was no time to lose.

I shrugged out of my hospitality vest and handed it to Jonette. "Cover for me. I'll be right back."

I stepped into the crowded reception room, scanned the room, and caught Charlie's roving eye. He loped across the room to greet me. It didn't escape my notice that he wore the charcoal suit I'd bought him for Daddy's funeral and the tie clip I'd given him on our last Christmas together.

My nails bit into my palms. I was doing this for Mama.

"You're looking delectable, Mrs. Jones." Charlie sniffed my ear. "Smell good too. Sassy. Sexy."

Thank God I had on my spiky sandals and towered over him. "Give it a rest, Charlie. I need to talk to you."

Charlie put his hand on the small of my back and steered me into a vacant corner of the reception hall. He leaned one arm against the wall, blocking me in. "Excellent. Because I wanted to talk to you, babe."

The fluorescent lights seemed overly bright, the roar of conversation in the room too loud. What did Charlie want? The only thing I had that he wanted was custody of the kids. My blood pressure spiked. He was not getting full custody of the girls. He was the adulterer. Not me.

"I want Lexy to have the digital camera she needs for the yearbook staff," Charlie said.

I allowed myself a small breath of air, releasing my fear. Indignation followed. "You dragged me over here to tell me that?"

His smug smile made my blood boil. The girls were my Achilles' heel, and he knew it. He'd punched my buttons, and I'd let him. Now I had to deal with his inflated male ego. "That camera is too expensive. I can't afford it, even with the child support you pay."

"I wasn't asking you to pay for it. I'll buy it. I wanted your approval first."

That wasn't how Charlie operated. I scrutinized the face I knew so well. The angular jaw, chiseled lips, humped nose, blue eyes, and lady-killer eyelashes. The face that had shattered my heart into a million pieces. "Who are you, and where is the real Charlie Jones?"

He sobered. "I've changed, babe. I'm on a mission to get my family back."

I shook my head emphatically. "Not happening."

"You've gotten your way on everything, Cleo. All I'm asking is for you to give me a chance."

He thought a few apologies would make me forget he'd brought another woman into our bed?

No way in hell. "You can't turn back the clock on this. I'm not stupid enough to trust you again."

Charlie took my hand and cradled it gently. "I'm not asking you to blindly believe. I want to show you the kind of man I am. Give me this chance. That's all I'm asking."

His familiar scent filled my senses, and, against my will, a flood of good memories returned. Memories of us holding baby Charla. Of Charlie smiling at me on the porch swing as if I was more precious than the rarest diamond.

I tried to withdraw my hand, but he must have sensed my softening attitude. With the pad of his thumb, Charlie traced small circles on the back of my hand.

I prayed for divine intervention. A lightning bolt setting the church on fire would be nice. A moment passed, and nothing untoward happened. Drat. "Buy her the camera, then. I'm not stopping you."

"That's not all. I want to help you with this."

"This?" I blinked in confusion.

"Your mother. Erica. The whole thing. Like we talked about in the Tavern on Saturday. Only, no rain check. I want to be involved. What can I do?"

I snatched my hand away. Letting him help wasn't caving in. I'd come out here to ask him for his help. "I understand Erica had money troubles. I want to know what happened to her money."

"No problem."

"Thanks. I appreciate it. I have to go." I moved to duck under his arm, but I misjudged the clearance needed and smacked my head into his rigid arm. I reeled and would have fallen flat on my face if Charlie hadn't steadied me. His hands rested heavily on my waist.

Heat poured off me. Why had I thought these stupid heels were a good idea?

"You forgot something, sweetheart." Charlie's blue eyes twinkled with mischief.

I narrowed my gaze and shot him my death glare. He seemed entirely too pleased with himself. Was it possible he'd set me up so that he'd have reason to grab me?

"Is there a problem here?" Rafe asked.

The testosterone level in my corner of the room bounced off the chart with Rafe's arrival. Though his outfit of khaki trousers, white Polo, and navy blazer looked less formal than Charlie's suit, I thought he looked just right. Perfect, in fact. I smiled brightly at him and shrugged off Charlie's grip. "No problem. None at all."

Charlie's gaze darkened, but he let me pass. I thanked God for that small miracle. The last thing I needed was to start a brawl at Erica's funeral reception. "I need some punch," I said to Rafe.

He accompanied me over to the punch bowl. Muriel dipped us two cups of punch, but I couldn't meet her questioning gaze. I downed a cup of punch in one gulp. Rafe refused his.

Tension radiated from Rafe in unrelenting waves. My heart hammered. Would Rafe give up on me because I couldn't delete Charlie from my life? I slipped out the side door into the empty corridor linking the parish hall to the church.

"What was that all about?" Rafe asked.

"It was about nothing." It was nothing because I said so. It couldn't be anything. I wouldn't let it be anything. I was not going down that road again.

"It didn't look like nothing. It looked personal. Intimate, even." Rafe's voice flattened. "Are you getting back together with your ex?"

Even with heels on, I was shorter than Rafe. I hugged my arms to my chest to ward off the chill in the aseptic corridor. "Charlie wants to reconcile. I don't."

Rafe watched me behind hooded eyes. "Don't play games with me, Red."

The hurt in his voice tore at me. I touched his jacket sleeve. Electricity flashed between us. "I'm not playing a game."

"I'm getting a mixed signal here. I want you to be happy, but I don't know what you want."

"I'm not interested in Charlie. Don't you see? He's trying to stir something up, but there's nothing there to stir."

"You didn't give me an answer. Does he make you happy?"

"He makes me mad. And sad. And to be honest, there are times he surprises me with a good deed. But you're missing the point. I don't trust him. I'll never trust him again. Not after the way he hurt me."

"You sure?"

"With one hundred percent certainty, something an accountant rarely says. He doesn't make me happy. You do."

Light gleamed in Rafe's eyes. The corners of his lips kicked up. "Oh, yeah. That's the answer I wanted to hear." He kissed me until my knees went weak. Then he left.

My lips tingled as he roared out of the parking lot. I'd been honest with him, and he'd believed me. I hadn't had to raise my voice to be heard. He'd understood me, respected me. How novel. How exciting. He cared for me. Bunches. Happiness welled up inside of me.

It was a victory worth celebrating.

Except I couldn't.

Not when Mama was in trouble.

The crowd inside represented my primary suspect pool. I needed to get in there and gather more information. But first, I needed more punch. Evan and Eleanor stood talking to Muriel at the punch bowl. I slowed, uncertain of the protocol. Grilling them would be tacky, but Mama going to jail would be worse than tacky. I could live with being tacky.

Evan started guiltily as I approached. "Cleo."

"You have my deepest sympathies," I said.

"Thank you." Eleanor looked down her perfect nose at me.

Evan shifted uneasily on his feet. "I'm sorry about missing our Saturday appointment."

"No problem. Gen walked me through it," I said. "But she

wasn't as good a trainer as you are."

He shrugged. Eleanor stared at me as if she'd like to dissect my brain. I shivered under her icy glare. Rafe was right about her. She was cold through and through. Encouraged by that thought, I plunged into the realm of tacky. "I heard Crandall House is for sale."

Evan nodded, sorrow dulling his eyes, bending his shoulders. The tragic knight next to the stoic ice maiden.

"How can you bear to part with it?" I asked. "Crandall House has been in your family for generations."

"You couldn't pay me enough to live in this one-horse, know-nothing town," Eleanor said, depositing her empty punch cup on the linen-shrouded table. "I'm cutting my losses and getting out. Excuse me."

"What about you, Evan?" I asked once Eleanor was out of earshot. "Are you leaving, too?"

Evan stared after Eleanor for a minute before turning to me. An array of complex emotions flashed across his bereaved face. "I have nothing against this town. I grew up here. I make my living here."

I didn't get it. "Then why sell the house?"

Evan's face and neck flushed beet red. "You don't know?"

A cautious woman would shut up now. But I wasn't cautious. "Know what?"

"Mother wrote me out of her will years ago when I didn't choose the right career. Eleanor inherits everything. I've got the clothes on my back, and that's it."

CHAPTER 12

I opened an electronic spreadsheet template, renamed it, and keyed in data for Harlan's Ridge Community Homeowners Association. Numbers flowed in a steady, soothing stream. Accounting wasn't a fancy shoe I wore on special occasions. It filled me with purpose, charged my brain, refueled my energy reservoir.

Methodical, analytical, and doggedly persistent. These personality traits complimented my career choice and benefitted my clients. But they created conflict in my personal life. Worrying a problem into resolution worked great for taxes, not for relationships.

When all was said and done, was Rafe the man for me? He cared for me. I knew that. He'd even taken care of my kids while I waited at the jailhouse for Mama. That felt like commitment. But he had drawn a line in the sand about his family. Sure he'd told me some of it, but not enough for me to get the big picture. Bottom line, he didn't trust me with his family secrets.

Trust.

I craved it. He parceled it out. Unbalanced equations bothered me. The weight of my convictions wouldn't lessen. How long until my side bottomed out, and he bounced off to find someone younger with fewer demands?

Worse, how long until he realized accountants were boring?

It was a nail biter for sure.

When the phone rang, I startled, striking the zero key. Harlan Ridge's maintenance expenses grew exponentially. I fixed the error and saved the page before I grabbed the phone. "Sampson Accounting."

"Hey, Red." The sexy growl in Rafe's voice launched my pulse into orbit. "How are ya?"

Not the police coming for Mama, but a dangerous call nonetheless. My heart cartwheeled with teenaged euphoria because he'd called. I hugged the phone to my ear. "Okay. How about you?"

"I'd be better if you were here in my arms."

I fanned the rush of heat off my face with my free hand. A goofy smile crossed my lips, lifting my spirits. "Me, too. I mean, I wish I was there with you. But I have stacks of work to catch up on."

"I have this image of a green-eyed, red-headed vixen in nothing but black lace underwear looping through my head." Rafe's voice caressed the dark places in my soul, filling me with anticipation. "Do you know how hard it is to meet with sales reps when all I can think about is getting you out of that lacy stuff?"

I'd wasted countless hours fantasizing about his delicious bod, too. "Welcome to my world."

"You think about me in black underwear?"

"I think about you being naked and me having a can of chocolate whipped cream." The new Cleo lived on the edge. "I'd use it to cover your interesting points and then I'd help myself."

Rafe whistled long and low. "Not fair."

I laughed and was pleasantly surprised at how throaty my voice sounded. "Didn't want you to be stuck thinking of me in lacy undies. Thought a new visual might spice up your day."

Rafe groaned. "Take it easy on me, Red. I've still got to meet with the Callaway rep and the Titleist rep this afternoon. If we keep this up, I'll need a cold shower."

I grinned at the unaccustomed power I wielded. "I've never had phone sex before."

"Let me assure you it doesn't hold a candle to the real thing." He sighed. "Come over tonight."

Last time I went out with Rafe all hell broke loose at home. "Why don't you join us here for dinner instead? You're welcome any time."

"You won't sleep with me at your place."

I winced at the truth in his wry tone. "But at least we could see each other." And maybe figure out how to indulge our passion while he was here.

"How about if you slip out this evening after your kids go to bed? We could fulfill your wildest fantasies."

I sighed. "As good as that sounds, the answer has to be no. Mama is Britt's top murder suspect. I have to stick close to home right now."

There was a pregnant pause. "I have this fundraiser dinner for the golf course Thursday evening," Rafe finally said. "I've been meaning to mention it to you. Will you go with me?"

Would my answer be the final straw? "Much as I want to, I can't accept your invitation. Not while Mama has this cloud hanging over her head. Did you want to invite someone else?"

After his sharp intake of breath, prickly silence invaded the phone line and my veins. "You want me to ask another woman?"

My stomach burned at my horrible tactical error. "Of course not. I was trying to make up for disappointing you, but it didn't come out right. I know being alone sucks."

"I wouldn't be alone if you spent time with me."

He was pushing hard. Time for me to push back. "I don't have a key to your place, and even if I did, I wouldn't sneak around at night. That's not who I am."

"I see."

The hole I was in kept getting deeper. "If you don't come tonight for dinner, I'll see you at the course tomorrow for the ladies league. Thanks for calling."

I hung up and stared at the wood-paneled walls in my office. The new Cleo did phone sex. What a fun discovery. Nothing boring or dull about the new me.

However, the new Cleo couldn't flit around like a hapless butterfly. I had to find a killer. Since the funeral, I'd been thinking more about the money angle. I tried Charlie's number again. Earlier he'd been away from his desk, and I hadn't left a message. He picked up on the first ring. "Charlie Jones."

"Charlie, I have another favor to ask."

"I'll be right over."

"No!" Alarmed, I leapt to my feet. "Don't come over. I'm busy. I need more financial information. This time on Eleanor Hodges."

"Eleanor, but not Evan?"

It appeared that Evan didn't stand to gain financially from his mother's death, but he was a Hodges. What could it hurt? "If you have time, run him, too."

"What am I looking for?"

"Anything out of the ordinary."

"Okay. Three credit reports coming right up."

"Thanks, Charlie. I appreciate it."

"Anytime, babe. I'm your man."

His words rippled down my spine like a bicycle on train tracks. "Get that nonsense out of your head. We are working together to keep Mama out of jail. I have no hidden agenda."

"That's okay," he said. I sensed his smirk over the phone. "I have enough for both of us."

Jonette viewed the tangled mess on my bed. "The rags go inside the whelping box."

I grabbed an armful of my mangled sheets and dropped them back in the inflatable wading pool that was supposed to be Madonna's whelping box. "I dump the rags in the whelping box every morning, but every night they end up back in my bed. Madonna doesn't want to have her puppies in the whelping box. She likes the bed."

Jonette considered the problem as Madonna stepped on the upholstered ottoman beside my bed, then climbed up on my bed. The dog circled until she found just the right spot on the mattress. It had been Lexy's idea to use the ottoman to help Madonna get up on the bed by herself. "Do you have a waterproof cover on your mattress?" Jonette asked.

"No."

"Better get one or you'll be buying a new mattress soon."

"I'll put that on the list, Mom." Lexy scribbled on her clipboard, her dark head bending intently over the page.

"Are we done yet?" Charla checked her purple watch with an injured air. "I have cheerleading practice in twenty minutes."

"This won't take long, dear," I said. "Everyone needs to be familiar with the drill because we don't know when Madonna will go into labor."

"Grammy's not here," Charla observed with a flip of her curly red hair.

She had a point. Although I wasn't sure if Mama would see Madonna birth her puppies. I expected Britt to storm the house to arrest Mama any minute now.

I went to the door and hollered down to the kitchen. "Mama! We need you up here."

Madonna sat up on the bed, ready to leap down and follow me if I crossed the threshold. Her dogged devotion to me was an absolute nuisance. The only thing worse than a neurotic pregnant dog was probably a neurotic dog mother and a batch of newborn puppies.

Lexy cooed to the dog. "It's okay, sugar. Mama's not going anywhere."

With an exasperated huff, Charla flopped down on the bed next to Lexy and Madonna. In the blink of an eye, she wrestled the clipboard from Lexy and began reading aloud. "Towels, blunt scissors, alcohol, hydrogen peroxide, heating pad, baby bottle, powdered puppy formula. All that stuff is sitting in Mama's chair."

"Mom. She's touching my clipboard," Lexy said. "Make her stop."

Charla grinned and tossed the clipboard out of her sister's reach on the bed. "Unlike the rest of you people, I have a social life. Are we done yet?"

"Almost." Jonette checked the inventory of dog birthing supplies in my chair. "Notify me when Madonna doesn't eat well for two consecutive meals, when you see her acting nervous or panting, or when her temperature drops. Got it?"

Charla waved her hand. "Yeah, yeah, I got it. Done?"

The likelihood that Charla would deliver Madonna's puppies alone wasn't very high. I offered her a hand up off the bed. "Go on. Get ready for cheerleading. Jonette will drop you off on her way home."

"Cool." Charla jumped off the bed. "Can I back your car out of the driveway, Aunt Jonette?"

"No," I answered quickly. Charlie let Charla back his car up in his driveway, and I had yet to forgive him for unleashing this monster on us. "You may not."

Charla shot me a thunderous look, then practically bowled Mama over as she dashed through the door.

"Careful," I shouted after her.

"Is it over?" Mama asked hopefully. She smelled of meatloaf

and peppermints. Her rust-colored pantsuit flattered her thin frame.

"You, too?" I groaned. Sometimes Charla acted more like my mother than me. I had to remind myself that I'd carried Charla, that I'd given birth to her. Not Mama.

"We verified the supply list. Do you know what to do if Madonna starts having the puppies?" Lexy added as she stroked Madonna's broad head.

"Sure. Call one of you," Mama said.

"Great," Jonette beamed. "That's exactly what you're supposed to do."

A look of resignation crossed Mama's face. "Not much point in worrying about birthing. It either happens right or it doesn't."

Lexy's face fell. "Nothing bad will happen. Madonna's going to be fine and so are her puppies. Right, Mom?"

Lexy was only thirteen. Was I putting too much pressure on her young shoulders by allowing her to become so involved in such an adult matter? I wanted to protect her from the disappointments in life, but that wasn't what she wanted. She wanted to experience life in the fullest.

I sent her a reassuring smile. "I hope so, Lex."

"If we're done, I'm going back down to work on dinner. I've got a few more peppermints to crush for my meatloaf sauce," Mama said.

A heavy double knock sounded on the front door. With a racing heart, I crossed to the window and lifted the curtain. My worst fear had come true.

Two police cars blocked my drive, one a black-and-white cruiser, and the other Britt's nondescript sedan. There were no sirens. No flashing lights. Just a routine pickup of a murder suspect. I shivered out a breath and dropped the curtain. "Lexy, why don't you keep Madonna up here while I answer the door?"

I edged around Mama, with Jonette hard on my heels. "Britt's outside," I said, just loud enough for Mama and Jonette to hear. I breezed down the steps projecting calmness, but I kept thinking, *oh God oh God oh God.*

"I need Delilah to step out of the house," Britt said when I opened the door. Two uniformed officers stood behind him.

I wedged myself in the doorway. "I have new information about the night of Erica's death."

"Not now, Cleo," Britt cautioned. "Delilah?"

I planted both hands in the door jam, creating a human barrier. "She didn't do it." I liked hearing those words. Best of all, I believed those words.

"I'm not coming out," Mama said. "I don't care if you have the whole police force out there."

"Don't do it this way, Delilah," Britt said. "Don't let your granddaughters see you resisting arrest."

"They've seen worse," Mama said.

Mama tried to shove the door shut, only I was in the way and the door rebounded to fully open. In four steps Britt apprehended his murder suspect. Mama left under armed guard, head held high.

"I'll call Bud." Tears misted in my eyes as I followed Mama and her police escort outside. "Don't worry, Mama. We'll get this straightened out in no time." Those words didn't ring true, but we needed to hear them. Without proof of Mama's innocence, positive thinking was our biggest ally.

Lexy, Charla, Madonna, and Jonette stood on the porch with me. Lexy clung to my hand, Charla bawled and held on to my waist. Jonette and I exchanged a look. It was up to us now. We had to learn the truth.

"Is Grammy going to prison?" Charla asked between sobs.

Resolve energized me. "No. She's not."

"You shouldn't have put the house up for collateral." Mama

sank wearily into the passenger seat. Her eyes appeared dull, lifeless even. Her rust pantsuit looked like it had been trampled by an elephant. She hadn't taken the time to put her pearls back on, leaving her corded neck bare.

The weight of the world bent my shoulders. Our eighteen-hour tour through the arraignment process nearly broke me. I'd worried all night and half the morning. I slid into the drivers' seat and started the Gray Beast. Like Mama, I couldn't wait to leave this place. "I didn't have any choice. It's the only valuable asset we own."

"They're not getting my house," Mama insisted.

"They won't. Not unless you jump bail."

"I'm not planning on skipping town, but I'm not going to jail." Mama looked out the window at the grassy shoulder lining the road and sniffed noisily.

That tight feeling intensified in my stomach. "You run, they get the house, and the girls and I are out on the street."

"Shouldn't have put the house up," Mama repeated, defiance sharpening her tired voice. "I'm not letting that bitch ruin my life."

"She won't. I'm going to find out who set you up. Count on it."

Mama banged her fisted hand on the center console. "Damn Britt for arresting me."

My temples pounded. I pinched my nose to relieve the pressure in my head, wishing I carried ibuprofen with me. "He proved your car is the murder weapon. The paint chips on Erica's clothes and her DNA on the Olds confirmed that. He didn't have any choice."

"He knows me." Her pale chin jutted out. "He knows I wouldn't kill anyone."

According to Bud, the circumstantial case against Mama was strong enough to convict her. "Britt can't let his personal feelings influence his judgment. He ran the evidence through the system twice."

"Still, he didn't have to arrest me."

I concentrated on getting us home in one piece. It had been a long evening of jumping through legal hoops. Bud had demonstrated a credible familiarity with the system, and we'd navigated through the judicial maze. Without his help, I'd still be there. So would Mama.

Jonette and Madonna met us at the front door. I was disappointed about missing the girls, but it was good they'd gone to school. "Well?" Jonette asked. Her eye sockets were rimmed with dark circles, giving us the appearance of sisters.

Mama shuffled into the house. "I'm old as dirt, and I'm going to spend the rest of my life making license plates unless you two brainiacs figure this out."

I exchanged a glance with Jonette that said, *we'll talk later.* "I'm hungry. Do you want something to eat, Mama?"

"Hell, no. I'm too tired to eat. I want to go to bed and wake up tomorrow and find out this was a bad dream."

"Let me know if that works," Jonette said. "I've got a couple of mistakes in my life that I'd like to dream away."

After my divorce, I'd tried the Rip Van Winkle thing. "It doesn't work. Sleeping too much is a useless escape mechanism."

"Works for me," Mama said. "I need to escape any way I can. You young people figure this out today, you hear. I don't have a lot of time left. I'm not spending any of it in jail."

"Want me to help you up the stairs, Mama?"

"No. I'm old but I'm not completely decrepit."

Jonette and I fixed hot tea and toast. The steam from the tea wafted up and soothed my aching head. I slathered jelly on my toast. Sugar and caffeine fixed most of life's problems. I prayed they'd do the trick today. Between bites I said, "Thanks for staying with the girls."

"You couldn't have pried me out of this house with a crowbar. I was glad to do it."

It felt good to be talking about something other than Mama's arrest. "Did Dean find someone to work your shift?"

Jonette shrugged. "He managed."

Her flip tone sounded wrong. Was the entire world coming unglued? "Things aren't any better between you two?"

"No. I'm looking forward to him leaving tomorrow for that bartender convention in Ocean City. He watches me all the time, like he's afraid I'm going to bolt."

"Are you?"

"I don't know." Jonette's forehead furrowed. She rubbed her temples. "I'm thirty-eight, and I don't have any kids. Can't have any kids. I've been with six men and couldn't make it work with the first five. Things work with Dean. But the initial rush of excitement is gone. We're stuck in the old homebody routine."

I finished my tea. For the first time in hours my stomach didn't feel hollow or queasy. "That's what I miss most about being married."

"You're domesticated. You like the homebody thing."

"So do you. You just won't admit it."

"Let's not talk about my failures," Jonette said. "What's the deal with Delilah?"

The too-tight feeling in my stomach returned. "She's been charged with Erica's murder. Tests on her car conclusively proved that it killed Erica."

"Dang. Everyone knows about Erica and Delilah's heated argument on Monday. Delilah must feel trapped."

"Britt's sure he's got the right person."

Jonette snorted. "Detective Dumb-as-Dirt is clueless. What do we have?"

"The richest, bitchiest woman in town is dead. Run over

several times by Mama's car."

"I always knew that Olds was possessed."

"Last Tuesday, Mama drove Francine and Muriel to the seven P.M. hospitality committee meeting at church. Erica drove there in her Caddy. After the meeting broke up, Erica left first, then Mama drove Francine and Muriel home."

I paused to gather myself for the rest. "Mama drove over to Bud Flook's house and stayed there for a couple of hours. Then she came home and went to bed."

"Bud's house? What was she doing there?"

I fiddled with my empty tea cup before answering. "Visiting an old friend."

"Someone stole her car while she was at Bud's house?"

"That's the way it looks, yes."

"How did they know how long she would be there?"

My fingernail traced the gouge I'd accidentally made in the table while working on my science fair project in ninth grade. At the time, I'd been frustrated because science wasn't as straightforward as math. The tables had turned. Now I counted on science being nonlinear. "They knew her routine."

"Routine?" Jonette's head popped up. "She went to see that old geezer routinely? Is she screwing him or something?"

I closed my eyes against that image. "Or something."

"A couple of hours, eh?" Jonette chuckled herself into a deep belly laugh.

"Could we get past this part? Please?"

"Okay, spoilsport. We got senior citizen nooky, we got someone who knows how to boost a car, and we got a dead woman."

"A dead blackmailing woman."

"You're sure about that? Who would pay blackmail these days? Everyone's dirty laundry is already splashed all over the evening news and the Internet."

"The citizens of Hogan's Glen still believe in old-fashioned honor, integrity, and reputation."

Jonette appeared thoughtful. "You just described yourself."

I ignored her remark, though I privately agreed I'd been born in the wrong generation. "Erica wasn't blackmailing me, but she was into all of Mama's friends."

"Maybe they drew straws, and the short straw had to kill her."

"Mama didn't kill her. Francine and Muriel swear they didn't kill her, though they have strong motives. They claim to be night-blind, but that could be a ruse. They had to know about Mama and Bud. Do you think either of them can hot-wire a car?"

Jonette shrugged. "Who knows what's in their skill set?"

"Anyone could have driven Mama's Olds. I wish I already knew who did it and only had to prove their guilt. Doing both in a short time frame will be hard. Who's smart enough to pull off a premeditated crime?"

Jonette cocked her head to the side, considering. "What about the lawyer?" she asked. "Couldn't Bud drug your mother and run over Erica?"

"Hmmm. His medicine chest is probably loaded with pills, like Mama's. He would have had the means and opportunity, but why would he? Mama was already his girlfriend. What else could he want?"

Jonette leaned back in her chair. If she was as tired as she looked and I felt, we were in trouble. But I'd sat alone for hours at the jail thinking about this. "Men of Bud's generation want to be married," I said.

She shook her head. "Bud Flook is a confirmed bachelor. He's not the marrying type. He never dated any woman in town."

I swallowed hard and closed my eyes. "That's because he's

been in love with Mama ever since his college days."

Jonette whistled through her teeth. "Holy shit."

"My thoughts exactly."

CHAPTER 13

"Caroline's ball is the closest." Alveeta Wagner's orange poncho crackled as she pointed out the obvious.

Rain dripped steadily off the brim of my red golf cap as I picked up my ball and joined her at Caroline Chiu's ball in the rough. In this best-ball format of our league play, our foursome had naturally chosen the ball closest to the green. Thank God this was the last hole in today's nine-hole event.

I had better sense than to golf in the rain, but this chilly downpour had snuck up on us in the middle of our Chocolate Cake Scramble. With numb fingers, I squeezed the water out of my sodden pony tail, trying to slow the water channeling down my shirt collar. What I wouldn't give for a cozy fire and a cup of hot coffee.

Moisture permeated my water-resistant jacket and my navy-blue slacks. Rain wicked down my socks into my waterproof shoes and rubbed a blister on my left heel. But I wasn't calling it quits. Not when I'd already endured four holes of rain.

"You're up Cleo," Caroline announced.

"Hold your horses. I'm coming." I grabbed my wedge from my bag. Teeth chattering, I hurried back to the group. Raindrops pelted the brim of my cap. If only I hadn't decided I needed to do something fun for myself, I could be warm and dry right now, like Jonette who was covering the Tavern for Dean.

"Take your time," Thelma Kress advised. She had the luxury of time because she was waterproof from head to toe.

A gaping bunker stood between us and the pin. The sloping green fed down into a pond. A ball hit too hard would be lost. *That water isn't there,* I told myself. *There's no sand trap, either. Just swing through this thick grass and make solid contact with the ball. Easy.*

I shook the excess moisture off my sand wedge. I was too miserable to bother with a practice swing. The faster I played, the sooner I'd be done with this round from hell. Tall grass arched over my shoes, lashed at my ankles. My grip seemed strong, but I had no feeling in my fingers. I stopped to re-grip, lifting the club in front of me to verify my hand position.

Looked good. I committed to the stroke, taking the wedge back shoulder high, driving the club head forward. But grass caught my club face, decelerating my swing speed, and changing the angle of impact. My ball squirted into the poison ivy in the out-of-bounds area. My club sailed out of my hand and impaled itself in the sand trap.

"Jeez, Cleo. If you don't like your clubs, give 'em away. Don't throw 'em," Thelma said. Her bright pink vinyl raincoat shimmered when she moved. It amazed me that she could swing with that coat on.

"Sorry about that." I'd have been embarrassed if I wasn't so darned cold. I snatched my club out of the trap. Could this day get any worse?

Alveeta sashayed up to the same spot and dropped her ball. She shot me a superior glance, a glance that clearly said, *I'm better than you.* After my last disastrous shot, anything was certainly possible.

But the golf gods had a sense of humor after all. Alveeta whiffed. Missed her ball by a mile. I turned to hide my smile. Alveeta and I had a long history, none of it good.

I mouthed the right sympathetic phrases because her whiff was bad for our team. Only two chances left to hit the green.

But those were our best chances. Thelma was a fifteen handicapper, Caroline an eight. Thelma nailed her shot, leaving it twelve yards below the pin, so we had a run at the cup for birdie.

Caroline approached the shot like she did everything else. One hundred percent Asian precision. Her ball flew through the air, struck the pin, and rolled to a stop six feet past the cup.

"Nice shot," I said to Caroline.

Thanks to Caroline's skill, we lay two on the green with a birdie putt. If I played like Caroline, I wouldn't have any trouble beating Jonette. But I wasn't the precision golfing machine Caroline was. I was an overworked, struggling accountant with a grossly pregnant neurotic dog, two teenaged daughters, and a mother wanted for murder. A mother who swore she wouldn't submit to jail, whose evasive actions might very well leave me homeless.

"Morning, ladies," Rafe looked dry in his blue and gold waterproof rain gear. He sounded suspiciously amused.

I groaned.

Had Rafe seen my disastrous chip? I hadn't sunk a putt today, and my chances of sinking this one weren't great. As the highest handicapper in the group, I would putt first. My lack of golfing prowess had to be a flaming albatross around his handsome neck. Or at least a strong deterrent to potential students.

"Morning." I looked up. Laughter danced in his warm eyes. My heart stalled. I looked like a drowned rat, and my golf game was stinking up his course.

"I can fix that hitch in your swing, Cleo." He handed out warm, dry towels to everyone. "I've got a cancellation in my Saturday lesson schedule. Can I pencil you in at nine o'clock?"

How could I say no when we both knew I needed serious help? I draped the towel around my neck, snuggling into its warmth. "Sure."

"Where does your group stand, score-wise?" Rafe asked.

Thelma pulled the pin. "We're three under so far, with a birdie opportunity here."

"Sink this putt and the chocolate cake is yours," Rafe said. "Two teams are already in with scores of three under and the remaining teams aren't in the running."

My mouth watered for chocolate cake. I mentally mapped out the intended path of my ball to the cup with imaginary yellow dashes. That repaired ball mark was a good intermediate point to aim at. So far so good. I addressed the ball and took a deep breath.

"Are you trying to make that putt, Cleo?" Rafe asked.

Heat rose to my cheeks. "Yes."

"You're going to miss it right by the width of the cup. Aim a bit more to the left."

I adjusted my putter until he was satisfied, then struck the ball. I didn't lift my head until I heard the ball plop into the cup. My team high-fived each other, and I got a breathtaking, toe-curling hug from the golf pro.

"Nice job, Red," he said, his lips nuzzling my neck.

I shivered with delight. "Thanks for lining me up."

"Any time."

As I rode back to the clubhouse, I got to thinking there was a lesson here. Relying on Rafe wasn't such a bad thing. We were a good team. A force to be reckoned with. I hugged that knowledge close.

After golf and chocolate cake, I went home, took a warm shower, and dried my hair. The wonderful smell of oatmeal cookies filtered upstairs. I snagged a handful for lunch and walked over to the office. Mama said she would bake the last pan and then she'd be over.

I checked my office phone for messages. There was one from Charlie. "Call me," he said.

My jaw clenched, and my spirits plummeted. Stop that, I chided. You asked him to help you. You gave him a reason to call. Be a grownup.

I dialed his work number.

"Clee. Got something you want." Charlie sounded tickled with himself.

I crossed my fingers, hoping he'd done what I asked. "What?"

"Three credit reports, but it's going to cost you."

My sigh of relief turned into a huff of exasperation. "Oh? You didn't mention a fee when you agreed to run the credit reports."

"I want a home-cooked meal with you and the girls. Tonight."

I ran my fingers through my dry hair. Dinner with Charlie. With the girls present. "Tonight?"

"Tonight. One meal. That's not asking too much."

It was asking a lot, and he knew it. "And if I don't agree?"

"You want this information? Dinner's the price you have to pay."

"What about wanting to help Mama out? What happened to your concern for her?"

"I am helping Delilah, but I'm helping myself, too."

He had information that would help Mama. What choice did I have? None, and he knew it. "Okay. Dinner. Six o'clock sharp."

"Thanks. You won't regret this, Clee."

From his distracted tone, I sensed he was ready to end the call. "Wait. What did you find out?"

"Erica Hodges' estate is flat broke. There are three dollars and eighty-one cents in her checking account. The house is mortgaged to the hilt, and her leased Caddy was repossessed. She owed money all over town."

That confirmed what I'd suspected after learning about her unpaid bill at the beauty shop. The richest woman in town had no money, which led to my next question. "Where did her money go?"

"Can't tell. For years, she took large cash withdrawals from her trust funds. Some of that money ended up in her checking account, the rest she spent. Payments through her checking account here at the bank were for routine expenses. Lights, water, garbage, phone, newspaper, that sort of thing."

"Her account balance isn't enough to pay for her funeral expenses. No wonder Eleanor is selling everything."

"Funny you should mention Eleanor. Her credit score isn't good, either."

I sat up straight. "Eleanor has money problems?"

"She poured her income into her clinic. Lawsuits and malpractice insurance are killing her. Plus, her credit is tied to her business partner, who is heavily leveraged. If she doesn't get a fresh infusion of cash immediately, she'll be bankrupt."

That must gall the perfect Eleanor. "What about Evan? Are the Hodges all headed to bankruptcy court?"

"Evan has a great credit score. He has steady employment at the gym, and he's living within his means. I'd consider him a good credit risk."

"You'd loan him money?"

"I would. Only he doesn't appear to need money."

Excitement skittered through my veins as I put the puzzle together. "But his sister does. What if she thought killing her mother would solve her money problems? According to Evan, Eleanor inherits everything. Erica cut him out of the will years ago. I'd say that gives Eleanor a strong motive to kill her mother."

"Sounds good to me."

My hopes soared. I danced out of my seat. Once Britt knew about Eleanor's money problems, he had to drop the charges against Mama. "Thanks, Charlie."

"I'll be home a little before six tonight."

Not even dinner with Charlie could change how excited I

felt. "See you then."

I called Britt's cell number and told him the news.

"I told you to stay out of this," Britt said.

I ignored his grumpy tone. "You arrested my mother. I can't sit back and do nothing. She didn't kill Erica Hodges. Eleanor has tons of motive."

"Motive isn't everything. Eleanor doesn't live here. How would she obtain Delilah's car?"

I hadn't thought about that part. I ran a scenario in my mind that worked. "She's a smart woman, and she's been trained to conduct intricate, complicated procedures. I bet she followed Mama before the murder and learned Mama's schedule. Mama is a creature of habit. Every Tuesday night is the same for her. She takes her friends to the hospitality committee meeting. Then she drives over to Bud's house. Whoever planned this would have known that."

"Too farfetched. Even if I buy the concept, Eleanor didn't have access to Delilah's car keys. And no one hot-wired the car. You can't convict on motive alone."

My theory sounded weak when he shot holes in it. "What about fingerprints in Mama's car? Did you have any extra ones that didn't belong?"

"The driver's side of the car only had Delilah's prints."

I brightened. "I drove her car not too long ago. My prints should have been there. What if Eleanor broke into Mama's car, killed her mother with it, then wiped her prints off?"

Britt sighed heavily. "You're making this up as you go along, aren't you? There were no signs of forced entry to the Olds."

"Mama didn't do it," I asserted. "I swear she didn't kill Erica."

"Her car was the murder weapon. We have solid proof."

"Someone else used her car. Besides, Mama has an alibi. She was with Bud Flook."

"She drove herself home. Alone. She had an opportunity to kill Erica."

"I know you think Mama is guilty, but her activities that night don't sound like the agenda of an angry woman bent on murder." I glanced into the outer office to make sure I was still alone. "Mama told me that they fell asleep afterward and that a phone call woke them up. If she was so relaxed and happy, why would she leave Bud's place and run over Erica? It doesn't follow."

"Bud got a call that night?"

"Yeah. Mama said it was a wrong number." I'd forgotten about that call until just now. "What if it was the right number? What if the killer needed Mama to get back in her car and drive home?"

Britt sighed again. "I'll check the phone records. If that leads anywhere, I'll look into it as a favor to you. But I'm not dropping the charges against Delilah. Her car is the murder weapon."

"Then you should arrest her car. Not Mama."

"Are you finished? I have other cases to work on."

"You promise you'll check on that call?"

"Promise. Bye."

Progress. About damned time. That phone call was important. It had to be. Once Britt saw it, too, he'd drop the charges. Mama would get her life back. I'd get the deed to my house back and a shot at having a sex life again. Not bad for an afternoon's work.

"How many places am I setting at the table?" Lexy asked.

I'd commandeered the kitchen. After talking to Britt, I'd run out and bought a roast. I'd even made Charlie's favorite sour cream mashed potatoes. Without his running the credit reports, I wouldn't have cause to celebrate. He deserved a feast for helping.

194

Back to Lexy's question of how many place settings. There was an outside chance Rafe might take me up on my open-ended dinner invitation, but I didn't want to count on it. If he came, we'd add a place for him. "Six. There's the four of us, Bud Flook, and your father."

Lexy stared at me through a handful of forks. "Daddy's coming to dinner? Here? At our house?"

Sunny cheer infused me from head to toe. I was too happy to be mad at Charlie for insisting on dinner. "He asked if he could come. I said yes. It's no big deal."

Lexy shook her head. Her brown eyes rounded. "It is a big deal. He'll think you've forgiven him. Is that what happened? You're going to marry him again?"

"What's this?" Charla came flying in the kitchen, her curly red hair springing in every direction. "You're getting married?"

I stirred the gravy. If you didn't pay close attention to gravy making, inedible lumps formed. "I'm not getting married. I invited your father to dinner. That's all."

Charla whooped for joy. Then she hugged me twice. She happily danced around the kitchen. "Thank you. Thank you. Thank you. I knew you and Daddy would get back together."

I'd been so worried about Charlie's reaction that I'd overlooked how the girls would view this. "We're not together. I'm dating someone else now, remember?"

"Rafe Golden," Lexy said, as if Charla had forgotten.

"But you're not married to him," Charla declared. "Daddy still has a chance."

Charla's optimism rubbed me the wrong way. I put down my wooden spoon, moved the gravy pan off the burner, and faced her. "The chances of me getting back together with your father are zero. He cheated on me. He slept with another woman while he was married to me. That's the worst kind of lying there is. I won't ever forget the pain he caused me."

"He didn't mean to hurt anyone," Charla said loyally. "He told me so."

"He's an adult and he knew what he was doing. I want you to have a good relationship with him, but you need to understand that our marriage is over and done with. Once trust is broken, it's almost impossible to repair it."

"You didn't say it was impossible," Charla insisted. "There's still hope."

My shoulders slumped. "Charla, wake up. I'm not the naive woman I used to be."

"That's okay, Mom. Daddy's not the man he used to be, either. He wants us back."

I raised my hand in protest. "It's not going to happen. You aren't listening to me. You are setting yourself up for a major disappointment."

"Don't worry about me, Mom." Charla flashed me a sparkling smile. "Nothing can be more disappointing than my parents getting divorced. I believe you guys will get back together again."

God save me from bright-eyed optimists. "Lexy? Do you understand?"

She grabbed a handful of knives. She brushed her chin-length dark hair behind her ear. "I understand just fine. Daddy screwed up. He cheated on you. Now he's alone, and it sucks to be him."

I patted her back, reassured I'd communicated the truth to someone. "Good girl."

Charla shot us both disapproving looks. "You spoilsport pessimists are all alike."

If you didn't count the seating arrangements, dinner went well. I'd put the men at opposite ends of the dining room table, thinking Charla and Lexy would sit beside their father while

Mama and I flanked Bud Flook. Charla had other ideas. She'd snagged the seat by Bud, leaving the only open seat next to Charlie. Madonna lay next to the far wall where she could keep an eagle eye on me.

I could have demanded Charla switch places with me, but I felt so good about today's progress that I didn't want to ruin the occasion by making a scene. I endured Charlie's smug satisfaction through the main course. After bowls of mint chocolate chip ice cream, Charlie surprised Lexy with her digital camera.

Her face lit up like Mama's last birthday cake. She dashed over and jumped in his lap with youthful exuberance. "Thank you, Daddy."

I couldn't remember Lexy acting so carefree and happy in recent months. Joy had been conspicuously absent from her life these last two years. That realization stung. Our divorce had hurt the kids in ways I hadn't realized. Tears misted my eyes, blurring my vision.

Charlie had the gall to smile at me. As if I would fall for that dimple in his cheek. Not hardly. I collected the empty bowls and headed to the kitchen. Staying busy would keep the past at bay, keep the present safe.

He followed me. "Would it be so bad, Cleo?"

I shot him a frosty glance as I opened the dishwasher. "Not going to happen. Fool me once, shame on you. Fool me twice, shame on me."

He stepped closer, trapping me between him and the sink and the dishwasher. His familiar scent filled my lungs. "I'm not giving up."

Headlights flashed on the kitchen window as a car pulled into the driveway. I stared him down. "You're wasting your time," I said.

"I saw the longing in your face when Lexy saw her camera,"

he said. "Admit it. For that moment, we were a family again."

It sucked that he was right. "I appreciate what you did for Lexy, but you can't buy your way back into my good graces. It won't work."

He touched my arm, caressing it lightly. "It will work. You'll see."

At the sound of a brisk knock, I skirted around Charlie to answer the kitchen door. A large bouquet of wildflowers greeted me. I glanced through the fragrant blossoms to see the man I loved scowling at me. I reached for the flowers and his hand before he could turn away. "Rafe. How wonderful to see you. Wow. Flowers."

"Sorry I'm late. I got hung up at the course." Rafe hovered on the stoop, indecision stamped on his angular face. "I didn't realize you'd made other plans."

I glanced over my shoulder to see Charlie standing right behind me. He wasn't going to mess this up for me. Not wanting to take a chance on Rafe getting away, I grabbed the front of his golf shirt and pulled him close for a hello kiss. "Please come in. I've got a ton of food. I'll fix you a plate in a jiffy."

The men exchanged last names and eyed each other. The tension in the air escalated as if these two dogs were fighting over one bone. "Oh, for heaven's sake, Charlie," I grumbled. "Go see if Lexy needs any help with the camera you bought her."

For once, Charlie obeyed.

Rafe stuck his hands in his pockets while I loaded his plate with food. He sniffed appreciably. "Looks like someone went all out on dinner. All the food's the right color."

"I cooked." I smiled up at him, brimming with goodwill and cheerfulness now that we were alone. "We're celebrating."

"Oh?"

I stuck his covered plate in the microwave and poured him a

glass of iced tea. "Charlie came up with a lead that might clear Mama. It seems that Eleanor—you remember perfect Eleanor?"

Rafe smiled. "Child genius, prom queen, Virgin Mary–hogging Eleanor?"

"Yeah. That Eleanor. Well, you're never going to believe this. She's broke. More than broke. She's deeply in debt. So deep her clinic is gonna fold. We think she killed her mother to get her mother's money, only her mother didn't have any money. Perfect Eleanor isn't so perfect after all. I called Britt, and he's checking it out."

"Sounds good." Rafe studied me.

His close scrutiny worried me. Was this about Charlie being here? I thought we'd already cleared the air on that. "Would you like to eat in here or join the family in the dining room?"

He shrugged. "Here's fine. Dinner smells great."

I joined Rafe at the kitchen table. "Thanks. I'm glad someone appreciates my boring cooking."

"Tastes delicious," Rafe said between bites. "I love your cooking."

Warmed by the compliment, I stuck my nose in the flowers and breathed deeply. The fresh scent reminded me of summer sunshine and carefree days. A smile welled up inside me. "I really appreciate the flowers. I can't remember the last time anyone brought me flowers."

"Glad you like them. You look a lot drier than this morning."

"Ya think?"

"Good to see you smile, Red." He reached across the table for my hand and held it.

I squeezed his hand in reassurance. "I'm fine. We're fine."

"Are we? I keep tripping over your ex."

"Charlie wants you to think that, but there's nothing there. I'm in love with you, Rafe Golden."

Rafe's eyes heated, and he kissed the underside of my wrist. I shivered in delight. He cared. Boy, did he care. Joy spiraled through me.

"Mom, have you seen my cheerleading shorts?" Charla burst into the kitchen at full speed, slowing to a crawl when she saw Rafe. "Oh. Hello."

"Hello," Rafe said. He shoveled the last of his meal into his mouth.

"My shorts. Mom, have you seen them?"

If Rafe had come here expecting quiet time with me, he was in for a disappointment. Even so, I wouldn't abandon him to search for Charla's cheering duds. "Sorry, dear. I haven't seen your shorts. Did you check the floor of your room?"

"Not yet. Daddy said he'd drop me off at cheerleading practice tonight."

"Daddy seems to be scoring points all around today," I said flippantly.

Beside me, Rafe stiffened. I chewed my bottom lip. Why had I opened my big mouth? Even though we were dating, Rafe wasn't family. That's what I kept coming back to. Family. Charlie was scum as a husband, but because of our mutual love for our children, he was still family. Rafe wasn't. But I hoped he would become family.

"Daddy's the greatest," Charla said. "He's getting me a laptop."

My mouth dropped. "He is?"

"Yeah, but I have to share the color printer with Lexy." Charla ran out of the kitchen.

A laptop and a color printer. Charlie was letting out all the stops. The girls would think every day was Christmas around here.

The kitchen door opened again. This time it was Lexy. "Mom, you and Mr. Golden want to play Monopoly with us?"

I glanced at Rafe. He shrugged. I interpreted his gesture to mean why not. "Sure. We'll both play. Give me a minute to put the food away."

"Okay. What piece would you like, Mr. Golden?"

Rafe bit back a chuckle. "The car."

The door swung shut. "I hope it was all right to say you'd join us. We played a lot of board games . . ." I paused to find the right words. "When the girls were younger."

"I know Monopoly," Rafe said, interlacing his fingers with mine. "It's the one game my family mastered."

The dancing lights were back in his bedroom eyes. I didn't know if it was because Charlie was leaving any minute now or because Rafe's belly was full. Either way, harmony ruled my household again. I leaned over and kissed him.

Rafe gave the kiss his full attention. My blood heated, and my thoughts ran wild. Would anyone notice if we did it in the laundry room? The kitchen door opened. I realized someone was watching us and broke off the kiss.

Mama snorted from the doorway. "Just as I thought. Smooching in the kitchen. Bud, come in here and help me get this kitchen cleaned up. Otherwise we'll be waiting all night on these love birds."

Love birds.

Was that what we were?

I clung to that thought for the rest of the evening.

CHAPTER 14

Jonette, Mama, and I stared in rapt fascination at the *Washington Post* spread out on the back corner booth of the Tavern. Jonette had turned up the lights because lunch was over and it was too soon for happy hour. With Dean away at his bartender convention, Jonette was running the place. She'd called us as soon as she'd opened the newspaper.

"See what I mean?" Jonette tapped the black-and-white photo. Two men were hauling a gurney full of machines out of a door. Overhead, the weighty block letters proclaimed CRANDALL BRAIN CLINIC.

"Looks like Britt's got a new suspect all right." I leaned close to read the fine newsprint. James Taylor's song about friendship faded as I digested the article. According to the reporter, the prominent Crandall Brain Clinic in Washington, D.C., was kaput. One of the partners had skipped the country. The remaining partner, Dr. Eleanor Hodges, couldn't be reached by press time.

"Hot damn! I might get to see my grandchildren grow up after all." Mama raised her arms in a victory salute, straining the fabric and the buttons of her pink jacket.

"Don't get too excited, Mama," I cautioned. "We still don't know if Eleanor was in town that night, or if she would know how to break into your car and start it without a key."

Mama toyed with her pearl necklace. "I wasn't completely honest about this before, but that night I left the car unlocked with my keys in the ignition. Bud's house is off by itself. I didn't think anyone would even know the keys were in there. Eleanor didn't need any criminal skills to borrow my car."

I was appalled. "Mama, why didn't you tell us this before?"

"Because I didn't want another lecture from you about leaving my keys in the car. I left them in the car for a reason. It takes too long to hunt them up in the dark."

I couldn't believe she didn't grasp the importance of the information she'd withheld. I reached over and grabbed her by the shoulders. "You would've gone to jail rather than tell anyone you left the keys in your car?"

Mama scooted out of my grip. "I wouldn't let it go that far. I'd rather have a lecture from you than serve a prison term. I didn't mention the keys before because I didn't want anyone to know I'd been over at Bud's house. Then when I did tell you about Bud, I forgot to tell you about the keys. I'm a senior. I'm allowed to be forgetful."

"Don't move." I whipped my cell phone out of my pocket book and dialed Britt. He answered on the first ring. "Radcliff."

"Did you see the *Washington Post*?" I asked.

"Got it here in front of me. Just got off the phone with the reporter who wrote the story. You were right about Eleanor Hodges. She's in serious financial trouble."

"Told you so. And another thing. Mama just let it slip that her car wasn't locked while she was at Bud's. And her keys were in the ignition."

The line seemed to go dead. "You still there, Britt?" I asked. Jonette leaned close to listen in.

"I'm here." He swore under his breath. "Why didn't she mention that before?"

"Because she didn't want me to give her hell for leaving her keys in the car."

"She's not making my job any easier."

"Of course not. She's still spitting mad at you for arresting her. Charging her with murder didn't help, either."

Britt groaned. "God save me from opinionated women."

I let that slight slide. He was helping me clear Mama's name. "Where does that leave us with Eleanor?"

"It leaves me checking her out more thoroughly. If something comes of this, I'll let you know."

I hung up. "Britt's definitely looking at Eleanor for the murder. Let's keep our fingers crossed."

"The hell with that," Mama said. "Bud and I have been wanting to get away for the weekend. I'm going to tell him that we can go."

My stomach burned. If Mama jumped bail, we could lose our house. "You will not leave town. Not unless the charges against you are dropped. If you so much as think about it, I'll clip your wings so fast you won't know what hit you."

Mama scrunched up her brow. "See why I didn't tell you about the keys? You're no fun at all. Everything has to be done your way. Who made you queen of the world? You don't know anything. The best time to take a trip is right before you're stuck in jail forever."

"You won't be stuck in jail forever. Britt will find the real killer."

"Hmmph." Mama stormed off to pour herself a fresh cup of coffee.

Jonette folded the newspaper section and handed it to me. "Here. You guys keep this."

I tucked the paper in my purse. "Thanks, Jonette. How's it going with Dean away on his trip?"

Jonette made a face. "I miss the old fart. Who knew that he did so much around here? All he ever seemed to do was get in my way. Now that he's not around, I hardly have time to think, I'm so busy."

I leaned close to Jonette and whispered, "What about the other?"

"What other?"

"You know. The other part of missing Dean. The personal part."

Jonette sighed with great feeling. "Yeah. That part sucks, too."

"When's he coming home?"

"Tomorrow." Jonette shoved her fisted hands in her apron pockets.

"You'll be happy then."

"Yeah, but he'll have won."

I chugged the rest of my lukewarm coffee as America started singing about sister golden hair surprise. "You're wrong. You both won. Caring about someone who cares right back is never wrong."

Jonette arched a well plucked eyebrow. "You're not going to lecture me about love, are you?"

"Hell, no. Not when I know so little about it. All I'm saying is give it a chance. Dean's a good guy."

Twelve hours later, I was ready to retract my kind words about Dean. Because of his inconsiderate behavior, I was on the Bay Bridge at three in the morning. Not my idea of how I wanted to spend my night.

"Tell me again why we're going after Dean?" I asked Jonette.

From the muted fluorescent glow of the Volvo's dash instrumentation, I barely made out the smile on Jonette's face. "Because he called me and asked me to come bail him out of jail."

"What about his car?" I asked. "Didn't he drive it to Ocean City?"

"No. He rode with a friend. Dean's car is in the body shop

getting painted, or I wouldn't have bothered you tonight."

I heard an odd sound. It took me a minute to place the noise. From the direction, it had to be coming from Jonette. Humming? She never hummed.

"Why are you so happy about this?" I asked. "It's the middle of the night, and you've been on your feet for over twelve hours. Aren't you exhausted?"

"Not tired," she said.

"Why's that?"

"Because Dean's not dull."

"Dull?" I'd had two hours of sleep before Jonette called me for this road trip. Not enough sleep to come up with a snappy retort.

"Like an old slipper. He's not dull. He did this for me."

"You weren't even in Ocean City. How could he have done this for you?"

"To prove he wasn't dull. When his friend suggested running naked down a busy Ocean City street, Dean jumped at the opportunity to streak."

I blinked away the mental image of a naked Dean jumping around. "How many men did this?"

"Two of them. The rest of their group was apparently pretty dull. But not Dean."

I'd take dull any day, especially if it got me a good night's sleep. My cell phone rang. "The dog is in labor," Mama said. "What should I do?"

"Just a minute, Mama." I turned to Jonette. "Madonna is having her puppies right now. What should Mama do?"

Jonette snatched the phone out of my hand and fired off a bunch of questions at Mama. I reeled from the rapid pace of the conversation. This was too much for Mama to handle alone. She needed help, and not just help from Lexy and Charla.

I had two choices when it came to help. Rafe or Charlie. My

gut instinct said to call Rafe. I didn't know what he knew about birthing puppies, but I sensed he had a cool head in a crisis. I snatched the phone back from Jonette. "Wake up the girls, Mama. They'll know what to do. As soon as we hang up, I'll call Rafe and ask him to come over to help you."

"Suit yourself," Mama said.

I phoned Rafe. No answer. I dialed again. This time he picked up. I explained the situation.

He yawned into the phone. "You want me to do what?"

"I want you to help Mama and the girls with the dog."

"Where are you?"

From his sharp tone, I gathered he expected me to be home in the middle of the night. "I'm about an hour from Ocean City. At the very earliest, it will be four hours before I can get back."

"How am I going to help?"

"I need you to be the voice of reason. Lexy knows what to do, but she's only thirteen. That's too much responsibility for her. Mama doesn't count as an adult. She might dye one of the puppies blue."

"You convinced me." Rafe yawned again. "I'm on my way."

I hung up.

"Dang," Jonette said. "All that planning and I'm gonna miss the big event. Dean better appreciate the sacrifice I'm making for him."

We sped through the dark night.

At the police station, Dean was sloppy drunk and a little sheepish after he put on the jeans, T-shirt, and sneakers Jonette had brought. "Sorry to be a bother, but at least I'm not *dull*," he said. Jonette and I had our hands full keeping him upright the rest of the way to the car.

"You're not dull, Dean. I never thought you were." Jonette patted his butt.

The three of us leaned against the Gray Beast as I fumbled to unlock the door. I could see Mama's point about not wanting to waste time looking for her keys in her purse when it was dark outside. At last, I found the keys and gained entry.

"You aren't leaving me?" Dean asked, suddenly standing straight and tall.

"Not a chance." Jonette slid into the back seat with Dean. "It takes a lot of nerve to run naked in public at forty-eight. I admire that about you."

He scrunched up one eye. "You do?"

"I do. And if you ever do it again, I'll kill you."

"I love you, Jonette."

"I love you back, wild man."

We headed home, missing the morning rush-hour traffic around Baltimore by skirting through back roads. My phone didn't ring again, and I trusted Rafe was taking care of everything. Dean and Jonette slept while I drove.

I parked in the driveway and ran into the house, Jonette hard on my heels. "Hello?" I called anxiously. "Where is everyone?"

"Up here, Mom," Lexy's excited voice sailed over the balcony.

I dashed into my bedroom, fearing the worst. Lexy sat in the whelping box with Madonna. Nearby, Charla and Mama held puppies in their laps. From the grim set of Rafe's face, I owed him big for this favor.

"How'd you get her to use the wading pool?" I asked.

"Mr. Golden put Madonna there, and she didn't argue," Charla said. "Isn't this the cutest puppy you ever did see?"

The puppies were adorable. "Sure is." I turned to Rafe. "You all right?"

"Doing good. I believe this is the last one."

An hour later, it was finally over. Jonette took Madonna out to relieve herself. I moved the whelping pool down into the kitchen, and the girls kept the puppies warm until Madonna returned.

I went back upstairs to my bedroom to find Rafe sound asleep in my bed. With all that he'd done for me, he deserved an undisturbed rest. So did I, for that matter. I yawned big, locked the door, and joined him.

CHAPTER 15

I decided to knock off work at four o'clock Friday afternoon. My client calls had been returned, two more homeowner association audits had been completed, and the billing was caught up. Not bad for a half day's effort.

I had been walking on air all afternoon, a big goofy smile on my face. Sleeping with Rafe tended to do that.

"You're certainly in a good mood today." Mama leaned a trim hip against the doorjamb. She'd dressed in a cotton-candy pink sheath and jacket, but the colorful outfit didn't brighten her tired air.

I filed away the materials from the completed audits, smiling inwardly at her observation. "Go ahead. I know you're dying to say it."

Mama laughed, her worried expression fading. "You're right. I told you so. I told you so. Getting laid this morning did you a world of good."

I blushed. Sex wasn't a topic I discussed with Mama. "That's certainly part of it. I feel like a million dollars."

She drifted closer. "It shows. That Rafe Golden is not so bad."

He was magnificent. I had trusted him, and he hadn't let me down. It didn't get any better than that. "I love him, Mom."

Mama halted. "You certain?"

"Absolutely." The knowledge swelled up in me like heated popcorn, pushing at my reservations, seeking release.

210

"He seems fond of you."

"I want to be with him all the time, but I have a responsibility to set a good moral example for the girls. Only, neither of the girls said anything about us sleeping together this morning. Do you think they didn't notice?"

Mama settled in a guest chair, dismissing my question with a flip of her wrist. "Not a chance. Believe me, they know exactly what's going on between you and Rafe."

I clasped my hands to my chest, daring to hope. I could have it all, a boyfriend and a family. "Do you think they're all right with it?"

"Ask them."

If I couldn't talk sex with Mama, no way could I discuss it with the girls. "Right." Time for this conversation to end. I stood.

"Anybody back here?" Britt called from the outer office.

At the sound of his voice, Mama lurched to her feet, the color draining from her face. Heart in my throat, I went to her, cinching my arm around her waist. "Come on in. We're back here."

Britt's strong legs ate up the ground. All too soon he stood next to us, thick forearms bulging from his hunter-green polo, gun and badge visible at his waist. His close-cropped hair, steely eyes, and inscrutable face all painted a picture of a tough cop. "I have news."

I dared to hope for good news, but his serious demeanor worried me. "Let's sit down over by the window." I steered Mama into a chair and sat next to her, holding her trembling hand.

Britt perched on the edge of his seat. "The charges against you have been dropped, Delilah."

Mama gasped. I clutched my heart. Hope flared, sparkled, and burst across my thoughts. "Eleanor?"

Britt nodded, his features hardening once again. "You were right about her, Cleo. She had us fooled. She was in Hogan's Glen that night. Ate dinner at her brother's house, bought gas at the minute market, and made a call on her cell phone to Bud Flook."

"Perfect Eleanor." I closed my eyes momentarily as another wave of relief swept through me. How the mighty had fallen. "She was always a little too good to be true if you ask me."

"The feds are questioning her. They think she colluded with her business partner to defraud their lender. Her partner took four million out of their business account and fled the country. Left her to face the music. She was desperate for money."

Britt's gray eyes darkened with concern. "I'm sorry for what you went through, Delilah. I had no choice. Your Olds is the murder weapon."

Mama finally found her voice. "Will I get my car back?"

"I'll see to it," Britt said.

Mama sighed deeply.

Britt's news tumbled through my mind. Curiosity reared its ugly, whiskered head. "Did Eleanor confess to killing her mother?"

He stiffened. "She hasn't confessed to anything except hating her mother."

Hate was a strong word. I shuddered. Her Crandall ancestors must be mortified. "Is she out on bail?"

"When Evan came in to post bail, she spit on him. Told him not to bother. She started yelling at him about what a big disappointment he was to the family, and she wouldn't calm down until he left. She's staying in jail until the trial."

"If they have a Christmas pageant in prison, she'll already know the part of the Virgin Mary." It was a mean thing to say, but I felt mean. Perfect Eleanor had nearly framed Mama. Eleanor wasn't so perfect anymore.

Britt rose, touched his gun and badge in an unconscious motion. "I haven't seen my family in two days, but I wanted to tell you personally that you were exonerated, Delilah."

"This is for real? You won't change your mind?" Mama's voice cracked with emotion.

"Not a chance," he said. "The DA says the case against Eleanor is rock solid."

"Well, hallelujah! It's about time you came to your senses, young man." Mama stood up, her face wreathed in smiles. "Excuse me. I've got calls to make."

"She's got grit," Britt said as Mama hurried outside, leaving the front door wide open.

Grit was a family trait. I rounded on Britt. "She's got a heart condition, and you put her through hell."

Britt raised his hand, his wedding ring tight on his thick fingers. "Don't start on me, Cleo. I had no choice. My wife has been giving me grief nonstop ever since I arrested Delilah."

"Good for her," I said. "Nice to know the whole world didn't go crazy at once. You tell Melissa I owe her one."

Britt nodded. At the doorway, he looked over his shoulder. "Thanks for your help, Cleo."

I hadn't expected him to say anything. His humility touched my heart. "You're welcome." I sat for a minute in my office, enjoying the peace and quiet. Satisfaction purred through me. I couldn't remember when I'd felt this wonderful.

Mama was off the hook for Erica's murder. Our home was secure. Madonna's puppies were healthy. And I'd slept with my boyfriend at my house. Not bad for a day's work. Not bad at all.

Saturday morning dawned with clear skies. Dew glistened on the grass surrounding the practice tee at the golf club. I made a pendulum stroke with my putter. The ball rolled directly across the smooth putting surface and clinked into the cup. I grinned at my hot teacher.

Rafe smiled back, his eyes warm and knowing. "You've got the basics down, Red. Practice will increase your consistency."

We'd practiced a lot of things last night. We'd been so absorbed in each other that we'd forgotten to eat. I hadn't minded the lack of food one bit. However, certain muscles were letting their presence be known today. A long soak in a hot tub sounded like just the thing to round out my Saturday morning.

"Easy for you to say." I hooked the head of my Ping putter over my shoulder. "You practically live at the golf course. When I get the time to come here, my mind is on playing, not on practicing."

Two golfers smacked balls on the range behind us, and another woman putted on the far side of the putting green.

Rafe's sandy eyebrows waggled. "Practice makes perfect."

"Don't even say that word." I shivered. "*Perfect* Eleanor almost ruined my family."

Rafe moved closer. His husky voice resonated deep within my bones. "But you didn't let her. You kept digging until you found the answer."

"Does this mean you approve of my nosing around?"

His expression sobered. "It means I'm relieved you gave Britt the information and let him handle the dirty work."

Not a ringing endorsement, but I'd take it. "Doesn't it seem odd that the killer turned out to be a woman? What does that say about Hogan's Glen?"

Rafe extracted another golf ball from his front pocket and rolled it toward my feet. "It says know your woman or you could wind up dead."

I gave up the pretext of putting. Conscious of the others nearby, I lowered my voice. "Am I your woman, Rafe?"

"Most definitely."

I snorted delicately. "That sounds like a caveman attitude."

He held my gaze, heating my blood. "When it comes to women, men think like cavemen. Don't let any guy tell you different."

An older gentleman joined us on the putting green. Rafe acknowledged the man with a smile and a nod. "My ten o'clock lesson is here, Red. Are you going to stay and practice?"

"Heck, no," I said. "I'm starved, and I'm looking forward to soaking in the tub."

To my surprise, Rafe blushed. He turned to his other student. "Go ahead and hit a few balls on the range, Nelson. I'll be right there."

Rafe scooped up my golf bag and caught my hand. At the casual contact, electricity arced between us. I wanted to jump him, but that was poor course etiquette. Definitely not allowed in the *Rules of Golf.*

He stowed my clubs in my trunk and pulled me close for a lingering kiss. We drew wolfish whistles from men loading carts in the parking lot. I didn't care. My blood sang a happy tune.

"When can I see you again?" Rafe's fingers combed through my hair, which had somehow come out of its customary pony tail.

"Tonight. Come over tonight. I'll figure something out."

He kissed me again, long and slow. "Tonight."

After he left, I sat in my Volvo, thoughts humming in my head. I loved him. He called me his woman. I trusted him. Did that mean we were becoming a family? It sure felt like that was the case.

And that made me happy.

Very happy.

I rummaged through my purse, looking for my calendar, to double-check that my schedule was clear today. I'd crossed out my personal training session with Evan to make the golf lesson appointment with Rafe. I'd called the gym yesterday to cancel today's session.

Cars whizzed by on the highway, but I sat rooted in place. Poor Evan. His family had imploded. His sister had killed his mother, and his sister didn't want anything to do with him. He had no one. For years he'd lived under his big sister's shadow. Living with Erica and Eleanor must have been awful.

Britt said Eleanor had yelled at Evan in the police station. About what a big disappointment he was to the family. Had his mom and sister expected him to rake in the dough?

If not for my nosing around, I could be in Evan's shoes. Without that new evidence, Mama would be looking at prison. I would have spent every penny I owned on her defense. For her freedom, I'd have given up my house and financial security. Luckily fate had intervened.

But fate had dealt a rough blow to Evan. How was he holding up? He must feel like a broken man, bereft of family, isolated by shame. Poor, poor Evan. He was alone in the world now. I bet he could use a friend.

I needed food. Wouldn't it be nice if I got enough for two and dropped over to cheer Evan up? He was my personal trainer, after all. I might be the closest thing he had to a friend.

My stomach growled urgently. I needed food and I needed it fast. At the drive-through window, I got two big breakfasts to go. With juice. A health nut like Evan probably drank juice with every meal. Even if he turned his nose up at the greasy food, he'd go for the juice.

I drove to Evan's apartment and knocked on his door.

Loud Jimmy Buffet music pulsed through the opening when Evan opened the door. Surprising musical choice, given Evan's hard-work philosophy. I would never have pegged him as the Caribbean party type. He was more the poster child for a health infomercial.

Nor would I have guessed he owned a Hawaiian shirt, bright red shorts, and flip-flops. The definition in his leg muscles drew my eyes down to his tanned feet and nicely trimmed toenails. I'd never seen Evan's toenails before, but they were trimmed as if he'd had a pedicure. The man was full of contradictions. I couldn't imagine Rafe or Charlie going to a nail salon.

"Cleo! What a surprise." A dark look crossed his face. "I didn't forget your session today, did I? The gym said you cancelled our appointment."

"I did. But I need to talk to you about that."

In the background Jimmy crooned about fins to the left and right. Evan's shoulders moved to the feel-good Caribbean beat. A wall of heat and coconut oil wafted out through Evan's doorway. He was really into this tropical thing. I half expected a parrot to fly up to his shoulder.

"I'm sorta busy," Evan admitted.

His personal inconsistencies intrigued me. Why was he in tropical mode? My curiosity flexed its muscle, and I waved the paper bag of food at him. The aroma of fresh, hot fries encircled us. "I brought food. Breakfast. I hope you'll share it with me."

Evan hesitated, so I waved the bag of food again. My stomach growled at the enticing smells. "All right," Evan said "Come on in." He cut the volume on his stereo and invited me to sit in his living room.

When he disappeared into a hall closet, I took stock of my surroundings. Precision-aligned black-and-white artwork decorated the plain white walls. A cluster of coconut-scented candles flickered on the walnut coffee table. A leather sofa and chair faced off against a massive entertainment system.

The National Anthem of Margaritaville filled the air. Curious. The austere furnishings fit with what I knew about Evan's personality, but I liked the laid-back, less intense Evan better. Was he taking antidepressants to combat stress? With all he'd endured, poor Evan deserved the lift.

The good vibes from the stereo infected me. I sank happily into the overstuffed buttery-soft leather sofa. My toe tapped along with the fun music, while my brain danced around the paradox of Evan.

From outward appearances, he was the perfect male. Handsome, successful, single. Why hadn't some woman snatched him up and married him? Did Evan date? I couldn't remember his name being linked with anyone recently.

Evan returned with two TV-dinner tables. Sturdy and walnut-toned, they matched his gleaming coffee table. The glossy tropical brochures next to the flickering candles struck me as odd. But what did it matter? I'd hate for anyone to analyze the things on my coffee table.

I set out the food, my brain refusing to settle. A litany of data streamed through my thoughts. Travel brochures. Jimmy Buffet music. Tropical atmosphere. Fun things. Vacation things. "Going somewhere?"

Emotions flickered across Evan's face as he sat down across from me in the matching overstuffed chair. "This has been such an ordeal. I need to get away for a few days."

I nodded, sympathy welling. "This week hasn't been easy for any of us."

We shared a look of understanding over our egg sandwiches. I wolfed my food down too fast. Evan ate his food deliberately, as if he were savoring each bite. With a buff physique like his, this meal must be a real departure from his standard diet. I hoped I wasn't leading him too far astray.

On the stereo, Jimmy Buffet switched to a Cajun tempo and sang about gypsies in the palace. In the song, some house-sitting friends threw a wild party. Chaos ensued.

I couldn't help but draw an inference to the festive mood in this place. Evan's apartment had a celebratory feel to it, not one of mourning and despair. My curiosity kicked into high gear.

"What did you want to talk to me about?" Evan asked.

Now that my stomach was full, I felt positive I was doing the right thing. "I'm canceling my personal training sessions and giving up my gym membership. I wanted to tell you in person."

He glanced up sharply. "Because of mother and Eleanor?"

"No. It isn't them. It's me. I thought physical fitness would help my golf game. Only, I need to practice my golf game to get better at golf. I don't have time for both activities. This has nothing to do with you or your family."

Evan folded the waste paper into flat rectangles, every corner perfectly square. "You got something good going with the golf pro?"

Did I ever. But I wasn't here to talk about my hot sex life. Jimmy Buffet sang about a volcano blowing up. The reference to hot molten lava in the midst of thinking about Rafe and sex made me blush. "We've been dating for a couple of months."

Evan started gathering up the trash.

I beat him to it. "I'll take care of this. Where's your trash can?"

"Under the kitchen sink." Evan folded up the TV tables and headed back to the hall closet.

I dashed into the kitchen, intending to deposit the trash and get the heck out of here, but Evan's calendar lay open next to his phone. I slowed on my way past it, observing his extensive color coded notations on various recent dates. That stopped me altogether. I flipped back to the previous month and saw similar markings. Mama's name was there. So was Eleanor's.

Warmth fled and a hard chill filled the void. I shivered against the cold. The hair on the back of my neck snapped to attention. My brain seized on one thought: *Why would Evan record Mama's schedule?*

The date of Erica's murder was circled in red ink.

A bitter taste pervaded my mouth. Air leaked from my lungs. *Think,* I told myself. *Think this through. There's probably a rational explanation.*

But what if there wasn't anything rational about this? What if the calendar notations were the blueprints for murder? If that were true, I was in big trouble.

Was Evan Eleanor's accomplice?

I couldn't imagine her letting him walk. Her reaction had been the polar opposite. She'd wanted nothing to do with him.

That brought up another, more chilling possibility. Eleanor wasn't the killer at all. Evan was.

My heart stopped for a long minute.

Lord, Lord.

I'd stepped in it now.

My brain kicked back on. I had to get out of here. Fast. Get out of here and call Britt. He'd know what to do.

Air seeped in my lungs. That was a good plan. Quickly, I shoved the remains of our breakfast in his trash can and whirled on my heel to leave the kitchen.

What I saw pushed my elevated heart rate into overdrive.

An aquarium on steroids occupied the entire interior kitchen wall. The wood-framed glass structure had a hasp and combination lock securing the mesh top. Two lights were mounted in the rear corners of the aquarium. The entire bottom of the glass case was filled with a multicolored snake.

Loops and loops of big, fat, slithery snake.

Enough snake to hurt someone.

A scream boiled out of me, the shrill sound piercing my eardrums. I clapped a hand over my mouth. I didn't hate snakes, but I didn't like them either. Afraid, I checked the floor for more snakes. The spotless white floor gleamed.

No snakes in sight.

"What is it? You okay, Cleo?" Evan poked his head in the door.

"S-s-snake." I pointed across the room. The jumbo reptile opened his slitted eyes and studied me. "What kind of snake is that?"

"Monty is a Burmese python."

Monty looked like he could crush me and swallow me for a midmorning snack. I took a step backward. The sharp edge of the kitchen counter pressed into my lower back.

Knees trembling, I tried to hold it together. Bad enough to be cooped up in here with a Hodges who might be a murderer. The snake added another dimension to my fear. Seeking solace, I shoved my hands in my pockets, palming the golf ball I found there. My fingers traced over the familiar dimpled surface. "How'd he get to be so big?"

"I've had Monty since I was a kid."

I shuddered.

I couldn't imagine having a reptile in the house with my kids. How had Eleanor and Erica tolerated Monty?

Evan joined me by the sink. He casually closed his appointment calendar. His action reminded me he'd had my mother's whereabouts on his calendar.

I was so unnerved by the huge man-eating snake that words babbled out of my mouth. "God, Evan. That thing is huge. How do you keep him from eating you?"

Evan's spine stiffened. "Monty is tame. He's not dangerous. What is it with women and snakes? Mother and Eleanor were scared to death of him."

"Because he's a predator. A reptile. Women are predisposed to dislike snakes. That Adam and Eve thing, you know. It's not our fault." No wonder Eleanor had perfect attendance for everything. She didn't want to stay home with the monster snake.

Inside his glass cage, Monty shifted position, his coils bulging and squishing as he moved. His oblate head cruised the top half of the cage, as if testing for an exit point. In the silence, I noted the music had ended. Now the place felt hot and close and oppressive. A thick musty smell filled the air.

Keeping one eye on the snake and another on the door, I asked, "He can't get out, can he?"

Evan regarded me steadily, much like the snake had done. "Monty is quite an escape artist, but I've got him locked in there pretty tight right now."

I couldn't imagine perfect Eleanor sharing a house with a supersized snake. I exhaled slowly. "Have you always kept him in the kitchen?"

"No. I had to keep him in the basement when I lived at home. Otherwise, Mother and Eleanor would flip out."

"You didn't like them very much, did you?"

Evan's eyes narrowed. "They hated Monty. Mother kept trying to kill him by turning off his light while I was in school. So I let him have free range in my room."

I gasped in a puff of snake air. "I bet that went over real big."

"Kept them out of my room and off of my back. You have no idea what it was like to grow up with them belittling everything I wanted to do."

"Hey, I went to school with Eleanor. I know exactly what you're talking about. Teachers constantly compared us to her. It was annoying, wasn't it?"

He nodded and rubbed his buzzed head. "It used to drive me crazy. If I got a ninety-eight on a test, Eleanor got a hundred. No matter what I did, it was never good enough."

He was opening up to me. More questions bubbled out. "So you stopped trying? Is that why your mother disinherited you?"

"She hated me because I didn't do what she wanted. I was supposed to grow up to be a banking whiz like Grandfather

Crandall. She cut me out of her life when I didn't stay the course. I'm the only Crandall ever to work their way through college." He snorted. "Get this. She said fitness wasn't a career. It was a rich man's hobby."

"That's harsh. It's obvious you like what you do at the gym."

"Thanks. It wasn't an easy choice."

"You stood up to her though. You kept your snake and studied the career you wanted. I had no idea you'd struggled so hard to be yourself."

"Mother had no respect for anyone. When she found out she couldn't manipulate me the way she could Eleanor, she wrote me off."

"Didn't that put a wedge between Eleanor and you?"

"We were never close."

His statement clunked in my head like a rock stuck in a tire tread rolling down the highway. "Funny. I thought she had dinner here the night your mother died."

He shot me an inscrutable look. "How'd you know about that?"

"Britt told me. Did she tell you about her brilliant plot to frame my mother?"

Evan barked out a harsh laugh. "Eleanor's never had an original thought. Mother told her what to think, night and day."

Another inconsistency. And his neck was bright red. I recklessly plunged ahead. "I disagree. Eleanor's plan was brilliant. It must have taken weeks to plan the frame job."

Evan shook with emotion. "Eleanor is not brilliant. She's a stupid bitch, and she's going to rot in prison the rest of her life."

I'd hit a nerve. The snake's tongue flickered in the glass cage. I ignored the snake and concentrated on the new information. The schedules I'd seen on his calendar. Evan knew them. Eleanor didn't. Evan couldn't stand Eleanor being smarter than him. I seized on that. "She is quite clever. It took a keen mind to coordinate the schedules so Mama took the blame. How did Eleanor know about Mama and Bud anyway?"

"All she had to do was to follow them around."

"Follow them?"

"Yeah, follow them," Evan said. "People do the same dumb things over and over again. They're stupid cows."

"It must really gall you Eleanor figured that out."

Evan's hands clinched into tight fists.

Interesting. He didn't like it when I pushed him a bit more. I used that. "I wonder what it must have been like to sit in that big powerful Olds and aim it at your mother. I wonder what Eleanor thought as she punched the accelerator."

A faraway look came into Evan's eyes. Like he was in the zone. The killing zone. "Die bitch. You can't hurt me any longer."

An icy chill ran through my blood at the smoldering rage in his voice. I'd gotten it wrong. Evan killed his mother. Not Eleanor. I knew it sure as I knew my name but I couldn't prove it. Britt needed proof. "How did it happen? What did Eleanor see as she drove at your mother? Would your mother have been blinded by the approaching headlights? Did she roll up on the windshield?"

Evan slid deeper into the weird zone, his body quieted in an almost hypnotized trance. "She stood there, shielding her eyes. She called out, Delilah, why are you stopping out there? Why did you ask me to meet you here? The car rammed her, and her head struck the hood before she fell to the ground. One of her sequined gold shoes flew through the air like a sparkling firework."

I thought of the discarded shoe I'd seen beside the body. That information had not been released to the public. I sensed victory. "And then Eleanor drove off?"

"No. The car backed up and ran over Mother again."

"She struck her twice?"

"Three times. The car hit her three times."

Britt would be keenly interested in how Evan knew these details. "I don't understand why Eleanor killed her. Your mother would have given her the money to save Crandall Brain Clinic."

"Not hardly. Mother gambled our fortune away. When Daddy tried to stop her, she killed him for interfering. She said she'd kill us if we ever told. Eleanor and I have been afraid of Mother our whole lives."

My eyes rounded in horror. What a terrible burden to carry for a child to carry. "She can't hurt you now, Evan. She's gone."

Evan blinked. His eyes focused on me, the same way Monty's had. Like I was dinner.

Oh, shit.

Think, Cleo.

Get out of here.

I edged sideways, slow and crab-like. "I have to go."

"I don't think so." Evan moved between me and the door. The muscles in his arms flexed. "You know too much."

I tried to downplay what I knew. "You had a terrible childhood. But your Mother can't hurt you now. Eleanor, either."

"Damn it." He smacked his palm on the granite counter. "You know. How did you figure it out?"

I eyed the distance to the front door. Could I escape? I was not in top physical shape. Evan was. In a foot race, he'd beat me. In hand-to-hand combat, he'd beat me.

I had no gun, no large Saint Bernard to save me this time. I was in a deep pot bunker with no easy way out. Evan stalked closer. The only way to avoid him was to walk closer to Monty's cage.

Oh god. Oh god. Oh god.

The golf ball in my pocket.

I could throw it at Evan.

It wasn't much, but it was something.

My fingers closed around the familiar dimpled ball just as Evan grabbed my left arm. "You can't leave, Cleo. I'll kill you and hang your death on the dumb golf jock."

A golf ball to the noggin wouldn't phase someone as crazy as Evan. Luckily I'd come up with a plan B. I spun around and hurled the ball at Monty's cage, striking it soundly in the center. The glass broke with a loud pop and splinters of glass flew everywhere.

"Monty!" Evan released me and ran to save his precious pet.

I bolted out the door and called the cops.

Chapter 16

The storm came out of nowhere. A black whirling monster of epic proportions. I walked faster and faster on the unfamiliar golf course. A black snake fell from the sky. Startled, I steered clear of it. But a striped snake fell to the right. Then a rattlesnake dropped on my left. Oh, God. It was raining reptiles. I clutched my collar close and hurried along the narrow fairway bordered by ominous woods.

The light dimmed to twilight levels. More snakes fell. They hissed as they landed and slithered to cover. One gray snake hit my shoulder as it fell, and I yelped with fear.

I had to get out of here, fast.

Why couldn't I get my bearings?

Lightning arced across the leaden sky. A giant python coasted down the lightning bolt in a thunderous roar. Its bloodred eyes fixed on me. I froze. Oh God, I was going to die.

A chime sounded.

Angels? Would I be rescued?

The chime sounded again.

I surged from sleep, blinking in the drowsy sunshine of late afternoon. With one hand on my racing heart, I scanned my surroundings for slithering creatures. Nope. No snakes.

Just me and the living room. I sighed in relief.

The doorbell chimed insistently. Rubbing the sleep from my eyes, I padded to the front door and opened it.

"I brought the beer." Dean and Jonette strolled in arm in

arm. Dean looked strong enough to best a lumberjack. More importantly, he was smiling. Who wouldn't smile with a "Moore for Mayor" button pinned on his ball cap and another on his black T-shirt?

Jonette looked smashing in her wild pink getup. Infused throughout her steady regard of me was a liberal dash of happiness and relief. She waved a bag of donut holes at me. "This will cure what ails ya."

"I'm not sick," I protested. "My arm's a little sore, but other than that I'm fine."

"You need donut holes," Jonette said.

I groaned. I could eat the whole bag, and she knew it. "Maybe I should rethink my decision to quit the gym."

"You look fine to me." Dean regarded me warmly. "Not as fine as Jonette, but I'm slightly prejudiced."

"You better be." Jonette gave me a brisk hug and glanced around. "Where are the puppies?"

I waved in the direction of the kitchen. "In there."

Jonette's hips twitched as she strolled to the kitchen. In her bright fuchsia sundress, she was a vibrant orchid amidst the dark neutrals in my house. I couldn't imagine how blah my life would have been without her friendship.

"You guys all right?" I asked Dean.

His gray eyes gleamed. "Never better."

His statement sparked my curiosity. In the space of a few days they'd gone from being on the verge of breaking up to making gooey eyes at each other. "What turned the tide? How come things are good now?"

The corners of Dean's lips twitched. "I'm not dull."

I'd been called dull plenty of times, by Mama and Charlie. Jonette had worked her magic on my life, and I'd become less dull. Seemed she'd transformed Dean, too. He stood tall, radiating confidence. I smiled. "You're getting a lot of mileage out of running naked in the street, aren't you?"

He rolled up on his toes and back down. "I'm milking it for all it's worth. Then I'm getting me a Harley."

The image of Jonette in fringed white leather, seated on a big hog rumbling over the lush Maryland countryside, came to my mind. She'd love the freedom of the bike. "Live the dream, Dean. Life is short."

"Don't I know it." His expression sobered. "I'll take good care of her. You don't have to worry about that."

His promise confirmed what I suspected. Dean was the best Jonette had ever landed. I couldn't keep my smile inside. "How do you feel about Saint Bernards?"

He nodded. "Anything Jonette wants."

Lucky woman. I hoped they'd always feel this special connection. I took his arm and guided him to the kitchen. "Let's get that beer refrigerated."

Charla, Lexy, and Jonette each held slumbering puppies in their arms at the table. Mama manned the stove, stirring and baking. Cinnamon and nutmeg perfumed the air as two apple pies cooled on the counter. Before I could sit down, the doorbell rang again. No one else moved to answer it. I sighed. "I'll get it."

Despite the boxes of chocolate in his hands, Bud Flook's voice trembled with uncertainty when he greeted me. His glasses tilted to the right, and his rumpled business suit looked like he'd slept in it. "Is Delilah home?"

I stepped aside to wave him in. "She sure is. Would you join us for supper?"

"I wouldn't want to put you folks out. I wanted to borrow your mother for a few minutes."

"Good luck with that. I haven't been able to pry her out of the kitchen all afternoon, but you're welcome to try."

He handed me a box of fancy chocolates, his cigar-scented

clothing rustling as he moved. "This is for you."

"Thank you." My mouth watered at the pictures on the box. "That's so sweet."

Bud blushed. "You're welcome. I'm glad this matter is settled once and for all."

"You and me both." I tore open my chocolates and offered him one.

"No thanks," he said.

"Mama's in the kitchen, Bud." As he ambled away, I selected a chocolate for myself. I'd earned this reward, even if I did ruin my supper. The decadent treat melted in my mouth. I hummed with delight, savoring the rich flavor. All too soon it was gone. But there were eleven more. Which one would I try next?

Another car stopped on the curb in front of my house. A bright red convertible. My pulse leaped with joy at the sandy-headed, lanky man who strode my way. I stepped out on the porch and closed the door. With any luck, the crowd inside wouldn't miss me for awhile.

Rafe approached with a giant crystal vase of roses. Dark red roses. Twelve of them. Lots of white babies' breath and fern leaves in between. I liked.

The flowers and the man.

"Thank God you're safe." His lips met mine.

We'd only been apart for a few hours, but it felt like days. My body basked in his strength, warmth, and passion. I wanted a lifetime of his kisses. I needed our relationship to mean more to him than flowers or sex. Though I wasn't complaining about either one of those things.

I reached for the beautiful roses, but the chocolate box was in my hands. Placing the box on the porch railing, I accepted his roses and inhaled deeply. Heady floral elixir filled my lungs, my heart, my soul, fueling my dreams.

"Open the envelope," he urged.

Anticipation rioted in my blood. Carefully I set the vase on the wicker table. His expression sharpened, causing me to tense as I plucked the white envelope from the fragrant bouquet. A thin red ribbon the color of the roses was bunched inside. Tied to the ribbon was a gold key.

My breath hitched. Chirping birds and passing cars faded until we stood there alone, a universe of two. His brown eyes glittered. "For you." He placed the ribbon around my neck, the metal key sliding under my shirt to rest against my skin. His light caress shivered through me.

He'd given me the key to his house. My heart raced a mile a minute. Two months of dating, and he'd given me his house key. I pressed the key against my breast.

"Come see me anytime." He cradled my hand in his.

My heart swelled with emotion. A key implied commitment. It wasn't a ring, but it indicated trust and dedication. Energy surged. I jumped him. "Thank you."

Our teeth smacked together. He caught me, centered me, and chuckled at my eagerness. "Easy, Red. We've got all night."

After dinner, Charlie had the girls overnight. I planned to spend the entire night with Rafe. "You'll stay for dinner?"

His arms hugged me close. "I'm not leaving here without you. Did you cook?"

"It's all Mama tonight." I caressed his clean-shaven face. Frissons of awareness flashed between us, rioting my heightened senses. Tonight would be the best ever between us. "We have regular food, too. Dean brought beer, and Jonette brought donut holes."

"Two of my favorite food groups. I'm in." He glanced over at chocolates on the railing, and his expression clouded. "Where did those come from?"

"Bud Flook. He's over here courting Mama."

Tension ebbed in Rafe's face. "Sounds like you've got a full

231

house in there."

"It's a little crazy inside. You want to sit out here for a bit?"

"Sure."

The setting sun cast long shadows across the lawn, but on the porch it was all sunshine. We cuddled in the creaking swing, Rafe's arm around my shoulder. His masculine scent filled me with wonder and hope. I could get used to this. I could so get used to this.

Rafe cleared his throat. "About this afternoon—"

I put my fingers to his lips to cut him off. "Hey, no fair fussing. It's over and done. If it weren't for me, Evan Hodges would be getting ready to kill again."

He brushed my fingers aside. "Why didn't you take me with you to Evan's? I could've taken him out easy."

Big macho-man talk. "You had golf lessons to give. Besides, it was a spur of the moment thing."

Rafe cupped my chin, held it fast. "Red, you almost got yourself killed."

Suddenly the key around my neck weighed a ton. It felt less like a precious gift, more like a ball and chain. In accepting the key, had I given away the freedom to make my own decisions? I pulled away from him. "I got myself out of there. I called the cops. Everything turned out fine."

He stroked the length of my hair, his hand coming to rest on my shoulder. "I don't want to fight, sweetheart. I want you to be safe."

I thought of Monty in his glass cage and shuddered at the prospect of being similarly caged. "This is who I am, a woman who thinks for herself." I slipped the ribbon off my head. My voice broke. "If you don't like it, take this back."

I dropped the key in his lap. Commitment, or trust in this case, wasn't enough after all. I wanted an equal partnership. If we weren't in accord on a basic level, this would never work. We had no future together. Despair kicked me hard in the gut.

Rafe blinked rapidly. "You're mad at me? For caring about you?"

"For trying to control me. I want to be with you, Rafe, but not at that price."

He stared right through me. I prayed he didn't get up and walk out of my life, but this heart-to-heart talk was long overdue. For once I held my tongue. Silent winds tore at my heart. I braced for the worst. I hoped for the best.

"One of the things I like about you, Red, is the starch in your spine. You don't let anyone walk over you. That's worth a lot in my book. I want you. I've made no secret of that. But I want you safe. That's not going to change, either."

"We're deadlocked? Both of us too stubborn to compromise." I didn't purposefully shift in my seat, but somehow my boat-neck top slipped off my right shoulder. My black bra strap stayed firmly in place. Rafe traced my neckline with his fingertips, his languid touch setting fire to my skin.

In a flash, the key was back around my neck and he held me tight. "We can work this out. I care about you, Red. I don't want anything to happen to you." Rafe's breath warmed my throat.

Hope rushed over the dam of frustration. "We're back to being a couple?"

"Definitely."

"You can't sleep over here routinely. I have the girls to think of."

"We'll make it work, Red."

I tucked the key under my shirt, hardly believing my good fortune. My opinions and convictions mattered to him. The new Cleo rocked. Even better, Rafe respected me for who I was. I'd dreamed of having someone accept me for who I was all my life. We held each other in contentment.

Dreams did come true. I happy-danced inside my head, twirling and humming with joy, until an unexpected sound caught my ear. A door slamming. The door of the vacant house. I had new neighbors? I strained forward to catch a glimpse, then wished I hadn't.

Charlie exited the vacant house next door. He strolled across my front yard, swaggering like royalty. His size-ten feet made short work of my steps. "Evening," he said.

With a heavy heart, I intercepted him. "What now, Charlie?"

The skin at the corners of his blue eyes crinkled. "I rented the house next door. We're going to be neighbors."

Alarm closed my throat. I gasped for air. "This is not a good idea."

"For you, maybe. It puts me right next door to my daughters."

Rafe pressed in close behind me. "Jones." Rafe's arm circled my shoulder.

"Golden," Charlie said.

I fisted my hands at my sides. "What are you doing here, Charlie?"

His chest puffed out. "Charla invited me to dinner."

I shook my head. Charla and her matchmaking were driving me crazy. I pointed to the front door. "The girls are in the kitchen. Go on inside."

He did.

A glance at Rafe's scowling face confirmed what I knew in my heart. Charlie's dogged persistence was more than a nuisance to Rafe. I found my voice. "I'm as stunned as you are. I had no idea he planned to move next door."

Current pulsed through the air. "Do you love him?"

Charlie was my past, Rafe my future. I gazed directly in Rafe's eyes and willed him to believe me. "No. I'm crazy in love with you."

Rafe searched my face for the longest time. His scowl faded, and he clasped my hand. "Then there's no problem."

Jonette scraped the rosemary-flavored popcorn stuffing out of her purple pork chops and over to the edge of her plate. "I don't understand how you knew Evan was the real killer. What gave it away?"

I swallowed a mouthful of stuffed pork chop. The stuffing wasn't bad. I rather liked the unusual flavor combination. "Great stuffing, Mama."

She beamed her pleasure. "Thanks, dear."

"To answer your question, Jonette," I said, "I didn't go there to grill him about the murder. I went to tell him why I'm dropping my gym membership. Only once I got there, things didn't feel right."

"Are you psychic?" Light glinted off Bud Flook's rimless glasses.

"Absolutely not." I shook my head vehemently. "I'm too much of a by-the-numbers person to believe in woo-woo stuff. All I can tell you is that it felt wrong."

"Sounds to me like you're psychic." Jonette leaned forward, a grin pasted on her elfin features.

Dean scraped Jonette's popcorn stuffing onto his empty plate. "Let her tell the story," he prompted.

"Yeah, Mom." Lexy gestured with her fork. "What happened next?"

After spending the afternoon at the police station telling and retelling the same story, I wanted to put this behind me, but I understood my family's need to make sense of today's events. "Evan was celebrating. That was the first thing that hit me wrong. He had Jimmy Buffet cranked up so loud I could hear it outside his door. It's a wonder his neighbors weren't complaining."

"Nothing wrong with a little Jimmy Buffett," Dean observed. "The best music of the century came out of the 1970s."

"When I think of Evan Hodges," I said, "I don't think Jimmy Buffett. I've never seen Evan wear anything festive his entire life. Even his body building clothes are drab colors. But today he wore an aloha shirt."

"You're a fine one to comment on Evan's boring wardrobe." Jonette waggled a finger at me. "You and I need to have that shopping trip."

I blushed. My navy-blue slacks and a burgundy boatneck couldn't hold a candle to Jonette's low-cut fuchsia sundress. Jonette had been threatening a wardrobe makeover for months.

"That is a really good idea, Red," Rafe said. The heat in his voice reminded me he'd glimpsed the black bra strap. Did he remember Jonette selected the black lingerie set?

"We'll see." I tore off a piece of my sprinkle-coated roll. "Anyway, the music was loud, his clothes were loud, and he didn't act like a man whose mother had been murdered by his sister. Everything about Evan shouted party time. He wanted the junk food I'd brought for breakfast, so he invited me in."

"Anybody want that last pork chop?" Charlie interrupted. When no one responded, he forked it onto his plate and sliced it up.

That was his third pork chop. I glanced around in hostess mode, assessing the dishes on the table. Charla's rainbow salad had hardly been touched. "I'd like some of your beautiful salad, Charla."

Charla perked up and passed the dish. I helped myself and passed it over to Rafe. He took the hint and loaded up on salad. By the time the bowl got back to Charla, it was empty. She beamed radiantly. "What happened next, Mom?"

"The more I talked to Evan, the more I realized something was up. From the extreme neatness of his apartment I knew he was detail oriented. He had good credit, good looks, and great taste in furnishings. I couldn't figure out why he was single. You know how it irritates me when things don't fit together. Evan was a puzzle. But I got a big piece of his puzzle when I saw his calendar. He'd been following you around for two months, Mama."

"That little sneak. He tried to frame me for the murder he committed. But my smart daughter saved me." Mama reached over and gave my hand a squeeze.

"I wasn't feeling too smart this morning, I tell you. I felt like I had fallen into an alternate universe. Eleanor had been arrested for the murder, and the case was supposed to be closed. The calendar suggested otherwise. At first I thought they were in it together. Then I realized Evan hated both his sister and his mother. And they didn't like him or his snake."

Lexy shuddered. "I can't believe he kept a fifteen-foot python in his kitchen."

"Owning a large snake didn't make him a bad person," I said. "Evan told me he'd had Monty since he was a kid. That's more of a commitment than some men make to their wives."

Charlie avoided my gaze and stuffed blue ricotta cheese in his mouth.

I took a small delight in his discomfort. "Then I found out how controlling Erica was."

"I could have told you that," Mama said. "Everything had to be her way. She was impossible to deal with."

Everyone stopped eating to look at Mama. Baffled, she stared right back. "What?"

"Never mind," I said, eating another bite of rainbow salad. "Anyway, I started thinking about that calendar and how much Evan hated his family. Put that with his being disinherited and you have a boatload of resentment. I started praising Eleanor's brilliant strategy in planning the murder, and Evan came unhinged. He told me what it had been like to run over his mother. He was very convincing. I had no doubt that he was telling me the truth."

"But what about the call from Eleanor's phone the night of the murder?" Bud Flook asked.

"Evan lifted her cell phone at their private dinner earlier that night. Later, he returned it to her car. She didn't miss it because she frequently left her phone in her car."

"Evan must have been pretty clever to frame not one but two people for his mother's murder," Lexy observed.

Clever or desperate? Regardless, I didn't want Lexy to idolize a killer. "I felt sorry for him. He claimed his mother killed his father and threatened to kill her children if they told."

"I hope you didn't feel sorry for him when he decided to kill you," Rafe said.

"No." I glanced over at Rafe. He'd stopped eating to listen. "Evan planned to set you up as my killer, Rafe. That's when I used my Noodle."

Lexy frowned. "Your brain?"

"My Noodle brand golf ball. I shattered the snake cage with it and ran for all I was worth. I'll never play golf with anything but a Noodle after this."

"What about perfect Eleanor?" Charla bounced in her seat. "Is she still in jail?"

I squared my fork and knife on my plate. "Britt is releasing her and dropping the charges."

"What happened to the snake?" Lexy asked.

Why was she so fixated on the snake? "We are not adopting Monty. One Saint Bernard with puppies is all I'm willing to take on."

Lexy wasn't satisfied with my answer. "Did Eleanor inherit the snake?"

My eyes wanted to roll. I closed them instead. Gathered

myself. I gave Lexy a reassuring glance. "Animal control has Monty. They'll find him a home."

Charla propped her chin on her hand. "You're good at this figuring stuff out, huh, Mom?"

"My Cleopatra is super-smart, I tell you. She was right on the nickel when it came to saving my sorry butt." Mama raised her glass. "I propose a toast." Everyone lifted a glass. "Here's to family. And to sticking together through thick and thin."

"Here, here," Jonette said.

I basked in the warmth of our gathering. Sharing a meal with family was the best part of life. During the past few weeks, I'd learned a lot about family. Blood ties were the strongest, but so were shared experiences. Though Jonette wasn't blood kin, we were sisters just the same.

As for the men, I had high hopes but realistic expectations. Which of the four men at our dinner table would be here in a year? I smiled wistfully at Rafe. *Let him be the one with staying power,* I silently implored.

The sparkling lights in his brown eyes hinted at mischief. Bedroom mischief. For now, that would suffice.

ABOUT THE AUTHOR

Maggie Toussaint's golf game formed the basis of her protagonist's golf woes. While tromping through the forested rough, she realized there's something about trying to hit a white ball into a small hole that brings out dark thoughts and murderous possibilities. With that insight, IN FOR A PENNY, the first book of the Cleopatra Jones series was launched. ON THE NICKEL, the second installment of the series, puts Cleo's sleuthing to the test once Mama's car is identified as the murder weapon.

Maggie writes both mystery and romance. Her first published book won a National Readers' Choice Award for Best Romantic Suspense. She's active in writer's organizations, freelances for a weekly newspaper, and leads a yoga class. Visit her at maggie toussaint.com.